BEYOND THE
WHITE CURTAIN

SHIRLEY McGRATH

 FriesenPress

Suite 300 - 990 Fort St
Victoria, BC, V8V 3K2
Canada

www.friesenpress.com

Front Cover Illustration and Design by Codrut Miron

ISBN
978-1-5255-2184-3 (Hardcover)
978-1-5255-2185-0 (Paperback)
978-1-5255-2186-7 (eBook)

1. FICTION

Distributed to the trade by The Ingram Book Company

Chapter 1

––––––⤳∘⟨⟨⟩⟩∘⤶––––––

I LOST MY dear Matka in the spring of 1936 when I was 12 years old, days before my birthday. As anyone would expect, my world was never the same.

I can still remember the soft, steady breathing from behind the white curtain. Over the years I'd heard many sounds coming from behind that curtain. I knew when there was laughter; it brought me a feeling of joy. Through the curtain I heard soft sobs, Matka not wanting us to hear her crying. On rare occasions, there were the ones that I knew were wet with her tears—louder, more intense sobs. I could feel my own heart breaking as I knew hers was. Then there were the most familiar noises, which my brain couldn't comprehend: the moaning and sighs filled with sweetness. All the while, the bed did its own talking: rather loud and annoying metal on metal, nut to bolt; *squeak, squeak, squeak.*

It was easy to hear sounds through the white curtain; after all, it didn't hang right down to the dirt floor. Yes, it was dirt, but no mistaking it was well kept. Each day, it was swept with a corn broom, the same broom that made us cover our behinds when we saw it coming to discipline our misbehavior.

When Matka got sick, towards the end, she never left the bedroom. Our weekly bath didn't happen because we didn't have the use of the bedroom for privacy. Usually, the metal tub was set in the bedroom. Starting with the oldest, down to the youngest, we took turns in the tub; hot water added as needed from the pot on the stove. It was the only time the filing order was oldest to youngest. All other times, the youngest went first. Even when we stood by the stove to do our daily sponge bath, the youngest went first.

1

The evening was approaching, when from the bedroom, Tata yelled for us to come in. I knew, all day, the sounds coming from Matka were ones I had never heard. My brother pulled the curtain to the side, then gently touched each of our backs as we filed in. My little sister was the closest to Matka's face, then me. There were nine siblings all together but only eight here, just enough to encircle the bed. It couldn't be Matka who lay there, for her pale skin didn't represent her cheerful, loving, and vigorous spirit. Her eyes were different. Although still recognizable, they were cloudy and filled with intent—still the prettiest green, but with dark circles beneath them; she had eyes like no one else. When looking into her innocent eyes, one could feel the kind and gentle, pure being she was.

Her voice sounded the same; it just wasn't coming through her usual soft pink lips. My heart broke to see her dry, cracked lips, which should've been pink or reddish to match their soreness but instead matched the color of her pale gray skin.

She started by saying she was going away to be with "her" Matka and Tata. My little sis's eyes lit up. She asked if we were all going back to Poland with Matka. There it was, that sweet smile that always signified her glorious being.

"No, my angel. I'm going far beyond here with God. My flesh will be gone, but don't let that trouble you, as you'll forever feel me inside you. Through the birdies' songs, the wind playing with leaves on the trees, and in each other's voices, you'll hear me. When you look into each other's eyes, and your own eyes, you'll see me. Something stronger than our flesh connects us."

I doubt that my little sis understood, but it was enough to stop the questions. Then Matka started talking about how she expected us to live after she went on her journey. That was the reason she wanted us here. She felt the need to guide us, which didn't come as a surprise to me. I wouldn't have expected anything less for she was the most selfless being and was mine for eternity.

Her first words made sense to me. I understood when she said that we needed to have God occupy every bit of our hearts, so the Devil could never enter and do his damage. If we felt him creeping in, all we had to do was call God. He would protect our souls and keep them pure.

Next, Matka called us all blessings and said that we needed to look after each other. She said we were blessings to each other, and we were to show our love by guiding each other through life.

"Feed the younger ones as I do. Make sure they don't go to bed hungry," she said. "You'll feed each other's hearts when you have fewer words but instead listen. I mean listen with your heart. Then you'll be soft with each other. This is what I want from each of you."

I didn't grasp what she was saying in her last request. They were just words to me. If they wouldn't have come from her, the one who gave me all I needed, I wouldn't have embedded her words in my head.

Matka said, "You'll all grow, and in time you will find someone special with whom to share your life. I need you to listen to me, as I know what will bring you the happiest, sweetest life. When you find this person, the connection you feel will be unique. It'll be a feeling not *from* your heart, but *beyond*. You'll feel connected deep down in your whole being, in your soul, for eternity. There will be tough times. Even if you're torn apart, you will always find your way back to each other."

Marie, my oldest sister, who was named after Matka, asked if this person would have a face that she would think was handsome.

I could see Matka's face wrench in agony as she said, "Maybe, and maybe not. That won't be the actual way of knowing though because you're speaking of physical desires and earthly wants. This person will feel connected to you and you to him, as though you've known each other forever. Your two souls will be attracted to each other, bonding you while on earth. When God calls you home, you'll still be connected to each other, as our spirit

3

never dies. Your body, mind, spirit, and soul will be in alignment with each other's for eternity."

Matka's tired eyes never looked away from me. We were eye to eye except for blinking. The whole time she talked, it seemed as though it was meant for me. That was what I felt at the time, but later I questioned my thoughts. Maybe it was just the angle she was lying at on her bed, too weak to move. Perhaps her eyes couldn't focus anywhere else. I knew that she loved each of us equally but differently. That visit with Matka stayed with me. Her words protected and guided me through my life journey.

Tata then waved his hand toward the door to signal us out. Youngest to oldest, out we went. Part of me wasn't ready to leave. Many times, when looking back to this treasured time, I wish I'd stayed beside her, feeling the love emanating from within and looking at her beautiful face.

It was time to light the lamps. For then, that was a job for my older brothers and sisters, but one day it would be my turn to take on the important task. Tata was exhausted. To help, our closest neighbor Nelly had brought fresh bread over earlier in the day. Tata made us a pot of soup. I could smell the delicious aroma as it simmered on the stove. It went perfectly with the bread. He got the metal cup out, and that was all we needed to prompt us to get our bowls and spoons. It didn't matter who got their bowl first; the lineup never changed. Anna was first in line, then me—always youngest to oldest when it came time to feed us.

It usually didn't take much time to eat our supper, though this meal was different. It was like we were eating in slow motion. Once everyone finished what was in their bowls, my oldest sister filled the dishpan with hot water from a battered pot on the stove. The rest of us stacked our bowls and spoons off to one side of the table to make room for the dishpan. Dishes were washed, dried and put away in the usual fashion.

It was bedtime, so we stripped down to our underwear. The four of us girls knelt, resting our elbows on the side of our bed. Our prayers were silent and never took long. That night, I knew we all had the same prayer.

The boys had their bed across the room. When they did their praying, we could usually hear them quibbling in fun. On that night, their corner of the room was dead silent. They were stripped down and in bed before us girls.

I got to sleep with Anna at the head of the bed and my two older sisters, Marie and Alice who slept at the foot.

I had a tough time getting my mind to shut down—sleep didn't come easy. When it finally did, I slept soundly, until my bladder woke me up. I swung my feet out onto the floor and bent down to reach the piss pot from under the bed. The proper name for this divine bowl was the chamber pot. Our brothers teased us about it, saying that we were too afraid of the dark to go to the outhouse, but the teasing never bothered me. I could relieve my bladder without getting dressed, without getting cold and without waking my older sister to accompany me out into the dark. I still believe to this day that jealousy was behind the teasing. I didn't understand why they would be jealous as they seemed to enjoy going outside before bed. I'd often hear one say, "I'm going out to pull my dong." The others would chuckle.

It didn't matter much if it was winter or summer, 6:00 a.m. was when our eyes popped open. Tata took the pail to the outdoor well and brought in water. More wood went into the stove to heat the water. Some water would be put into the wash basin. The rest would be used to make porridge or to boil eggs for breakfast.

Once our bellies were full, we had our chores to do. On this day, the boys went out to pick tree roots from a nearby field they had cleared in the fall. My older sisters collected the dirty clothes that were heaped up in a corner over by our bed. Enough water was put on the stove for the dishes, as well as washing the clothes. As it was a warm, sunny day, the clothes could be washed outside and then hung on the line to dry.

Right after breakfast, Tata went back into his and Matka's room. I heard the bed squeak when he lay down. I could always tell if it was Matka or Tata getting into bed by the sound of the squeak. I suppose we were all familiar with the noises each of us made, and for that matter, to all the sounds in our home. Our space was limited, but it worked. We had to be good at sharing as there were only two rooms and one of them was off limits to us kids. It made us close physically, as well as mentally.

I thought I heard her soft whisper before Tata got up. He came out from behind the curtain and flung open the door, yelling for my brothers to come quickly. As we filed into the bedroom, I knew the time had come. It was time for her to go, her eyes locking onto each of ours for a few seconds. She wanted to make sure to look at each of us so that we could feel her love through those kind eyes. Then it happened. Her beautiful eyes closed.

You can't imagine the agony and pain that came into our bodies, right from our toes up and out through our mouths. Each of us in our way was letting out what occupied our hearts.

I remember begging her, "Matka, Matka! No, no, no! Don't go. Don't go. Matka. Matka!" Beside me, little sis was screaming, and the tears were dripping. Across the bed Peter, my oldest brother reached out to cup her hand in his, while begging God not to take her.

Then a miracle happened, Matka opened her eyes, but it only lasted a few seconds. In all my years, I've never had an experience where so much commotion turned into silence. We all needed this, short as it was. I recognized, and I'm sure the others did too, that Matka wanted to go. There was no doubt. We saw it in her eyes at that moment. They closed and never opened again, but it was enough. We understood that God and our dear Matka were together now.

Night came, and I found it strange that Tata went behind the curtain and slept with our sweet Matka for one last time. I never did understand why. I guessed he still wanted to feel her, even though there was no warmth. In later years, I realized this was necessary for both. Tata's beating heart needed to be as physically close to her soul as possible.

The following day Nelly came to us with a full meal, complete with sweet cakes and homemade strawberry jam. Tata opened the door to let her in. She said, "I know that she is with God now. We could hear the children crying out in pain. God bless all of you." Nelly was a kind and gentle soul.

Nelly's husband Pete came with a few other men, and they took Matka to be put in the ground at the graveyard which was down the road from our house. We went the next day and stood beside the fresh dirt, each of us saying our silent prayers.

It didn't take many months before I knew it wasn't that Matka couldn't have her head at a different angle because of pain or her position in the bed. As I think back to the day Matka died, I understood her words were meant for me. She knew it was me who needed to hear those words the most. That was why my Matka never took her eyes off me.

Chapter 2

THE FOLLOWING MONTHS were a sad time for all of us, but our family stayed close, talking about Matka and how much we loved and missed her. The neighbor ladies brought meals and even some fruit on occasion. We knew there was talk as well as questions about Matka's passing on to be with God.

Our family had two very hurtful times, and both happened the year before Matka died. One was a family secret. We were told to never talk about it to anyone, or Matka and Tata would get into trouble. The other was about our brother Tim, and the surrounding countryside gossiped about it until their jaws were sore.

Tim didn't live with us anymore. He was sent away after working on a farm as a hired hand for a woman who had a reputation for crushing people with her filthy tongue. Even though Matka and Tata were warned about her, the idea of more money coming in won out. Tim wasn't there for too long when he did a horrible thing.

Tim was busy cleaning out a barn when the woman came in. Her rude, crude words became unbearable, and he flung the pitchfork her way. It caught the side of her head splitting it open. Tim ran home and told us what had happened. A short while later, a police officer showed up and told us that the cut required stitches.

Tim was taken away and held until his court appearance, which was an excruciating day for our whole family. The judge considered him a danger, so he decided to deport him back to Poland. The neighbors had varying opinions on if he should have been taken from us. Most saw it as tragic and unfair, with only a few in favor of the judge's decision.

He left us two weeks later, only fifteen years old. I'll always remember taking him to the train station. Matka held on to him, his chin resting on her shoulder. His eyes were shut, but the tears flowed in streams down his cheeks and onto Matka's back. I found it the hardest watching him; slumped over, crying openly as he pulled himself up the steps of the train. It was heart-wrenching when we saw him appear in the window seat, a look of desperation and disbelief on his face. The train slowly moved away from us.

The following days, we lived in a fog. Matka was never the same, and we found ourselves crying along with her. Losing our brother was a sorrowful time for us. We looked at each other and tried to understand why he'd been taken away. For most of us, time healed all wounds, and finally, our tears dried up. But for Matka, even after the visible tears didn't happen as often, her body told us she was broken inside.

Our friends and neighbors thought Matka died because Tim was forced to leave us. In truth, it was only part of it. Our family secret was heartbreaking. There was a baby in Matka's stomach. A few weeks after Tim left, the baby came, prematurely, stillborn.

Matka asked Tata to put together a small wooden box. Each of us gave a piece of our hair, although I'm not sure why. I suppose it was because that was all we had to give our baby brother. We put our black, blonde, brown, straight, and curly locks of hair into the bottom of the small box. It was enough to make a soft, thick layer for the little one's eternal bed. Matka kissed his little face then gently laid him on his forever bed. The memory is so clear; the hair was all around the tiny white piece of material he was wrapped in, leaving only his face visible.

Tata dug a hole on the side of the field close to the bushes, not far from our house. Matka had planned it that way. We all gathered around, and Matka led with prayers to God before the dirt was put back on top of him. Each of us put a rock around the freshly dug soil, making a circle to mark where he was. We were told never to talk about him, or Matka and Tata would be in trouble. Tata said that legally the baby should be put to rest in the graveyard, but Matka needed him close. She couldn't bear the trauma of losing another son.

In the evenings, for many weeks, Matka went out to be with him before bed, praying over the fresh mound of dirt. This went on right up until she took sick, and her lack of strength didn't allow her to visit him anymore.

I believed that Matka couldn't bear the pain of losing two of her boys. She left us because of the heartache and stress of it all. Tim was far away, and we suspected that we would never see him again. Baby boy was on the land close to our home. Dear Matka was down the road in the graveyard. At times, I wished the baby was in the graveyard with Matka, but I couldn't answer why. Deep down in my heart, I knew that the location of the flesh didn't matter.

Chapter 3

⸺◦◦⟡◦◦⸺

TIMES WERE TOUGH, but we managed to hold our own. We had chickens to give us eggs or to butcher for meat. Our three cows gave us all the milk, cream, and butter we needed. The pigs not only fed us but before slaughter, when they got big enough the boys took turns riding them. Entertainment was never better than watching my brothers straddling the pigs.

Fresh vegetables from our garden were plentiful in the summer months. In the fall, the root cellar was filled with potatoes, carrots, onions, and turnips, along with our canning.

My older sisters and I learned how to make bread. Sometimes we had it fresh out of the oven for our noon meal, unless our chores kept us too busy to bake in the morning. On those days, we would have it for our evening supper. It didn't matter when we ate it. We loved it.

We picked wild berries growing on our land. Across the field, there was a plentiful raspberry patch. Picking the berries was the most fun for me. I loved the stillness around me, imagining the berries were our only food. That was what kept me going even on the hottest afternoons. I could spend more time in the berry patch than any of my sisters.

Tata seemed to be doing a lot better in those days. A few months after Matka died, our world changed forever. I loved hearing Tata's cheerful whistling happening again, to his favorite tune, "Happy days are here again, the skies above are clear again, so let's sing a song of cheer again, happy days are here again."

On a late afternoon, as we were getting our supper together, Tata shared some important news. We were going to have another room built onto our house. My brothers and Tata would start to build the much-needed room in a couple of days. We were pleased to hear this news. It was the topic of conversation all through supper, the cleanup, and while getting ready for bed. Once the lamps were turned off, I heard the door open. I could see Tata's shadow leaving. I didn't know where he was going but thought he needed some fresh air and alone time. I never paid much notice as he was always there in the morning, stoking up the fire and heating the water. But I would soon find out.

Chapter 4

———⊶∘⟨⟨∞⟩⟩∘⊷———

TATA AND MY brothers worked on building the room every spare moment they had. As the walls went up, I got more and more anxious for it to be done. Finally, there was only the roof to put on. I would stand in the partly finished room trying to picture where the beds would go, and where our clothes would be hung.

There wouldn't be a window in this room, but that was practical. Windows, not without a purpose, could be a problem. We had two windows in our house, one facing the east field and the other facing to the south beside the door. Our windows had cloth hung over them when the weather allowed. If there were few flies, we'd pin the fabric back to let in fresh air. When it turned cold, we had to board the windows up, as it was necessary to keep our house warm. When the wind got bitter, we could feel the draft from the two windows, even more so than that from the door.

The boys thought they'd have the roof on in two more days. Tata said that once the room was complete, he would make a special announcement. We girls were told that we should prepare a feast and set the table for three more. I was excited to hear about who was to occupy the new room. The boys or the girls?

The guests were a puzzle to me. I worked my brain hard trying to figure out who they could be. After much thought, I decided it would be the people who lent tools and gave a few logs for our new room. At last, I thought I had it.

The day finally arrived, and the roof was finished. All of us felt blessed. My sisters and I were anxious to make our favorite foods to celebrate. While rolling little dough balls, I thought about Matka and how proud she would be of us mastering our home country dish, called perogy. The dough balls were flattened into a circle and then filled with cooked potato, onion, and cottage cheese. The filled dumplings were then put into boiling water until the dough was cooked. The perogies were finished by putting them into butter to keep from sticking together. We roasted pork and cooked fresh carrots and greens from the garden. Dessert was fresh raspberries with cream. It was going to be a wonderful celebration.

Our visitors came by horse and wagon. I could hear them as they came up the road. Tata went out to greet our guests. I thought that was strange, as normally he would let visitors in after they had knocked on the door. While the rest of us waited inside, we could hear them talking in pleasant tones, with a bit of laughter.

The door opened. In came a woman with a smile that showed her teeth, mousy brown hair that fell to her cheeks, and a face that was enough to keep my attention. I couldn't make my eyes go past her face. It was her awkwardly long and skinny nose. That nose looked like it belonged on someone else's face—for that matter, on a man's face. My interpretation was confirmed when behind her followed a young man with the same nose, which suited him much better. A girl came next, a little younger than the boy. There was no mistaking they were brother and sister, with their mother in the lead. All that was missing was the father.

The food was ready to be put on the table. Tata told us to sit down and introduce ourselves to our guests, saying a little to explain who we were.

First was Anna. Quietly, with a shyness about her, she said, "I'm Anna," then looking down, she said, "I'm the youngest."

Next was me. "My name is Stephanie. We have a very kind neighbor named Nelly who lets me ride her horse named Meg."

Henry and David, the boisterous twins spoke next. Both said they liked straddling the pigs because it made everyone laugh. They were the family comedians.

"I'm Thomas. I like to play a game called kick the can." Thomas made it uncomfortably obvious that he wanted this introduction to be over. I bet he was hungry, but that wasn't unusual as he was always hungry.

Peter's introduction was only meant for the girl; I was sure of it. He stared at her throughout the whole grueling task. Still looking into her eyes, he said he liked to go into town, drink soda pop, and listen to the jukebox; of course, this was when all the day's work was done. I almost lost control but kept it to a silent grin. Peter had no money to get into town and buy soda pop. It was clear that she liked his answer. He impressed her.

"I am Alice," said my second oldest sister. "I love to help my younger brothers and sisters." What that meant was how she wasn't happy unless she was barking out orders to all of us. She had a way of getting things done with her mouth. She would go on and on until it was easier to give in and do what she asked.

Finally, Marie, the eldest, introduced herself. She said that her favorite part of the day was when we got into bed after our prayers and shared the day's adventures with each other.

We listened as Tata said, "I'd like all of you to meet Agnes."

The woman's hand was resting on the table, and Tata laid his hand on top of hers. She looked at him and then turned so I could see the toothy smile. This time I picked up on how phony her smile was, and a terrible one at that.

Tata then looked at her daughter, who was sitting on the other side of her mother. "This is Beth."

I wasn't sure Peter heard Tata say her name as he couldn't seem to take his glazed-over eyes off her.

The young man sat on the other side of my Tata. I watched as Tata's hand reached up to his shoulder, where it rested while he said, "And this is George. He is Agnes's son and Beth's older brother. Once we're done eating, I'll have more to tell you. The food smells delicious. Let's get it onto the table."

Tata's words were almost the last spoken throughout the meal. Other than "Please pass the perogies," or "This is delicious," not a word was spoken. Not even the usual weather conversation.

Marie, Alice, and I got up to start clearing the table while Agnes and Beth watched. I'd never been in the presence of ladies who didn't pitch in to help wash dishes. I found it odd, and I wondered if my sisters were thinking the same. When the clean-up was done, Tata asked us all to come and stand in a circle. I sensed it was time for the announcement. I couldn't believe my ears as I listened to what came next.

Tata looked into Agnes's eyes. "Agnes and I got married over a week ago. We are husband and wife. The reason we added to the house is so Beth and George can have a room to share."

I was paralyzed, numb with disappointment. My plans for the room melted away.

Trust little Anna to question where the lady would sleep. Tata turned a rosy color and replied, "Her name is Agnes. She will be sleeping in my room. She is your stepmother. Beth is your stepsister, and George is your stepbrother. We are family and are blessed to have each other. They will be bringing their belongings and moving in over the next couple of days."

At that moment, I'd had enough. I wanted to go outside. I asked Tata if I could go out to milk the cows. He nodded his head. That should've been my perfect exit, but no. As I was opening the door, I yelled back, "One of our cows' name is Agnes." That broke the silence. My brothers and sisters snickered.

Tata yelled, "Wait a minute, Stephanie. Why did you say that?"

My answer was an honest one. "I don't know why, Tata. I guess because I am going to milk Agnes. I realize there will now be two Agneses. I meant no harm."

Tata came toward me and held me in his arms. He pulled away and put his hand under my chin so our eyes would meet. "I believe you, Stephanie. I know you have a kind heart. You wouldn't hurt a soul."

I was always told how much I resembled Matka. I had her green eyes that revealed my kind nature. My hair was black with curls like hers, hanging down a little past my shoulders. Most people were drawn to it, asking if they could touch it. The usual comment would be that it felt so soft but thick, and how they wished their hair was like mine. Looking back, my simple, honest comment, and Tata's reaction to it sealed my fate with my stepmother, Agnes. She determined how I was filed in her heart, and there was no changing it.

When I was finished pulling Agnes's teats, I heard everyone outside talking about the move. The plan was to transport beds, chairs, and some personal belongings the following day. The three of them would stay at Agnes's close friend's house one night. The next day, they'd move in. It didn't seem real to me. I wondered what the others were thinking. *Could this be happening?*

The following morning, the furniture arrived. Two beds were put into the new room, and a small wooden table with a lamp was placed between the beds. Filling the room should have been a joyous time, but it wasn't. I had hopes for that new space, and they'd been crushed. I hoped it wouldn't be off limits like Tata's room. Maybe our new stepsister and stepbrother would let us come into their bedroom. The thought cheered me up. It would be our last night as the family I knew. It tore me up to think about it. *It could be worse,* I told myself. *No one is leaving, we still have each other, and there has always been room in our hearts for others.* Between hearing Matka's words about keeping God in my heart, and my self-talk, it helped me deal with my inner conflict and turmoil. I was part of a new family. I had to get used to it.

Not long after the breakfast dishes were washed the next day, they arrived bringing the last of their clothes. George and Beth seemed cheerful as they arranged their belongings. Agnes went into her new bedroom. Tata followed her. Even though the white curtain was pulled closed, it didn't hold in the sound of their laughter. My body ached to hear Matka's sounds—any of them, even her saddest cries. It was sinking in that Tata had replaced our Matka. When I thought back to this time, I realized it was the start of my nonacceptance that Tata's heart belonged to Agnes.

Chapter 5

━━━━━━━━━━━○◦◖◗◦○━━━━━━━━━━━

DINNER WAS READY to dish up. We had prepared our native beet soup of borsch while our guests moved in. The soup consisted of carrots, green beans, peas, potatoes, and of course whole beets, leaves and all, from the garden. Hard-boiled eggs and fresh bread were placed on the table. That's when Tata told Beth to get her soup first, then George, and then Agnes. The lineup order had changed.

Little Anna didn't say anything on that day, but when she got more comfortable around them, she would ragingly ask why she wasn't going first anymore. Tata would answer, "Never mind, stop making a fuss, and be happy your stomach is being fed." Looking at Agnes while this went on, I could tell she was enjoying it. Her smile wasn't fake, but more of an annoying, satisfied smirk.

One week later we were told that a wooden floor would be built throughout the three rooms. Agnes was going to pay for the wood. The boys would work on putting it down. It was great news as we all knew the winter months would be much cozier with a wood floor to walk on.

We learned that Agnes was a widow, a well-off widow. Her deceased husband had worked on the railways, which meant a steady income. It wasn't hard to see that Agnes and her children were in a different class than we were. The quantity and quality of clothing they came with told us something.

Most of our clothes were sewn from gunny sacks that the flour and wheat came in. The sacks had various designs and colors. Some were dark and used for the boys' shirts, while the flower-patterned ones would be utilized for our dresses. I remembered saving the sacks, matching patterns so we would have enough of the same pattern to sew a new dress or shirt. Nelly sewed for us, and we wore our new outfits with pride.

We always made do with what we had. Thank God for our land, which provided all we needed. We had vegetables and meat to sell to friends and neighbors for cash, which paid for our flour, sugar, salt, beans, and a few other supplies. As women of the house, we had the essential task of growing and preserving vegetables and fruit. Our livelihood depended upon our ability to produce, preserve, and stretch what we had. Matka had taught us well.

Tata and my brothers would slaughter a pig in the fall, skin it, gut it, and take it over to Nelly and Pete's to cure in their smokehouse. We always shared the meat with Nelly and Pete, as it was just the two of them. Once the meat was cured, it was hung in our shed, which was used for this purpose. Butchering was done the end of November. We had no problem keeping our meat from spoiling, between the salt used and the bitter temperatures of the cold winter months.

Chapter 6

NELLY AND I had a special agreement. When all my chores were done for the day, I was allowed to go over to ride Meg, Nelly's horse. Nelly and I enjoyed riding together. She told me I could think of Meg as my own, even though she would stay at Nelly's farm and they would supply the feed. I was thrilled with the arrangement, as I knew Tata would never let me keep Meg at our place.

The plan for this day was to harvest the cabbage, which might sound like a minor job, but there was a lot of work involved. I wanted to do the job so Nelly and I could go riding. The cabbage was cut off from its roots, its outside leaves pulled off, and then the cabbage heads washed in a tub of cool water.

Some of the heads were shredded, pounded, salted, and put in a crock; this was how we made sauerkraut. Our root cellar would hold sacks filled with whole heads. They would be used through the winter months for salad and delicious cabbage rolls, another Polish dish. To make them, we'd first soften the cabbage, so it would be easy to roll. Cooked white rice and fried onions were rolled up in the cabbage leaves and then baked. Even years later, it was still one of my favorites.

We were almost done filling the crock with cabbage for sauerkraut when Agnes opened the door and waved for me to come inside. I wondered what it could be about as I hadn't interacted with her much. Once inside, she told me to shut the door behind me and sit down at the table. She sat across from me and asked me why I was always bringing up Matka, and talking about her as if she were still alive.

It took a few seconds before I could find the words to answer her. Puzzlement must have shown in my eyes as I tried to make sense of her question.

I told her honestly, "Matka taught us everything we know. I feel closer to my Matka now, more than ever. I feel our souls are one."

Agnes's big nose turned a crimson red. She stood up and leaned over me as she let her words fly.

"Stop with the Matka business. Matka did this! Matka made this! Matka was this!" Her hands were waving angrily, "I am sick and tired of hearing your talk about her. You're a Bohunk from Poland. You live in Canada now. It's not Matka and Tata anymore. It's Mother and Father. That's how you need to address your father. Remember that your mother is dead, as your talk of her must be." Her eyes were filled with hate. She shook with anger.

I stood up in horror and made my way out of the house. There was no indication that my sisters knew what had happened. Our house wasn't soundproof, but they were working in the garden far enough away that our voices hadn't carried out to them.

After my work was done, I took off down the road to Nelly's as fast as I could go. Meg saw me coming and followed me along the fence line. Nelly came out of her house to greet me with a freshly baked bun covered with strawberry jam. Nelly's bread was as good as ours. No surprise there, as Matka was the one who'd taught her how to make it.

I asked if she'd like to join me for a ride on her horse, Blue. She was happy to oblige, so we started down the usual trail. That was when I felt the need to ask her a question that was burning inside me.

"Nelly, what is a Bohunk?"

When Nelly stopped her horse, Meg also stood still.

"Where in God's name did you ever hear that word?" she asked.

I stumbled for an answer. "Humm, I'm not sure. Probably my brothers." I lied.

I could tell by the way she was shaking her head in disbelief that she didn't want to answer me.

"Stephanie, it is not a kind word to use. It means a person from another country who is unskilled and stupid." Some silence passed. "Anyone who uses that word isn't with God. It's the Devil's way to puff a person up by calling another down. If you hear that word again, you should tell your Tata."

"Alright, I will. But can we use Father instead of Tata? George and Beth call him Stepfather. It's important to keep names the same. I have decided to call him 'Father' from now on." A surprised look crossed her face.

The rest of our ride was in silence. Both of us were comfortable not talking. Instead, we enjoyed the quiet stillness of the beautiful nature around us.

Before I went home, I thanked Nelly for the time we'd shared. I put my arms around Meg and snuggled up to her neck. "Have a blessed evening, and see you soon."

Walking home gave me time to think about Agnes and her words. *Why me? Why is she so set on hurting me?*

Marie and Alice were finishing up making supper when I came through the door. I would do most of the clean up since I didn't help prepare.

We filled our plates with stew and salad. The bread and butter were on the table, along with a big pitcher of milk, and another with water. Lots of conversation was going on, but when I said, "Father, would you pass me the butter, please?" They all stopped and looked at me in a way that showed their surprise.

"Stephanie?" Tata quizzically asked, "Why 'Father' instead of 'Tata'?"

My eyes turned from his and moved onto Agnes. "Agnes told me I had to start calling you 'Father.' It's the Canadian way."

Agnes jumped up from the table, so fast her chair tipped. Glaring at me, she blurted out, "I've never told you how to address your Father. You're making this up." Then she put her hand on Tata's shoulder and bent down close to his ear. "She's lying. I don't understand why. I don't know what she thinks she'll gain by saying this."

Tata put his arm around Agnes and coaxed her to sit back down. In a soft persuasive tone, he said to her, "Don't let this upset you, my dear. It's okay. Sit and finish your supper."

I hoped he would look at me, but he didn't.

Chapter 7

—◦◦◦◦—

MY MATKA CAME to me the same night that Agnes spewed her horrible words. I woke, feeling her presence, but not in the way you might think. I didn't feel her flesh near me. No, what I felt was different. It wasn't a dream. It was hard to explain because it wasn't an earthly occurrence. I knew her message was brought to me through my soul.

"Do not wonder anymore, Stephanie. Let your brain rest and use your heart. Your heart is a garden that is flourishing with all the nourishment it needs. You sowed the seeds, and now your garden is full of life and ready to give back.

"But wait; the heat is taking over, and it is going to destroy what you sowed. Your garden needs water, Stephanie. Water will cool the hot dirt and stop the burning. Water always finds a way. It will make your garden full of forgiveness. It will forgive the heat for trying to destroy its pureness, and its devotion held within. This is the only way your garden will stay healthy and bring you much joy. Remember that you cannot fight heat with heat, nor can you win over the Devil by becoming his twin."

I thought about Matka's words, and her message became clear to me. I understood what my path would be. I knew it would take incredible strength to follow it.

Comforted, I relaxed and fell back to sleep. Later I awoke when I heard the floorboards creak. I could tell someone was up walking around. Peter surfaced out of Beth and George's bedroom. I sat up in my bed. Marie kicked me gently before I could say anything. I looked at her with surprise. She signaled me to be quiet. Beth and Peter had special feelings for each other, but at the time I was too naïve to understand why they would sneak to be together in the night.

Chapter 8

—◦◦⟋⟍◦◦—

AFTER OUR MORNING chores were done, Marie asked me if I'd like to go for a walk. Our walks usually followed a path on the edge of the field. On one side of the field, there was a road. On the other side, the railway tracks. The trains went by a few times a day, and I loved their messages. The loud rhythmic *puff, puff, puff* at the same time of day told me how reliable they were. The clatter of the iron wheels on the track implied mighty strength.

What I loved the most was how the train brought visitors to us. All kinds of interesting people arrived, mostly men, all having a story to tell. It wasn't by mistake that they got off the train by our house. They had a marking on a tree at the edge of our property. The mark showed that a kind lady lived here, and there would be food given to them. These people were labeled as hobos who rode the rails, and Matka felt sorry for their situations. Most were looking for work, others a home-cooked meal. My Matka always gave something, depending on what we had. At the very least, we would make porridge, and there was always bread. We were told that we could listen to their stories but cautioned not to get too friendly with any of them. We were taught to have compassion for our visitors, as they had even less than we did. After some food and a drink, they would leave, walking along the track until they could jump onto the next train.

Some of them we saw more than once. They were the ones who had nowhere to go. No job, no money, merely riding the rails and depending on the kindness of others. The odd time Matka would allow a hobo to stay a couple of days in the woodshed, but never in the house. Looking back, the ones that got to stay were the ones that seemed to need the most help, walking toward our house, so frail and worn down.

Marie and I got close to the end of the field. "Can I talk to you about Peter coming out of Beth's bedroom?" I was interested in hearing what she had to say. I'd been thinking about it all morning. Marie was always full of information. I was all ears. "Peter and Beth are more than stepbrother and stepsister, more than friends. They are like husband and wife, and more than likely will be married one day." Marie let out a boisterous laugh, and I joined her. When I got control of myself, I had so many questions that I didn't know what to ask first.

"What would that make Beth to us?" I asked, "Stepsister and sister-in-law? What about their babies?"

What Marie shared next was almost as unbelievable.

"Then there is George. He told me that I was all it, and how much he wanted me to be his doll," said Marie. Her head was turning from side to side indicating how disgusting this was to her.

"I made it clear that he had zero chance of having me. Remember, Stephanie, what Matka wanted for us? She said that we would know when our soul connected. We would know this person to be our true partner for eternity, here and beyond. I'm willing to wait for my true love. George will give up on any notion of making me love him. Alice is putting the squeeze on him, and I can tell he is getting close to settling for her."

What Marie said puzzled me, so I asked her, "How do you know that Alice wants George?"

Marie snickered, "Alice is acting like a cat in heat around George, and he's picking up her scent."

I thought I understood, but still asked, "Do you mean George likes the way she smells? Is she using special soap or something?"

Marie bent over, and her laughter went on long enough for me to be annoyed. She wanted to answer me but couldn't get it out. Finally, composing herself, she looked straight at me and said, "When a woman acts like a cat in heat around a man, it means she wants to have his baby!"

"Nooo. You're telling me silliness, aren't you, Marie?"

"Stephanie, a man can pick up a woman's smell when she wants him the same way she can pick up on his manly body odor when he is ready to plow her. It's no different than the animal world when it comes to sex and reproducing. If it happens and Alice gets George to bed her, my world will be quiet again. I don't believe they would be a joining of two souls, but I hope they would treat each other with respect and kindness."

My sadness must have shown because when we got home, Tata asked me if I was upset. I told him no. I couldn't figure out whether I was angry or disappointed in myself. How could I have missed this? Before Agnes, Beth, and George moved in, life was predictable, with no secrets hiding in the corners. I realized going into that room had become unimportant to me. I vowed that I would start paying more attention to everyone around me. Thoughts of Agnes would have to diminish. I could do that with Matka's help. When Matka came to me, she told me that I didn't have to wonder anymore. No more wondering why Agnes was treating me the way she was. Matka knew that Agnes's evilness occupied my mind those days, and she had given me the answer to protecting myself. I needed it.

Chapter 9

I SHOT OUT the door with speed I never knew I had. Agnes was quick to come, not far behind with a knife in her hand. Marie was outside, bent over weeding. She glanced up and looked toward me, then returned to her gardening task. It only took seconds to register, and when it did, Marie stood up and yelled at Agnes to stop chasing me. I'm not sure if that was when Agnes retreated, as I didn't look back or change my speed.

When I got to Nelly's, I didn't see anyone except for Meg. I jumped on her and rode through the open field, my heart still pounding with fright. Unexpectedly, Meg lost her footing, and I lost my balance. I remember falling off the horse and hearing the loud thud when my left side hit the hard ground. Fortunately, I didn't hit my head, but the pain in my left hip was enough to keep me from moving too quickly. I perched myself up on my left elbow. My darling Meg came close enough to rub her nose on my cheek. She knew I was in pain.

Nelly, who was standing out by the barn, got a glimpse of my misfortune. It didn't take long for her to come running. She knelt beside me. Her eyes were intent as she checked my head, my arms, and all the way down to my feet. "Stephanie, do you hurt anywhere?"

"My pride more than anything," I replied. She helped me get into a sitting position and supported me while I made it up onto my feet.

It wasn't until we got close to Nelly's house that I broke out in sobs. She thought I was crying because of physical pain, and I debated leaving it that way, but I didn't want her to worry about me. My hip did hurt, but my crying wasn't from that pain, but from sadness, my heart had never felt.

We went into the house, and my composure slowly returned. Nelly put some milk, bread, butter, and strawberry jam on the table. When I saw the jam, the heavy, uncontrollable sobs started all over again.

Nelly knew me so well. She could tell there was something besides the fall bothering me and asked what it was. Getting my sobs under control, I shared the scary events of the morning.

"It all started when I decided to take a break from weeding the garden. I headed toward the house for a drink and a snack. When I got inside, Agnes was coming out of the bedroom, and she looked at me, not saying a word. No smile, no "Good morning," no "How are you today?" I made my way over to the table, grabbing the bread and jam on my way. I sat down, picked up the knife, and cut a slice off the loaf. When I reached for the spoon to get some jam out of the jar, Agnes yelled that there would be no jam for me. She said the plain bread would do because she knew I'd already had my share of jam this morning."

As I told my story, I could see the horror on Nelly's face. She held my hand, encouraging me to continue.

"Agnes told me the rest of the jar was supposed to be for the others when they came in for their break. She said we were using the jam up too quickly. As my hand was still holding the spoon, I ignored her words and stuck it into the jar. I was pulling out a right amount to spread on my bread when Agnes leaped toward the jar, trying to grab it off the table. About the time the jar flipped out of Agnes's hand, even before it hit the floor and shattered into pieces, I knew this would end up being my fault.

"Agnes's hateful eyes were on me, but then she turned her head toward the table. My eyes followed hers, and I realized both of us were staring at the knife that was laying there. She picked it up and pointed it at me. Then she told me I was nothing but a troublemaking little bitch, and she was going to cut me into pieces if I didn't stop causing trouble.

"Oh, Nelly. I jumped to my feet and belted out the door. Agnes was quick on my heels, but I never stopped until I made it here, and I prayed she would run out of energy. All this over a spoonful of jam."

Shaking her head, Nelly reached over and embraced me, and even though I couldn't see her face, I knew she was crying. Then she became outraged.

"I'm going to go back with you and give Agnes a piece of my mind."

"No, please leave this alone. It'll be okay," I pleaded.

That wasn't what she wanted to hear, but she agreed to keep quiet. When I was ready to go back, she wanted to walk me part way home as she could tell that my hip was causing me a fair amount of pain. When we got to the halfway point, Nelly gave me a warm, comforting hug, and we promised to see each other the next day.

As I rounded the corner of the house leading to the door, I got a glimpse of Marie walking toward the far end of the tree line. I debated yelling out to her but decided not to bring any attention to myself. It turned out to be a wise choice because once inside, I knew that Agnes was in her room, resting. I went back outside to check if there were any eggs to gather. I kept myself busy long enough to see Alice and George coming down the road, hand in hand. When Alice saw me, she barked out orders for me to dig some potatoes for our supper.

I considered myself lucky and was thankful that we made it through supper without Agnes making eye contact with me, not even for a second. Father asked me why I was limping, and I explained what happened while riding Meg. Agnes's reaction was a content little grin. It was getting more and more difficult for me to keep my pureness, but I knew Matka would never guide me in the wrong direction. I replayed her message many times during the day, over and over in my head, making sure it was planted firmly in my heart.

Peter and Beth were in the open by then with their love for each other. There was no doubt they were very much in love. It seemed everyone accepted their relationship; Agnes was even promoting it. Often, she would tell them to go off by themselves for a walk or into town for a dance.

I noticed that Alice was always trying to please George. She wanted to bring him closer to her, and Marie seemed happier than ever that it appeared to be working.

Chapter 10

—⊃०∈∞⊃०⊂—

MID-AFTERNOON, I LOOKED through the window and saw a hobo. He was coming along the tree line between our house and the railway tracks. When he cut across the field, I recognized his stride. I knew that he'd been there many times previously. His name was Bill, and I remembered him to be a soft-spoken, friendly sort. As I opened the door to his shy, smiling face, I was already thinking about what we had to give him. After our greetings, even though it was difficult for me, I told him that our dear Matka had passed away. He was surprised and saddened to hear about our loss. I told him to wait outside, and that I'd bring him some food.

Agnes was alongside the woodshed. It didn't take long before she came into the house, crushing any idea I had of giving Bill anything to eat. She warned me specifically not to give him sandwiches from the leftover pork we'd had for dinner. Agnes said we needed it, in case someone got hungry before supper.

She went back outside, and I followed. "Never stop here again. You'll be wasting your time because we don't have anything to give you." Agnes's rudeness made Bill take a step backward. She turned away from him and headed back over toward the woodshed. I saw Bill's confusion when he looked at me for answers. Before he hung his head in disappointment, he gave me a half-smile.

I made the decision right there and then to listen to my heart. I whispered to Bill to wait for me at the far end of the field over by the trees. His slight nod told me that he understood. Ten minutes later, with my hands full of sandwiches and some milk in a tin cup, I took off after him. I saw him standing back a couple of feet into the bush. I imagined how much he was going to enjoy the lunch I'd brought. I watched him devour the first few bites. That alone told me how hungry he was. He stopped chewing long enough to thank me, showing his sincerity and gratitude.

As I turned to leave him, I caught a glimpse of something unusual farther into the bush. I went closer and discovered it was a brown blanket with a man's shirt laying on the edge of it. The dark blue shirt looked familiar. I was almost sure it belonged to George.

When I stepped out into the field, I saw Bill heading to the tracks, ready to jump the next train. I spun around to my right, and there was Agnes, taking long quick strides toward me. I'd been caught. As she approached, her fist went up in the air, going back and forth as though she was practicing for a boxing match. She was winning, but the air isn't a challenge for anyone. As she got closer to me, I prayed to God and Matka for protection. I couldn't move from the spot.

Please, please dear God stay with me. God and Matka, you're in control of my mind, heart, and soul. There's nothing stronger than your presence.

Her hand came swiftly with a loud smack as it connected with my cheek. Even though I felt the stinging pain and the ugly words registered in my mind, they didn't anger me. Instead, I had an overwhelming sense of pity for the broken woman, who was Devil driven. Agnes saw what I felt when she looked into my eyes. There was no hiding what was going on inside me. As the demon controlling her cowered, her body retreated farther and farther, before she spun around and ran from me.

"Thank you, Matka," I said out loud.

My heart raced. The thought of Agnes returning made me uneasy, but I needed to sit and rest for a few minutes before heading back to the craziness within my house. The grass moved gently in the slight breeze.

The flutter of the bird's wings was the first sign that I wasn't alone. It landed directly in front of me, only three or four feet away from my outstretched legs.

"Pretty, pretty, birdie," I whispered. "Did you come from afar to see me?"

Its tiny head tilted to one side as if to show me it was listening. Its wings each had a bold white patch; the rest of it was a silvery gray. What stood out the most were its eyes, which were a brilliant crimson. Two steps forward then one step back was the visitor's dance. Then three steps forward and two back. That brought the lovely bird ever so much closer to me. The desire to put out my hand so that I could test its trust in me was overpowered by my fear of scaring my timid friend into leaving.

My hip still ached bad enough that I had to roll onto my opposite side to maneuver onto my feet. As I rose, I watched to see how the bird would react. It never moved. Hesitantly I made one step, and then on my second step, my friend, the show bird, flopped over on its side, cooing the whole while.

This was the first time I heard the calming song it shared with me. When I took another cautious step, he took flight and circled above me, flying a short distance before coming to rest in the field again. His flight path was in the direction of home, where I was headed. When I stopped to rest my sore hip, so did my friend, once again flipping over on his side. He seemed to enjoy my response of laughter. Up he got, making a few little hops in the right direction as if to tell me it was time to go.

We stayed together all the way to the farmyard until my feathered friend stopped, tilted his head, and made the most delightful cooing sound, which I realized was his goodbye.

When he took flight, I yelled out, "Thank you!" I watched as he flew over the bushes and out of sight.

Chapter 11

—◦◦⊂⟋⟍⊃◦◦—

UPON WAKING, MY first thoughts were about the blanket and shirt. Alice and George didn't show their feelings for each other the way Beth and Peter did. *Had I found their secret hiding place where they could be together, exploring each other?* Asking Alice was out of the question. I decided to keep track of where they went, hoping I could pick up on a pattern.

The day was dulled with cloud covering most of the sky, only allowing temporary peeks at the sun. My mood was no better. Different emotions flowed in and out. One minute I was sad, yet the next minute I found myself smiling at the thought of all I had. Nelly came to mind, and my sister Marie. Most importantly, I felt Matka was guarding me. It filled me with a level of security that I could trust.

The clean clothes hanging outside were dry and ready to bring in. When I bent down to pick up a clothespin that had fallen to the grass below, I felt cramps. They were sharp pains coming from down below my stomach. I felt them in and around my *poochka*. Every bit of my flesh below my midsection, and down to my upper thighs, felt cursed. The pain made me nauseous enough to heave up my dinner.

Forgetting about the clothes on the line, I headed to the outhouse. The moisture between my legs felt like it was steadily increasing. Sure enough, once inside with the door latched, I pulled down my underwear and there it was. Fresh and bright red, like Marie told me it would be. What she'd neglected to share was that the blood was going to fight its way out of my body; the cramps nearly unbearable. I remembered that Marie had also told me to expect the bleeding to happen once a month; "Mother Nature's monthly gift." How cynical of her to call it that, and how naïve I was to believe her.

There were a few white dishrags on the clothesline, and not knowing what else to do, I decided to take one and put it to use between my legs. Back to the outhouse, I went. I folded the rag a few different ways trying to make it the best size to fit in my undies. Finally, thinking I had it, I pulled up the whole contraption but at once felt disappointed. The bulky rag didn't feel at all comfortable or natural. It was rubbing me in too many already tender areas, but I had no other option. Maybe I would be lucky, and the red flow wouldn't go on for too long.

I went searching for Marie, not sure where she was but knew she would help me. Then I noticed something, or someone sitting up against a tree. I looked down the tree line daily, so I was familiar with anything that didn't belong. I could tell there was an addition under one poplar tree that I didn't recognize. As I headed in the foreign object's direction, it became apparent it was a man leaning his upper body against the tree. Even though I tried to be quiet, it wasn't enough. He heard me coming. He got up quickly, heading into the thickest part of the bushes.

There wasn't much I could say about him at that point. His hair was dark, and he was tall. I didn't think I'd seen him before that day. My gut told me not to pursue the situation. Thankfully, I didn't because when I turned around, I saw Marie coming my way. I heard her yelling, asking me what I was doing. When she got closer, I explained that I was looking for her. I wanted to let her know about the red flow. She put her arms around me, squeezed me tight, and said, "Welcome to womanhood, little sister."

When we got back to the house, Marie provided me with a belt and a box of pads with wings. She explained the wings were to clip into the belt to hold it in place between my legs. I went back to the outhouse to remove the already blood-soaked rag I'd placed there earlier. Once the pad was in place, I had to admit I found myself in a better mood, or safer to say, I felt more hopeful. Marie had a lot to do with my calmer feeling. She always had a way of making life better.

After the supper dishes were done, I made one last trip to the outhouse. Marie told me to double up on the pads for the night. My body felt drained, so I was grateful that I only had to walk back the short distance to the house and get into my nightgown. I fell asleep quickly and hardly felt little Anna crawl over top of me to use the piss pot. Through the night, I was aware of the warm wetness between my legs. Each time I rolled over, I could feel the blood trickling out and onto my protective armor.

Chapter 12

———◦◦⟨⟨⟨⟩⟩⟩◦◦———

MARIE WAS RIGHT in saying I might feel more tired during that time of the month. There was warm water on top of the stove, so I poured some into a metal bowl that only had one purpose. I took it, along with a clean cloth and fresh pads to the outhouse. I felt so much better once I'd freshened up. I noticed the cramps had eased up, but I had no energy or desire to do my morning chores by the time I returned to the house. Marie and I were the only ones inside. I knew my body needed to lie down for a bit longer. Marie reassured me I would get used to my monthly visitor, and the pain might not be as bad the next time.

I was enjoying the comfort of my bed when Agnes came through the door. She gave me a look that was meant to instill guilt. In no way was compassion a part of her emotions toward me.

She asked in a disgusted tone if I was going to lie in bed all day. As I got up, I told her I wasn't feeling well. Marie, who was peeling potatoes for our noon meal, heard both of us but never said a word. Agnes spun around and walked out the door.

Little Anna's pee from the night before was still in the piss pot under the bed. Like every other morning, I reached for the pot with the intention of dumping it in the outhouse.

As soon as I opened the door to go out, there Agnes was, right in my face. Her mean words stung more than usual. "You're being lazy. Don't expect a free ride around here just because you're bleeding."

I wanted to block her cutting words, and I looked down so as not to make eye contact. I tried to pass by her, but she stepped in front of me, showing me the trouble was going to continue.

Marie came to the door yelling, "Agnes, get out of her way!" Agnes stood her ground, motioning to Marie to get back into the house.

What happened next can only be described as shocking and inconceivable. Coming from my beautiful, well-composed sister made it a most rewarding experience for me.

Marie made three quick movements, and Agnes became the victim of a flying piss pot. It all happened so quickly and yet so perfectly. Marie leaped off the doorstep, grabbed the pot from me, and swung it toward Agnes. First Anna's pee hit her in the face. Then the pot smacked her chest before hitting the ground in front of her feet. Fortunately for Agnes, for once her big mouth was closed. Wet pee droplets were noticeable on her red, enraged face.

Odd as it sounds, my first thought was that I would have to get Anna to drink more water. It was an obvious conclusion by the dark yellow drips coming off Agnes's ears and onto her shoulders. The yellow color was very pronounced as it splashed onto her white blouse.

I could see Tata, with little Anna trailing behind, coming back from Nelly and Pete's. Agnes, in an antagonized tone, yelled to Tata to come quickly. I wanted to flee, but I knew my aching hip wouldn't allow me to get far. Then my thoughts went to Marie and her bravery. There was no way I could let her take all the blame since I knew it was me she was protecting.

"Is everything alright?" Tata shouted. Agnes's mouth started to open. Before she could say anything, Marie blurted out to her, "I know about Alex."

All Agnes's facial muscles twitched in sync. Her eyes bulged. I knew Marie had shaken Agnes to her very core. I could tell Marie's words had control over her.

In a quiet voice, Marie told Agnes to expect they would have a discussion soon. It was clear, by the look on Agnes's face, how distraught and afraid she was. Tata, closer now, asked again if everything was alright.

Agnes, head hanging down, replied, "Yes, I'm okay. I tripped with the potty in my hands. That's all; nothing serious."

Marie and I both turned around and headed back into the house to finish making the noon meal. Standing together at the table, Marie finished peeling the potatoes, and I mixed a coleslaw.

Leaning closer to Marie, I said, "You must have something huge on her. I need to be in on it. Agnes needs to fear me as she fears you."

We both hoped that Father was naïve enough to believe Agnes would be involved in dumping anyone's bodily fluids. Never had Agnes ever put her hands on the piss pot, feeling it was beneath her. We never saw Agnes do any chores other than making a pot of tea. Even that was put onto us girls if we weren't already hands buried in other duties.

Chapter 13

—◦◦≪⊂◦≫◦—

A FEW WEEKS passed, and I was feeling secure. I could see Agnes acting like a lily liver. Whenever Marie and I came around, she got jittery and would escape to her bedroom. Even if she were outside, she was edgy and removed herself from our company. It was like we had the plague. Usually, my heart was soft, but I suppose the feeling of being free and not having to be on guard all the time blocked out any pity or sadness for Agnes. She was the one living in fear. Even though I was looking forward to listening to Marie's talk with Agnes, it was no longer in the forefront of my thoughts. I was enjoying being exactly who I was, and knowing that I didn't have to tiptoe in and around my own home.

I was hoping that time would heal my hip, but it was still giving me grief. I wasn't sure if it was my imagination, but I thought it was swollen, so I showed it to Marie, and we both concluded it was. Marie decided to ask Nelly to have a look at it. She was wise about all sorts of troubles life could throw at you, and we trusted her advice. Within a few minutes, I could see Marie and Nelly approaching. Marie was waving her hands, and her mouth was moving, but they weren't close enough for me to make out what she was saying.

Seeing Nelly made me smile, but my excitement was mostly from seeing Meg, trailing behind them on a rope. As they got closer to me, Meg stopped, raised her head, and pricked her ears in my direction. Apparently, Meg had missed me too. I heard her soft nickering sound as if to say, "Hi, good you are here." She came right over and nuzzled into my neck, showing her affection. She pulled back and held her head in front of my face as if waiting for my response.

"Good girl. I've missed you," I said. Meg and I shared a mutual trust. Our relationship was all about being kind and having respect for each other. Unlike humans, Meg was honest and never full of trickery.

Nelly and I took our time hugging each other. I felt safe being in her arms. It reminded me of being held by Matka. We broke our embrace, and she reassured me it was going to be alright as she cupped my face with her strong, warm hands. She always had a way of lessening my fear.

Turning back to Meg, I said, "See you in a bit." We decided to go into the house where it would be easier to examine my hip. I lay down on my good side but not for long. Nelly laughingly asked, "Do you think I can see your hip with your pants on?"

With that, she hooked her arm underneath mine to pull me up. I stood by the bed and pulled my pants down to my knees. She reached out and gently touched the reddened, hot flesh surrounding my hip. She quickly made up her mind.

"You need to see a doctor. There was damage done when you fell off Meg, and now perhaps infection has set in the area. Regardless of the cause, there is an issue, and it needs attention."

My first thought was about how we were going to pay for a doctor. For that matter, how would we pay for medication? Knowing me so well, she read my mind. Without any hesitation, she offered to pay the costs for treatment, as well as any travel expenses.

Marie thanked Nelly, telling her that offering money was kind but not necessary. I stared at Marie in disbelief. Had she lost her mind? There was no way we had extra money for medical fees.

Marie picked up on my questioning look, but I could tell she didn't want to deal with me in front of her. Before leaving, Nelly insisted we tell Father when he came home from town. There must be no delay in seeing the doctor. With Meg's lead in hand, Nelly started for home. They were halfway in the field when both stopped, and she turned around and yelled out her offer of money once again.

Marie yelled back, "Thank you, but we'll be okay."

I turned to Marie, and confessed, "You've lost your mind, Marie. You know darn well we don't have any money, and Father will feel horrible if we bring this to his attention."

Marie swung her arm up around my shoulder. "I have an idea that will solve all our money issues. I will always look after you, Stephanie. My love for you is strong and never-ending." I understood what she was saying, and I felt the same about her.

Chapter 14

ALL THE EXCITEMENT from the day before didn't keep me from having a solid nine hours of sleep. I was so tired those days because the pain from my hip was draining my energy. Months had gone by since the day I'd fallen off Meg, and I kept hoping my hip would get better on its own. Instead, it was only getting worse.

When Marie saw I was awake and ready for the day, she motioned for me to go outside. I wondered what was up. A few minutes later she joined me. "As soon as I get the young ones out of the way, I'm going to have the long-awaited talk with Agnes."

Father, Beth, Peter, George, and Alice were gone to town for the morning. Marie planned to send Anna, Thomas, and the twins to Nelly and Pete's on the pretext of borrowing some sugar. I noticed that Agnes was suddenly paying attention to what Marie was saying to the young ones. She sensed something was up. When Agnes offered to walk with the kids over to Pete and Nelly's, I knew she was running scared. Marie shook her head back and forth to let Agnes know that wasn't happening and she wasn't escaping.

The children were pleased to go without her. We knew Pete would entertain the boys by showing them some of the wood animal carvings he loved to make. He did the most amazing work creating dogs, horses, and wolves. Anna would take pleasure being in the house with Nelly, especially if Nelly were cooking or baking; she'd get Anna involved by allowing her to help. They'd enjoy a glass of cold milk and a few goodies before heading back home. It's hard to say if they would have the sugar with them, or if it would be forgotten. They might even get halfway back and remember, having to return to Nelly's. We knew this would give us a good hour alone with Agnes and I would finally hear Marie spill the beans. After they left, we walked side by side back into the house, and Marie put her plan to work.

Marie and I sat at the table across from Agnes. If anyone had walked into the room, they would've assumed we were about to have a visit over a casual cup of coffee. But when Marie pointed her finger at Agnes and told her to listen and not say a word until she was done speaking, it became clear this was no coffee party. As Marie shared her disturbing story about Agnes, it seemed to go on for an eternity.

Marie glared straight across the table at Agnes and blurted out a matter-of- factly, "Agnes, I know all about Alex. How you are using him in a way that is evil and sick. You put the Devil to shame with your cunning ways."

Agnes, with her eyes squinted and fixed on Marie, shouted, "I don't know what you're talking about. Alex? I don't know anyone named Alex. Both of you are always looking for trouble, and now you're making up lies. Why? What's your purpose? You're a pair of bitches."

Agnes pushed her chair away from the table and stood up as if to leave. Marie would have none of that; the talk was far from over. Marie was quick to get around the table in time to push Agnes back down into the chair. I could see the anger between the two of them escalating, getting to a level where I hoped it wouldn't get physical.

Marie loomed over Agnes, eager to make her point. With flared nostrils and clenched jaw, Marie was enraged like never before. She started letting it all out, not stopping her tirade until she felt satisfied.

"Listen to me, you stupid old bitty. You can't lie your way out of this; I know too much. Alex and his wife Grace left their Dukhobor community to start a new life with their young son. Alex wasn't able to find much work, so paying their rent and putting food on the table was becoming near impossible. Then he had the misfortune of meeting you in the general store.

"On that day, he was about to ask the store owner if he would be allowed to charge some items, such as milk, bread, and eggs. Alex was walking up to the owner when you dropped a bag of rice and Alex, being the gentleman he is, at once bent down to help you clean up the mess. You took the opportunity to befriend him, which made him feel comfortable in confiding his misfortune to you.

"That first day, you gave him money and tricked him into thinking you had a job for him. You told him to meet you the following day, right out here on our property. You met him at the far end of the pasture, by the thickest part of the bushes. I know because I followed you. When I saw you carrying a brown blanket out to the bushes, my curiosity got the best of me. Agnes, the brown blanket is still in the bush. Even though it won't serve any purpose out there now, I never want to see it back in our house again."

Agnes, head held high and neck stretched out, very heatedly asked, "Are you done?"

I was hoping Marie had witnessed more. By Agnes's confident demeanor I thought Marie was only going on suspicions about Alex, the blanket, and the meeting place. If that was it, we were going to be in big trouble when Agnes talked with our father.

"Well, Agnes, I may be done. If you agree to my requests, it will all be forgotten. Well, not forgotten, but I assure you it will never be talked about again."

Before Marie had a chance to put forth her demands, Agnes let out a soft snort and threw her head back in defiance. It was clear she wasn't going to agree.

"Okay I understand you need to hear more," continued Marie. "I saw you and Alex lying on the brown blanket down in the bushes. While you were lying on your back and Alex was having a box lunch on your demand, you displayed the most disgusting whoring behavior I've ever seen. Your legs were spread wide open, and Alex's head was down, right in between them. While he pleased you, he was sniffling. You heard him and asked if he had a cold. He replied yes, but that was a lie. I saw him wiping away his tears. You have lowered this good man with solid values to an appalling level of humiliation and disgrace.

"What about the time you told him how much you wanted to feel him inside of you, but no matter what you tried his manhood could not perform for you. Do you remember what you did to his cock, when you…?"

Before Marie could reveal any more shocking information, Agnes shouted, "Enough. What do you want from me?"

I was a little disappointed, as I wanted to hear more.

Marie made it more of a demand than a request. "Stephanie needs to see a doctor. You will tell Father to get her to a doctor tomorrow. The expenses for whatever care is needed are going to be paid by you. Keep paying Alex until he finds work and can make ends meet on his own."

Marie may as well have had her hands clenched around Agnes's throat judging by how Agnes's eyes bulged. From her neck up, she looked like she was about to explode. I was sure it was anger within her I was picking up on, as she didn't appear to be filled with fear, as I'd expected.

If our father ever found out what Agnes was up to, their marriage would be over. Father was a kind and gentle soul, but he was a proud man. If that secret came out, he would never lay his body close to Agnes again.

Chapter 15

AGNES WORKED QUICKLY to get me to the doctor. The very next morning, as I was enjoying my last bite of egg on bread, Father told me to get ready for a trip into town.

It was impossible for me to ride Meg, and there wasn't enough time to arrange transportation by the track-maintenance car referred to as the railroad speeder. Whenever neighbors took ill, they were often taken to the hospital on the speeder, often accompanied by a nurse. It was nowhere close to being as fast as the train. The name railroad speeder didn't make much sense. It was quicker than a handcar and didn't require manual power.

Father had decided to ask Nelly and Pete if he could borrow their Bennett buggy.

I could tell my father's heart was full of worry. Before closing the door, he turned back, his concerned eyes resting on me, and he told me to dress warmly for the trip. With the door open, I could feel the cool, crisp air on my bare feet. My wool socks, a gift from Nelly, would keep my feet from freezing.

It didn't take long before Father was back with Blue, Nelly's roan gelding, hooked up to their buggy. Father helped me get into my seat; then he walked up to Blue.

"Blue, we won't be traveling too far today, only about fifteen miles. You'll have a chance to rest while I look after Stephanie."

His respect for all living beings was clear in how he chose to interact with them. My father always showed respect, whether it was for people or animals.

"Our trip home will seem quicker; it always does. Good boy, Blue." He patted the horse's head. Blue let out a snort as he lowered his head, then lifted it back up as if to show us he understood and was ready to get moving. When we started down the driveway, I noticed the morning frost glistening on the trees that lined our short lane to the main road.

As we traveled, I could see the sorrow and concern in my father's dark eyes. He motioned for me to sit closer to him, putting his arm around me.

"Your lips are blue from being so cold, Stephanie. You'll be even sicker if you get a chill. Lie down here and put your head on my lap, out of the freezing wind."

I listened to him and used his right thigh as a pillow. He switched the reins to his left hand and gently stroked my face. Even though his hand felt rough from years of hard labor, I was comforted. My father told me, "I love you, Stephanie, my sweet girl." I don't recall him ever saying it to me in that fashion—*My sweet girl.*

My heart was filled. I had a firm hold on his heart. "I love you too," I whispered back.

The rest of our trip seemed to go by quickly. The cold air was no longer on my upper body, and his words warmed me from the inside out. I found myself drifting in and out of sleep.

When I opened my eyes, I saw rooftops and realized we'd arrived in town. While I was asleep, my hip went numb, which lessened the piercing pain. As soon as I sat up, however, the numbness was replaced with hellish pain that made me gasp and bite down on my lip. My father saw this, and he reassured me we were only a couple of minutes away from the hospital.

As we approached the long, white building, I noticed how neat and clean the hospital grounds were. There was little activity on the outside, and I was hoping to find the same calmness inside. I noticed a dark-haired, medium-build woman, wearing a white dress and nurse's cap, coming out of the front door. I'll always remember the first time I heard her friendly, bubbly voice.

"Hello. Please wait for me; I can help you get out of that buggy. Are you injured, missy?"

Before I could answer the beautiful lady, Father replied, "This is my daughter, Stephanie. She needs to see a doctor about her left hip. It's bothered her ever since she fell off a horse."

"Oh dear, my name is Viviana Gatti, but most call me Nurse Atti. I was finishing my shift when I saw you arrive. Stephanie, move closer to the edge of your seat and swing your right arm around my shoulder. Don't worry. I won't let you fall. You're one lucky young lady; our best doctor is here and should be able to see you at once. When we get you inside, things will happen quickly."

Grateful for her help, I responded, "Thank you, Nurse Atti. I can manage walking on my own once I'm down from the buggy."

"Okay, Miss Stephanie, if you insist. But I see no harm in walking in with you and your father. It'll give me a chance to introduce you to the doctor."

Realizing they had not been introduced, Nurse Atti glanced over at my father and asked, "Sir, what is your name?"

"My name is Joseph Sadowski." He opened the main door for us.

"Hmm, that's an unusual name. Would that be of Ukrainian descent? Or I suppose Sadowski could be Polish."

"Yes, Nurse Atti, Sadowski is of Polish descent. My wife and I were both born and raised in Sadowo, which is a village in east-central Poland. We moved our family to Canada so that we could have a better life. We have a farm fifteen miles north of here."

"Was Mrs. Sadowski unable to accompany you today?"

Our trip down the hospital corridor came to a halt, and Father swallowed so hard it was not only visible, but I heard it. His strong chin lifted high enough to show the tense muscles in his neck. He replied, in a sorrowful voice. "I guess I'm not making myself clear, Nurse Atti."

Looking directly into her concerned eyes, he struggled to get the words out.

"Marie, my beautiful wife of twenty-seven years, and the mother of our nine children passed away a while back. There isn't a day that goes by where I don't recall the glorious years we shared, but life goes on. I am remarried now and have a new life with a nice woman."

Father's attempt to conceal the lone teardrop on his cheek had failed, even though he turned his head away from us. As his hand went up to wipe it away, Nurse Atti and I bonded as our own teary eyes locked, and we both felt the massive pain he was trying to keep pent up.

"I'm so sorry to hear about your loss. I understand your pain," said Viviana.

Feeling the sadness in her soft tone, I knew her words were sincere.

As we continued down the hallway, Viviana removed the black bobby pins that held her nurse's cap in place. Her wavy coal-black hair was pulled back into a thick bun under the cap.

"My head hurts with my hair fastened up all day. It feels wonderful to free it," she said, smiling.

She removed the elastic and more pins, allowing her hair to unravel and fall past her shoulders. As she was reaching down to put the hairpins and elastic band into her pocket, I took the opportunity to study her in more detail. Nurse Atti's face was delicate, her skin a medium bright tone. Her nose was narrow and perfectly straight. But what made me think she was the prettiest lady I had ever seen were her almond-shaped eyes, which were an unusual golden-brown color, enhanced by high-arched black eyebrows. With her wavy hair hanging down along her face, I guessed her to be in her mid-twenties.

We heard a man's voice but couldn't see anyone as the sound was coming from around the corner.

"That's him; that's the doctor," announced Nurse Atti, "I'd know his velvety soft voice anywhere."

When the doctor rounded the corner and saw the three of us, his attention was at once focused on her. "I thought you'd gone home, Viviana. Why are you still here?" he asked puzzled.

"I was walking out the door when I saw Stephanie and her father, Joseph, arriving. I thought I should help them in," she replied.

"Stephanie, Joseph, may I introduce Dr. Robert Bentley, the best doctor we have on staff. I'll leave you with him now."

Viviana wished me luck and told me not to worry; Dr. Bentley would take good care of me. At that point, she turned her attention to the doctor and said she would see him the next day. His reply was a pleasant boyish grin for Nurse Atti. It was wasted, though, as her back was already toward us as she headed out the door. His grin made me realize that he too was very young.

Until then, I hadn't been nervous, but meeting Dr. Bentley got me thinking about why I was there. I wasn't looking forward to the exam. I wanted it over. The sooner I could return home, the better.

Chapter 16

———— ⇀∘⟨⟨⟩⟩∘↼ ————

IT DIDN'T TAKE long for Dr. Bentley to examine my hip, nor was it anywhere near as embarrassing as I'd been expecting. He quickly put me at ease. When I told him about falling off the horse, he shared some of his riding experiences. As he spoke, I realized he owned a few horses, and we shared a passion for riding.

I had x-rays taken, and blood was drawn. We sat and waited all morning for the doctor to come back. Finally, Dr. Bentley approached Father, and I could hear enough to know our wait wasn't over. He said he'd have more information when he got the test results, but that wouldn't be until after dinner.

We saw the food cart coming down the hall, indicating it was dinner time. My stomach was feeling empty, and I glanced over at my father who was thinking the same thing as I: we hadn't eaten since our egg on bread at breakfast time. The lady with the food cart asked, in a cheerful voice, if we would like something to eat. In unison, we replied, "Yes, please."

"Sorry for taking so long. I wish I could've gotten down your way sooner, but I needed to feed the in-patients first. I've got vegetable soup, ham sandwiches, and oatmeal cookies for a sweet," she said with a smile.

We thanked her and proceeded to devour the food on our trays. The soup was not as hearty as I was used to, consisting of broth with a few carrots, peas, and onions. It had no flavor, but I was so hungry that I choked it down. I silently scolded myself for being disappointed with the soup. My thoughts were ungrateful, and I knew better.

Many, many times, our Matka had said to us, "When someone gives you something, no matter what it is, let it fill your heart with gratefulness. People show kindness in many ways and for many various reasons.

"Sometimes people show kindness for their personal gain. But don't think about that. It's not yours to bear. Make sure your acts of kindness come with no conditions or expectations.

"When you show kindness for the right reason, how it makes that person feel will never be forgotten by them, and kindness will spread to others and live on forever. If there is no gratefulness in your heart, there will be no kindness either. They have to be there together keeping each other company."

I closed my eyes and lay my head back against the wall as I thought about my beautiful Matka. My neck felt relieved in this position, even though the back of my head wasn't comfortable against the hard wall. It felt good to stretch out, and I could feel the tension leaving my neck and shoulders. I felt sorry for my father though, all this time sitting in a chair.

It appeared our wait was finally over. With papers and a bottle of pills in hand, Dr. Bentley entered the room. He asked if he could sit down while he spoke to us. My father and I both nodded yes as the doctor reached for the chair beside me. My heart was racing, as he sat down. I was nervous in anticipation of his findings.

Dr. Bentley kept his eyes focused on me, and in a serious tone said, "I need you to understand that I am hesitant to make a definite diagnosis based only on the tests we did today. I made some calls to the university hospital, and after speaking to a couple of different doctors there, we concluded that you must be admitted for additional testing."

He paused briefly. "As of right now, I am about eighty percent certain of my findings, and I firmly believe you need the attention of specialists. I wish there were more for me to tell you, but I am reluctant. I have arranged for Dr. Douglas Huntley at the university hospital to see you the day after tomorrow. Stephanie, you did say you are fourteen years of age?"

I couldn't talk. I nodded my head. Even if this doctor wasn't one hundred percent sure about what was wrong with my hip, I was curious about his suspicions. My head was filled with questions, and I knew Father was thinking the same. Who wouldn't want to know?

"Dr. Bentley, I want to know your diagnosis of my hip. Please, will you tell us?" I pleaded.

Dr. Bentley looked at Father, then back at me. He saw the fear and tension within me, and I'm sure that was why he decided to share more.

"From what I see in the x-rays, Stephanie, you may have tuberculosis in your hip joint. Understand this is not a precise diagnosis; the doctors at the university will give us their results. That is why I made your appointment, and I want you to see the specialist as soon as possible.

"The x-ray of your chest was clear, so I know you do not have it in your lungs. You're not contagious; tuberculosis of the bone doesn't spread from person to person like tuberculosis of the lungs.

"For now, I'd like you to take the pain medication I've prescribed, and you need to rest. Let's have you take a pill right now, so you'll be ready for another dose before bed. If you follow the instructions on the bottle, your pain will stay under control, and you'll be able to get the proper rest. My colleagues will take great care of you at the university hospital," he said in a reassuring voice. "I don't want either of you to worry. Even though this is serious, you will be cured."

With Dr. Bentley's words reeling in our heads, Father and I thanked him for his time and said our goodbyes. Just in time, because as no sooner were we walking out of the room, when the nurse approached him and said he was needed down the hall in Room 102.

Back in the buggy on our way home, I started to digest what the doctor had said. I replaced my anxious thoughts with Dr. Bentley's words, "You will be cured." Those words played over and over in my head, doing a great job blocking my fear. With my head once again on Father's lap and his arm around me, I slept all the way home. The medication was working.

Chapter 17

—◦◦✦◦◦—

WHEN WE WALKED into the house, Nelly and Pete were there, along with my family. They all turned to us with concerned eyes. As Father told them about the doctor's assessment, I could see the shocked, worried looks they were throwing back and forth, from me to Father then back to me. Everyone was doing their best to capture our emotions, not wanting to miss out on any signs of fear either of us might be holding back. I was so blessed to have a family who cared, and the best feeling for me was that I knew I wasn't going through this illness alone. I felt the need to lessen their burden, as I knew their hearts would absorb whatever I was feeling.

I relayed the doctor's diagnosis that was playing over and over in my mind. "Dr. Bentley said that even if it is tuberculosis, they can cure me. I don't have it in my lungs, so that means I'm not contagious. Please don't worry about me. It'll all be fine."

Father announced, in an assertive tone, "Stephanie will need her rest, and Agnes's and my bedroom will be the best place for that. Stephanie and Marie will have our room for the next two nights."

Up until now, I hadn't paid any attention to Agnes, but hearing my father's words, I needed to see her reaction. To my surprise, her body language wasn't showing any disapproval. There was no frowning, no eye rolling, nothing. It wasn't what I expected. Could her heart be softening toward me in my condition?

"We need to find a way to get Stephanie to the university hospital. A horse and buggy won't do for that distance. She has to be there the day after tomorrow," Father said, with concern in his voice. We realized that living in a town without a vehicle wasn't a hardship, but being in the country with no vehicle was a different story.

Nelly spoke up, "We can go to the train station tomorrow and check the schedule."

Agnes interjected, "No, no, no, let me tend to it. I'll go to town tomorrow and make a phone call to arrange a ride for you and Stephanie. I can look into purchasing a Ford Model T or something reasonably priced."

Marie and I stared at each other in utter disbelief. Was Agnes turning over a new leaf? Or was she trying to be as helpful as possible, so Marie would not need to blow the whistle on her? That reminded me that I still had questions for Marie about Agnes's dirty secrets.

Father interrupted my thoughts when he suggested I go into the bedroom and have a nap before our supper. *Gladly*, I thought, as I grabbed the pillow from my bed and walked through the white curtain. I flopped down on the soft covers, and within minutes sleep came, along with the most vivid, beautiful dream.

I was floating on one of many vast, bumpy clouds, so soft and fluffy, and I couldn't see over the top of the bumps because they were so big. I'd sunk deeply into it, but it didn't bother me. I felt the need, from within, to let my body drift with them in the direction that was calling me. Even as I crested the larger bumps, my body never separated from them. I never felt unsafe or frightened, and my laughter echoed in testimony to the pure glory with which I was filled.

Next, I topped the highest bump and could see far, far ahead of me. A mass of pure white fluffiness surrounded me, and without hesitation, I drifted to where I knew I needed to be. That's when I felt her and knew that I had found my dear Matka. I didn't need any physical signs of her presence, for she was inside me. We were together as one, once again.

My disappointment crept in when I felt the end was near and it was time to leave. It was then that a piece of the cloud broke away and drifted toward me. I felt peace and tranquility as I took it in and as I began to wake up, my disappointment evaporated. My dear Matka knew what filled my heart and soul because she'd put it there. I had no more questions about what was going to happen to me.

Chapter 18

LYING THERE, I could smell supper cooking, and I found myself guessing what would be placed on the table. My senses told me sauerkraut was part of the meal. There was no mistaking its pungent odor. We always had sausages, mashed potatoes, and beans with fried sauerkraut. Yum, it was my favorite meal. It didn't matter how offensive the smell of the kraut was.

I saw the curtain moving and Marie's nose and one eye poked through.

"Oh Stephanie, you're awake. I was being quiet, but this is great timing. We have your favorite meal ready on the table. Can you guess what it is?" questioned Marie.

"Oh yes, the smell woke me up. The only odor that comes close to fried sauerkraut is when the twin's feet sweat in their socks and shoes all day," I said, laughing as I got out of bed.

After polishing off my first helping, I had more sauerkraut. I didn't feel guilty going for seconds as the younger ones didn't care much for the kraut, and there was a lot left over. That night, I wasn't allowed to help with the dishes. Marie told me to go into the bedroom, and when she was done, she would bring me a cookie and some milk to have along with a pain pill.

The light from the lamp in the kitchen was shining through the curtain, filling the room with enough light for Marie and me to sit on the bed with our cookies and milk. My pain was almost non-existent, so when Marie handed me the pill, I explained why I felt I shouldn't take it. Marie would have none of that, saying I had to do as the doctor instructed. Down went my second painkiller with my last gulps of milk.

Comfortable in our father's soft bed, Marie listened to my quiet whispering as I shared my dream with her. We were lying on our sides, facing each other, our heads only inches apart. When I finished, Marie hugged me and gently pushed my hair back from my face.

"I know Matka is with me all the time," I whispered. "We fill each other's souls, and I'm never without her. She won't ever abandon me."

"Now I'm certain you'll be alright Stephanie. Our Matka has indeed sent you this comforting message in that dream," said Marie.

The lamp was put out, and there were no more sounds from the others, except an odd cough or clearing of throats. It was important for me to tell Marie about Matka and my dream, but I also wanted to ask Marie about Agnes.

"Marie" I whispered. "I'm curious about what you said to Agnes, you know, about that man? I think his name was Alex?"

"Stephanie, I don't think it's a good idea to fill your head with Agnes's devilish ways. I don't want you dwelling on it," replied Marie.

"It isn't fair that you're keeping this from me. It'll be better if both of us know everything about what Agnes did. Please tell me, Marie," I pleaded.

With that, Marie divulged the whole inconceivable story.

"The day I followed Agnes and witnessed her and Alex in the bush on our brown blanket was the beginning."

"How do you know his name?" I interrupted.

"At that point, I didn't know his name, but let me explain the whole story." She paused. "After seeing them together in the bush, I got up the courage to approach Alex when I saw him in the general store a few weeks later. When I introduced myself and mentioned Agnes's name and her connection to me, he looked embarrassed, and his face turned a bright red. Next, I shared what I'd witnessed in the bush. He politely asked if I would come to his house so that we could talk in private. He could see I was reluctant to go with him, so he explained to me that he wanted me to meet his wife, Grace, and their young son. Alex brought me to their tiny apartment above the pharmacy store."

She took a deep breath, then went on, "Oh, Stephanie, it broke my heart to see how they were living, way worse than us. They slept on a mattress on the floor, and there was no table to sit at for meals. Grace offered me tea, but I declined. I could tell they were humble, very friendly. I was shocked when Alex started talking in front of his wife, telling me about Agnes. I realized Alex hadn't kept any secrets from Grace."

"That doesn't make sense, Marie," I uttered in disbelief.

"I was there, and I felt their pain. Both were breaking down when they recalled their horrific story. I listened, and with every detail, my heart was bleeding for them.

"You remember when I said Agnes met Alex in the general store after she had dropped some rice? That day, she told him to meet her out here because she had a job for him. Alex and Grace were so hopeful because they believed Agnes's job was the answer to their money problems.

"The first time they met, Agnes made it clear the only work she had for him was to satisfy her sexual desires. Sadly, and with much regret, he decided to become her gigolo, for which Agnes paid him well. Alex was honest with Grace right from the start. They cried together when he talked about his first meeting with Agnes. He felt so degraded. They both hated what he'd done, yet what choice did they have? The meager savings they'd managed to accumulate before leaving the Dukhobor colony were depleted. Alex couldn't find work, so it was either satisfy Agnes or have his family starve.

"Alex tried to take his family back to the communal dormitory, but the Dukhobors in the colony wouldn't accept them. I'm not sure about their reasoning, but once a family splits away, perhaps they're viewed as outcasts. I felt sympathy for them, Stephanie, because they had nowhere to turn for help, and that sweet little boy to feed and clothe. When you look at the circumstances, it's all about survival."

I finally knew Agnes's disgusting secret, or so I thought.

"I'm warning you, Stephanie, you must never talk to anyone except me about this. I haven't told you the worst part yet, but I will if you swear never to tell anyone. Do you swear, Stephanie?"

"Marie, you know you can trust me. Please tell me the rest. My dear God, I can't imagine what could be worse. Come on out with it," I begged her.

Marie's voice became excited, showing she was eager to share the next bit.

"Agnes decided she wanted Alex to please her traditionally, with his penis inside her. When it turned out he couldn't do it that way, things turned ugly. Agnes worked on his manhood with a passion, willing it to get hard. But, as soon as he was inside her, he would lose it.

"Agnes wouldn't have this. She told him he had a problem, but she was going to fix it for him. She got aggressive, you might even say forceful, with his penis. It took a long time and lots of physical effort on Agnes's part. He did eventually get hard, and she got on top of him. She straddled him and guided, or should I say misguided, Alex's erect penis. She came down hard on him with all her body weight, and his penis hit her pelvic bone. There is no other way to say what happened. Alex's penis broke."

Thinking I didn't hear correctly, I asked: "What did you say, Marie?"

"Agnes broke Alex's penis."

I started to howl with laughter, but Marie's hand came down hard on my lips to silence me. The pillow came up over my head because I knew there was no hope of me being able to contain myself.

"Stephanie, what the hell is wrong with you? You damned well better shut up right now. It's not a laughing matter; it's disturbing. I'm warning you, stop laughing, or I won't talk to you about this anymore." Marie said through clenched teeth.

I sobered up as I wanted to let Marie know how I was feeling, and why I found this broken penis story hilariously funny. The threat of her not continuing was becoming a reality, so I prayed I'd be able to keep it together long enough to share what I was thinking.

"Marie, do you believe this wild tale? Think about it. A penis would be like a rod all the time if it had a bone in it. How can you break something that doesn't have a bone in it? I think that Grace and Alex made this up so you would feel sympathy for them and their bad choices."

I managed to get this much out but feeling the uncontrollable laughter returning; I put the pillow over my head again. I stopped long enough to lift the corner to tell Marie I was sorry for laughing.

"Stephanie, it's true. There isn't a man on earth who would make this up. There is no bone, but there are blood vessels, and if those break, the pain is excruciating. When it happened, Alex had no choice but to visit the doctor. As embarrassing as it was for him, he told the doctor it happened during intimate time with his wife. I don't blame him for lying."

Now it was sinking in, and I was feeling a little guilty for my unsympathetic behavior.

"What did the doctor do?" I asked. "I hope Alex is okay, or I mean his manhood is okay."

"Alex had to have surgery, and he could have lost the ability ever to have children, but he fared out well. Agnes paid for his medical expenses, and she never tried to ride him again; she never bothered much with his penis after that. She still demanded to be sexually satisfied by Alex, but in other ways. I'm not sure how long this went on, but it came to an end when I found them out and threatened Agnes. Grace and Alex are praying that either of them can get a job. They're relieved to know that even though it will end the payments from Agnes, they will be free of her. I too have been remembering them in my prayers."

"Marie, how can we not feel sorry for Agnes? She's such a lost soul. Remember, Matka told us to keep God in our hearts."

Marie was quick to answer, as she had it all figured out.

"Save your sorrowful feelings, Stephanie. If and when the day ever comes, and Agnes is left all alone—I mean when the Devil vacates her, and she is empty—that's when she'll need our understanding and forgiveness. There will come a time when the Devil will turn on her. He'll leave, and Agnes won't be able to justify her evilness.

"This is when we will need to be by her, praying for her to find God. She will need to forgive herself and will only be able to do that through God. If Agnes doesn't accept God as her savior, her life might as well be over as her sins will eat her up."

Chapter 19

⸺◦○◦⸺

I WOKE, FEELING refreshed and ready to face the day. I thought about last night when Marie shared her thoughts about Agnes, and it made me think about all the havoc she created. Not just in my life, but in the lives of people I didn't even know, people to whom I now felt connected. Agnes established the connection, and I welcomed it. My hidden feelings that Agnes's abuse toward me was partly my fault lessened. I wasn't sure why she chose Alex or me, but it was her shame to bear, not ours. Even though I would never get to know Alex, I felt connected to him. I felt grateful knowing about him as his story helped me put the blame where it belonged. Knowing, hearing about, and feeling Alex's and Grace's pain gave me a sense of courage and respect for myself.

As I sat up in bed, at once the room started to spin. I thought it must either be the medication or from lying too long. With my eyes closed, I sat on the edge of the bed and hoped if I waited a few minutes, I could stand up. I slowly opened my eyes and with great relief noticed the whirling was gone. Even though weakness was present throughout my whole body, I got myself up by pushing with both hands on the top of the bed to help the rest of my body. It was a challenge, but I managed to stand on my wobbly feet.

No one heard my movements until I pushed the curtain aside, then all eyes were on me. Marie offered me her arm, and I knew I could make it to the chair by the table on my own, but I didn't want to be rude, so I latched onto it.

The lamps were lit. Our window openings were already blocked in preparation for the cold months ahead. I saw coffee cups and sweets on the table.

It took a while to register that it was already mid-afternoon. Was it possible I slept in, not an hour or two but half of the day?

"What time is it?" I asked.

Marie looked up from pouring coffee. "It's three o'clock. You are in time for a bite of lunch."

"What happened to my breakfast and dinner? Don't tell me I slept through it."

"No, you didn't. I brought you eggs and bread, with milk to drink along with your pain medication this morning. Stephanie, do you not remember me helping you eat? You spilled milk on your nightgown while taking your pill, so I got you a fresh shirt. I helped you change, and as soon as your head hit the pillow, you were back asleep. But you're right about missing your dinner. I tried to wake you, but you said you didn't want anything to eat, you wanted to sleep. You didn't even get your pain medication because I felt it wouldn't be good for you to take it on an empty stomach. Do you remember any of this?" Marie asked, worried.

"As you were talking about it, I do remember some. When the cold milk ran down the front of me, you got a stinky dishcloth and wiped my chin and neck with it. It had a sour smell, so I hope you aren't still using it." My eyes were panning the stove and table to see if it was anywhere around.

Marie laughing said, "Stephanie, look at the pile of dirty clothes, and you'll see it. Did you think I would continue using it to clean in the kitchen?"

"Well, Marie, with the hardships of washing and drying our clothes in the chilly weather, I never know what lengths you will go to save on the amount of laundry."

Marie bent over laughing, and my father joined her. The twins, Thomas and Anna, didn't pay any attention to us as they were on the floor engaged in playing a game of jackstraws. The others—Beth, Alice, Peter, and

George—were having a fun time in the bedroom. I could hear them; talk, talk, talk, then a mixture of the boys' laughter and high-pitched squeals from the girls.

Agnes sat at the table across from me. She seemed quiet, like she was upset.

My father was sitting at the end of the table and motioned for Marie to sit down with us. Before she sat down, Marie got me a big glass of milk. I thought she must be reading my mind. I was so thirsty that I downed half of it at once. We all reached for the plate of oatmeal raisin cookies in the center of the table. I could tell Alice had made them because they were huge and had way too many raisins for my liking. Marie and I made better ones, smaller and most of the time leaving the raisins out. I put the raisins I picked out of my cookie in front of my father. He knew my dislike of them and scooped them up into his mouth without saying a word.

"Stephanie, your ride is arranged for tomorrow morning, arriving here at 9 o'clock. I am going to let Agnes explain the details as she's the one who made the arrangements," he said.

I could tell as soon as Father looked at Agnes that there was tension in the air. Something wasn't right between the two of them.

Even though Agnes turned toward me, her eyes were resting on the table in front of me. She wouldn't look straight at me. Through pursed lips, and with tension in her voice, she spoke.

"Stephanie, I want you to know that I've done the best I could in such little amount of time. I made a call to a friend of mine in the city; they're coming to pick you up. Unfortunately, they aren't returning here as their business operates out of the city. What this means is that you will have to go alone. You are a brave girl, and you'll be fine on your own. I know your father is disappointed, and Marie also had hopes of going with you, but it won't work."

She paused. "Let's all be thankful you'll be there on time. Hopefully, if we can find a vehicle to purchase, we'll make a trip to see you; that is if you stay up there long enough. I imagine you'll be transferred back this way when the doctors decide the time is right."

I got up from the table, and with Marie by my side, thanked Agnes before going back into the bedroom. We lay down, and at once Marie got so close to my ear her mouth was almost touching it.

"That rotten old bitch is so mean," she whispered. "She could've paid the driver to come back this way. My hate for that woman is so deep inside me, and nothing will ever change it."

It was my turn, so I cupped my hand over her ear and my mouth. "We can't say for sure that she's being mean. She said this was the best she could do in the short amount of time."

"Oh, no, Stephanie she did this on purpose. When are you going to stop giving her chances to prove that she has one bit of kindness in her? Agnes is evil, and she preys on kind, gentle people like you and Alex. She sees both of you as being weak. I know better. I feel your strength, and I know what you are made of, and she'll never be able to destroy you. I am different than you because I can't help but get into her game and fight back. How I wish I could throw another piss pot at her. Remember the look on her face, Stephanie?"

We both burst into laughter. With our hands over our mouths, we hoped our laughter was muffled enough so they wouldn't hear us.

"Yes, I'll never forget it. I often think back to the day when the piss pot went above and beyond its line of duty."

We laughed until tears rolled down our faces. Many ideas came to us about how we would refer to our triumphant day, and we laughed some more. Finally, we agreed that we would refer to it as "the day the piss pot showered the Devil."

Marie and I had our differences. She was quick with her temper and stubborn; I was mellow and forgiving. But the clearest similarity was our sense of humor. We laughed at the same things, even if no one else found them funny. Marie's quick temper was what kept me from telling her all my encounters with Agnes. I hadn't shared the time when Agnes called us Bohunks, nor did I share when she'd slapped me across the face. Fear of what Marie would do to Agnes kept me from telling her it all, and if the consequences were the same as what they had been for our brother Tim, I wouldn't be able to bear it. The thought of never seeing Marie again made me afraid, especially with what I would be facing in the coming days. My thoughts ran wild, and sleep wasn't easy. Morning came, and even though I was exhausted, I was anxious to get up.

Chapter 20

MARIE CAME IN as I was dressing. I knew it was she who had laid out my prettiest pink blouse with black slacks on the end of the bed. I noticed there was a packed bag on the floor. As we went out of the bedroom together, I thanked her for doing all that for me.

Breakfast was on the table; my nervousness clear as we ate in silence. My hand shook as I picked up my glass of milk and if anyone noticed, not a word was said. I was relieved; no one should have felt sorry for me as it wouldn't make any difference. I was an emotional wreck. Hoping it would help as it had before, I preached Dr. Bentley's words over and over to myself, "You will be cured."

Agnes was busy over by the stove, making pork sandwiches.

We heard the car when it arrived at 9:00 a.m. sharp. We put on our coats and boots. Father turned to Agnes and asked, "Do you have the lunch for Stephanie made?"

"It's almost ready, but I need to add some sweets. Go ahead to the car, and I'll hand it out to you."

Marie and my father accompanied me out to my ride. A black hearse. I'd never ridden in a hearse before, but it was a common way to transport patients who didn't have an immediate life-threatening issue. The male driver jumped out and opened the door to the back seat.

He put his hand out. "Good morning, Joseph, My name's Andy. Be careful now, the skiff of snow that came down last night has made it a bit slippery."

Father replied, "Good morning, Andy. This is my daughter, Marie, and this is Stephanie. She'll be the one going with you to the city. We won't be coming, even though I'm concerned that she'll be by herself. It's a huge hospital. Would I be asking too much of you to go inside the hospital with her to make sure she's in the right department? She needs to see a Dr. Douglas Huntley."

Andy smiled, reassuring my father as he looked my way. "Of course, I'll go in with her. No trouble at all."

Father and Marie took turns hugging me. As I was getting into the car, Agnes came out of the house, carrying the lunch she'd made for me. Father went toward her to take the sack, but she shook her head, and her movement toward the car told us she intended to give it to me herself.

"Here you go, Stephanie. It should keep you from starving on the trip. Good luck."

I took the sack from her. "Thank you, Agnes."

Father said that if Agnes couldn't find a vehicle to buy, he and Marie would catch the train in the next couple of days. They would stay in the city to be with me during the day.

"Oh my gosh, thank you. I'm so relieved to know I'll have both of you visiting me."

My father kissed the palm side of his hand and reached through the car window, putting it up to my forehead. "Better get on your way now. Roll up the window before you catch a cold. See you soon." As I started to roll up the window, tears filled my eyes, but I realized they were grateful tears.

Andy had to turn around in the yard before heading down the driveway, so it gave us another chance to wave goodbye. Our drive would take about two hours. Andy asked me to let him know if I was cold and needed more heat, or if I needed to stop for a bathroom break. I thanked him; I wanted to lay my head back and rest.

The motion of the car relaxed me enough to doze off. I didn't think much time had passed when I woke to Andy's coughing spell. Looking at me in the rear-view mirror, he asked, "My coughing woke you, didn't it?" Then he started hacking again.

"Oh no don't worry, I was only dozing. How much farther do we have to go?"

"I would say we will be there in another half hour," he replied.

I reached for my lunch on the seat beside me. The drawstring was pulled so tight I had to fight with it to get it undone, but when I finally did, I could smell the pork sandwich while I searched for the sweets. I was hoping Agnes had packed enough cookies for me to share with Andy, as eating in front of him and not offering something would be rude.

I pulled out the sandwich and sure enough under it were four oatmeal cookies. Andy happily accepted the two cookies I passed to him. My pork sandwich was so delicious that I devoured it and I reached into the sack for the second half. With my eyes staring ahead at the snow-covered road, my hand went into the sack to retrieve it. Not taking my eyes off the road ahead, I got it unwrapped and took a bite. Mmm, it was so good that I decided to open the end to peek in. I wanted to figure out what Agnes had put inside to make it so tasty.

That's when I spotted it. A folded piece of paper lay on my lap. I unfolded it, read it, and instantly a shudder passed through me. My throat and chest became tight. Afraid to swallow what I had in my mouth, I let it rest there. I was sure my throat wouldn't allow the food to go down. Trying to do more than breathe would have been impossible. The ball of mush in my mouth made my stomach want to heave, so I had to get it out. I spit the glob into the sack right on the two cookies.

Before I put the note into my coat pocket, I couldn't help but reread it. Her poisonous message for me, printed in black ink, read: "THIS WILL BE YOUR LAST RIDE."

My head was a thick web of fuzz that kept my thoughts from escaping. My last ride. That's when I realized I was going to die.

Chapter 21

ANDY DID AS Father asked by going with me to find Dr. Huntley before he said goodbye and wished me luck. The hospital was busy with unfamiliar sounds. Beds were being pushed from one area to another. Men and women dressed in uniforms were chatting as they moved briskly. All of them walked as if they were on an important mission, but as they approached where I was sitting, in one way or another they acknowledged my presence. Some said, "Good Day"; others smiled and nodded their heads. Even though they were too busy to stop, they didn't ignore me, and my mind started to focus on what was happening around me.

Dr. Huntley was a quick decision maker. His nurse was in the examining room with us, writing down his comments on a notepad as he examined my hip.

I was going to be having many tests done for the first two days. A diagnosis would be made after the results were known. The three of us made our way out of the examining room, and I was told to sit down in the waiting area until someone came to take me to my room. Within a few minutes, a young man dressed in hospital clothes approached me.

"Hello there. I've come to help you find your room. My name is Jackson."

"Are you a nurse?" I asked, thinking he was done talking.

Sounding annoyed, he answered, "No, I'm not a nurse. I am a medical orderly, here to assist you to your room. Let me take your bag and please follow me. Your room is on the second floor."

Jackson walked a few steps ahead. I could see his slicked-back, black hair was long enough that it touched the nape of his neck. Unfortunately, he was wearing light green, and the hairs lying on top of his shoulders were impossible to go unnoticed. There amongst the hairs that had caught my eye in the first place, laid yellowish white specks.

Afraid I might get caught, but not able to stop myself from staring; I needed to see if these specks were moving. I focused in on a small area where they were most dense. Seeing no movement, I concluded Jackson had a nasty case of dandruff or dry skin. Surely to God he had family or close friends who would be comfortable enough to tell him about his embarrassing problem.

Funny how I would notice what seemed to be his only rather disgusting physical flaw. Otherwise, he was quite handsome; with his muscular build and dark features. He never said another word until we arrived at the door to my room. He pushed the door open and motioned me to go ahead.

"This is your room." He turned his head toward the white wall where a piece of paper hung. "There are the rules of the hospital you should read." Next, his eyes focused on the nightstand. "There is another piece of paper in the top drawer of the nightstand; it will explain mealtimes, visitor's options for meals, and visiting hours. The cord between the nightstand and bed has the button you push if you need the nurse. I guess that's about it." He said, looking away.

Out he went, shutting the door behind himself, without once looking at me. I found him odd. Was he so shy that he could only look at objects? I felt sorry for him and vowed if I got a chance to be with him again, I would encourage the poor guy to talk to me.

The closet was tiny but had enough hangers for me to hang my coat and extra clothes. A green nightshirt and housecoat were both laid on the bed. I changed into the gown and crawled into the bed, noticing how crisp and white the sheets were.

The following couple of days were going to be tiring for me, with all the tests that had to be done. What was wrong with my hip and how would the doctors help me get better played on my mind. I would be relieved once I knew the answers.

Chapter 22

IT WAS LATE afternoon on the third day after all the tests were completed that Dr. Huntley came into my room. Disappointment quickly followed when he informed me that he wasn't revealing the results of the tests until my father arrived. I was still waiting. I suppose, because of my age, it wasn't legal for me to make any decisions on my own. I never asked him to explain why he needed my father present. He assured me the tests had helped him and two of his colleagues agree on the cause of my hip pain and the treatment plan. I continued to wait for my father and Marie to get there on the train.

My pain level was low since I was started on the second type of medication the first day in the hospital. Three times a day I could walk up and down the hallways. It helped to pass the time, and I enjoyed the tiny bit of interaction with some of the nurses, who were now familiar to me. Jackson walked past me several times, but he turned his head. I was convinced he didn't want to acknowledge me. When I saw him approaching on my walk, I waited until he was practically beside me before I said hello. I know he heard me, but no response. He kept walking.

The day after Dr. Huntley came to talk to me, I returned to my room from my morning walk and saw my father and Marie had arrived. Marie had my coat in her hands, and I heard my father telling her to hang it back up in the closet. When they saw me walk through the door, they both gave me a big hug; it felt wonderful to have them there as I had never been away from either of them.

After our embraces, I asked, "Why did you have my coat out of the closet?"

Her answer came quick. "We didn't find you here, so we looked to see if your coat was gone. I saw it lying on the floor, so I was hanging it back up."

Right away it came back to me. Agnes's message was inside of my coat pocket. Sharing it with Marie wasn't in the plan, at least not then. I didn't want to add more trouble to all that was already happening.

"Stephanie, come sit down," said Father. "We ran into Dr. Huntley shortly after we arrived this morning, and he talked about your hip and the plan to make you better. You do have tuberculosis in your hip. Fortunately, it hasn't spread to other areas. The damaged part of the bone must be removed but will be replaced with metal plates and screws. The surgery is scheduled for the day after tomorrow. Marie and I will stay in the city while you recuperate." He was silent for a moment.

"You'll be transported by ambulance back to Mayley Hospital when the doctors agree you're ready. It's closer to home. That way, we'll be able to visit you more often. Agnes was able to buy a vehicle for us. Do you remember Dr. Bentley? You'll be under his care while at Mayley. He's an excellent doctor, and even Nurse Atti said he's a great physician."

"Yes, Father, I remember what the nurse said about him. But right now, I am disappointed Dr. Huntley didn't wait until I was present to talk to us together. The other day he told me he would discuss my hip when we were all present. I don't understand."

He replied, "He knew Marie, and I would share the information with you. Stephanie, don't be upset by this, he's a busy doctor, and we happened upon him at the right time when he could spare a few minutes."

"Okay." I reluctantly agreed. "I'm relieved both of you are here now. That's what matters the most to me." I said. My worries melted a bit; even the fear created by the death wish in my pocket subsided to a degree.

Chapter 23

—————⊸⊙◖⊂⊚⊃◗⊙⊶—————

I WAS STANDING in a field of golden wheat. The stalks were waist deep, and a gentle breeze caused them to sway gently back and forth. It gave me the sensation that the ground was in motion. I felt unsteady as I gazed across the undulating field. Suddenly, my eyes were drawn to a movement where the crop dipped below a small rise. Something green was moving toward me. It was small at first, but became larger and appeared as though it was rising out of the field as it moved up the hill.

I was transfixed, and couldn't take my eyes off it. As it continued directly toward me, it grew larger and larger. Then, I noticed the brownish-colored rotating blades that were chewing a path through the wheat. I was paralyzed with fear. It was almost upon me. I wanted to turn and run for my life, but it felt like my feet were frozen to the ground. I couldn't move. I squeezed my eyes shut and screamed at the top of my lungs.

"Stephanie. Stephanie—everything is okay. You're fine." The words seemed to come from afar. "Stephanie, can you open your eyes and look at me? It's Doctor Huntley. Everything is okay." His voice was calming and reassuring. I could feel light pressure on my shoulder.

Slowly, I opened my eyes. A blurry figure dressed in a green gown and cap was leaning over me. His hand rested on my shoulder. I started to survey my surroundings. Blades, brown blades. I closed my eyes and cried out, "No, God. Please, no."

Again, the soft voice. "It's okay, Stephanie. It's Doctor Huntley. You're in the recovery room in the hospital. You had your hip surgery. Everything went fine with the operation. You're safe. Can you look at me again?"

My head was full of emotion and confusion. I felt terrified. The hand on my shoulder gave a gentle squeeze. I opened my eyes. I stared at the figure dressed in green. My vision cleared, and I could see Dr. Huntley's kind face looking at me. I looked around the room. The walls were a pale yellow. Then I noticed the ceiling fan, with its brown blades turning slowly. I let out a small gasp.

"There, there, Stephanie. You're a brave young lady. Coming out of anesthetic can often be upsetting. You'll feel much better in a little while. We'll give you something for pain as it is needed. You need to rest now. Later, the nurse will bring you something light to eat. Have small amounts of water in the meantime. I'll be back to check on you in an hour or so."

The realization that I was safe overwhelmed me. I felt dizzy, and the lower part of my body seemed to be numb. I sighed and drifted off to sleep, feeling relieved that Dr. Huntley had said the surgery was a success.

∾

My entire left leg was in a cast. Nurses came in and moved it every few hours. I rang for them when Mother Nature called, as getting the commode in precisely the right position seemed to be an art. We had to make sure none of my body waste got on the plaster cast. They gave me a sponge bath every morning.

Father and Marie stayed by my side for a week after the surgery. Then they returned for a short visit two weeks later. That was the day Dr. Huntley gave us the news. He was arranging for me to be sent to Mayley Hospital in three days. My father and Marie both said they would be there, waiting for my arrival.

The worst part was behind me. The surgery was over, and I was going to be closer to my family. Nurse Viviana and Dr. Bentley were both so kind. Not that I didn't have nice people around me then; except for Jackson, who made a point of always being stuck up. Our little hospital with less staff was much more personable.

The nurse came in bright and early for my morning bath on the day I was leaving. My breakfast of perfectly poached eggs, with the yolks still runny, so that I could spread it on my toast, came early enough not to feel rushed. I was happy that nurses stopped in to say their goodbyes and wish me well before I left.

When Dr. Huntley popped in, he put his hand on my shoulder and said, "I am happy to release you today Stephanie. I know how much better it will be, closer to family and friends. My advice is to be patient and allow yourself time to heal; that will give you the best result. You have incredible strength, young lady, and I know you'll come back from this experience stronger than ever. Take good care and please pass a hello to Dr. Bentley for me."

All I could do was smile and nod at him. The lump in my throat wouldn't allow my words of gratitude to be spoken. This man had saved my life.

Jackson, along with a nurse I had never seen before brought in a stretcher. It took the two of them longer to agree on how to move me over to the stretcher than it took to do the actual task. I complimented them on how painless it was for me once I was settled. The nurse smiled, and I could tell she was pleased, even though she never said a word. She walked out of the room, leaving me alone with Jackson. I wondered about her working relationship with him because she showed no connection through her body language, and there was no verbal exchange.

"I'll get your belongings from the closet. Is there anything else I need to pack up for you?" Jackson asked in his loud, deafening voice.

"There are things in the top drawer of the nightstand. Thank you, Jackson," I replied in my most pleasant way.

I started making small talk as he pushed me down the hallway. I told him how happy and excited I was to be going closer to home. I shared my hopes with him about how my stay in the hospital would be relatively short, and I would return home good as new.

It seemed as though Jackson became agitated as he started pushing me faster toward the elevator. Once inside, as the door slid closed, his unbearably offensive words came crashing in on me.

"Don't you realize you'll be in the hospital for months with the cast on, from your hip down to your foot? Oh, they'll change it and x-ray your hip, but you'll wear a cast and be hospitalized for a long time. Don't expect to be the same as you were once you're released, or think you'll ever be treated the way you were.

"You'll be a cripple for the rest of your life. People will either feel sorry for you or look down on you because your body won't be as beautiful. Physically, you'll be limited. When little children see you, fear will make them shy away from you, and they'll innocently ask their parents why you walk the way you do, or why your legs aren't the same size. Some people will even think of you as being a freak of nature. I am telling you this, so you'll know what to expect."

My heart was breaking as the elevator doors opened. We were moving toward the ambulance that was waiting for me. As soon as I knew, I wouldn't be alone with Jackson ever again, as the two men were opening the back door of the ambulance, I took the opportunity to tell him how I felt.

I motioned for him to stand by my side. He walked over to me, and looking into his coal-black eyes it happened; I let my feelings fly. "Jackson, you're a lying bastard. Get your dandruff-ridden hair out of my sight."

He walked away with a smirk on his face.

Chapter 24

———∘◦⌾◦∘———

AS MY FATHER had promised, both he and Marie were at the Mayley Hospital. I saw them as we drove by the front entrance and I wondered how long they had been waiting.

I was embarrassed when Nurse Viviana greeted us because I couldn't remember her last name or her nickname—it hadn't been that long ago.

"Welcome, Stephanie. You can call me Nurse Atti. Everyone else does, and I'm quite alright with it."

"It's good to have you back, Stephanie," said Dr. Bentley who was also there. "Nurse Atti and I will be looking after you through your time of recovery."

I smiled and nodded. "I'm happy to be back."

Dr. Bentley shifted his attention to my father and Marie, and politely asked, "Do you mind giving us some time to get Stephanie settled into her room?"

As he turned to Nurse Atti, I couldn't help but notice his innocent, boyish grin, and the twinkle in his eyes. He touched her shoulder, and in more of a questioning tone than a demanding one, asked her to help get me settled.

She responded with softness in her voice. "Of course, Doctor."

Even if the two of them hadn't communicated a single word, I would've put the pieces together. Their bodies told me the relationship was more than a professional one. I thought back to what Marie told me about female and male attractions. How mutual chemistry is undeniable when two people are drawn to each other, and this was what I was witnessing. I guessed these two were in love.

Nurse Atti pushed me down the hallway, coming to a stop at the very end. As she maneuvered the stretcher through the door, she announced in a cheery tone, "Stephanie, this will be your room while you're with us. It's a private room and the nicest we have."

I perched myself up on the stretcher, so I could have the best view of what would be my new home for the next little while. The bathroom was to the left of the small entrance. I saw a bed with a nightstand and two chairs next to it, and then a short wall projecting into the room. I wondered why it was there. Nurse Atti must've read my mind because she explained that the partition was a narrow closet. I could see the foot of another bed on the other side of the closet. There was a large window on the wall alongside that bed. Nurse Atti must've been following my eyes as she was quick to explain that the bed wouldn't be used by anyone unless my family needed to stay overnight.

She explained there was a street lamp outside the window and it shone the perfect amount of light to my bed, but it was way too bright for the bed beside the window. The closet did a great job of blocking the daylight that was streaming in. Also, the window frosted badly in the winter months, and there was a problem with a cold draft on windy days. As a result, the bed was seldom, if ever, used for patient care.

Nurse Atti called for help to get me transferred to my bed. As we waited, I noticed my coat and bag of clothes were at the foot of the stretcher. Agnes's unforgettable note was still haunting me.

"Nurse Atti, could you please hand me my coat?"

"Of course, Stephanie," and with a little chuckle, "I don't think you'll need it for a while, though, but here you go."

"I want to search the pockets. There should be a piece of paper in there." I went through the two pockets twice, giving each pocket a good swiping with my fingers. The note wasn't there. If it was merely lost, that was one thing, but if Marie or my father had taken it the day they were alone in my room, I knew they'd eventually want to talk about the horrible message. Both would be hurt and angry with Agnes. I decided to wait to see if either of them brought it up.

I handed my coat back to Nurse Atti, and she hung it up along with my other clothes in the closet. She put my boots in the bottom of the closet. As she was closing it, in walked an older nurse. With a little effort, they worked together to shift me onto my bed. The other nurse left, and Nurse Atti stayed so she could check my vitals.

I got the conversation started with a simple question. "Nurse Atti, have you been working with Dr. Bentley for long?"

She smiled, "No, not really. I've only been here for a couple of months. I live with my aunt and uncle. I was sent here by my mother and stepfather, who thought it would be great for me to experience another country. I was fortunate to be hired here at the Mayley Hospital. I'm so busy that I don't miss my home near as much as I thought I would," she said, sighing. "My aunt and uncle are kind to me, and I can tell they enjoy me living with them. Sad as it sounds, I was in the way once my mother married my stepfather."

I couldn't help but hear the resentment in her voice.

"You asked me about working with Dr. Bentley, and I rambled off in another direction. He was here when I arrived, and he gained my respect within weeks. He cares about his patients and those of us who work beside him."

"I hope I am not too forward in asking, but do you know him on a personal level?"

"No, but he has told me enough, and from watching him, I know he is a passionate man. Being a doctor is his first passion, and I witness it when we work together. His feelings are genuine, and he has an earnest desire to help others. When he shares his stories of riding his horse, you can hear the excitement in his voice. He has a likable, quirky sense of humor. Settling down is not in his thoughts at all. He makes it clear. He's a free spirit. He likes to roam. It's a shame because he would be a great catch for anyone who is looking for a husband. Isn't he the most handsome man you've ever seen?"

Nurse Atti caught me off guard with her question.

"Well, I haven't had a chance to study his face much, but I did notice he has a particular way of looking at you. His face lights up with a boyish grin whenever you're in the room." I replied.

"I know what you mean," she said, smiling. "I'd be lying if I told you I hadn't noticed. The truth is I have his every facial feature etched into my brain. He resembles a famous movie star. Ummm, right now I can only remember the first name is Cary, and he is a dreamboat. Dr. Bentley has all the same features: light brown eyes, the dimple in his chin, the perfectly matched deep lines that start under his high cheekbones and don't disappear until they meet his jaw. His smooth, plump lips that I am sure bring hypnotic pleasure."

It was like Nurse Atti was in a trance when she described Dr. Bentley. Suddenly, she came back to reality and realized she was sharing too much.

"Please Stephanie, don't ever mention a word to anyone about what I shared." Her pleading eyes searched for my reassurance, and I gave it to her. I made a promise never to tell a soul. Nurse Atti thanked me and said, "I like you already. We're going to enjoy our time together while you are here getting better."

I smiled. "I knew when I first saw you Nurse Atti that you're a kind caring person, and because of this, you are a great nurse. How many weeks do you think I'll be here?"

"I can't answer that, Stephanie, but I'm sure Dr. Bentley will give you an idea. If he doesn't come by later today, he'll see you in the morning," she said, as she turned toward the door. "I'll tell your family you're ready for them to come in. If you need me, pull the call line; otherwise, I'll stop by before I finish my shift to say goodnight." She gave a wave as she left.

The head of my bed was raised, and I had two pillows stuffed behind me, so I was in a sitting position. It was only then that I noticed the mirror opposite my bed. Because of where it was placed on the wall, when I looked into it, I could see what was on the other side of the partition. There was a bed with two pillows, a nightstand on the left side, and on the right, a gray cloth-covered chair. So there were three seats all together for my visitors.

I could hear Marie and Father's voices coming down the hallway. When the three of us were finally alone in my room, there was no silence; they had a lot of family news to tell me.

Peter and Beth were planning to get married within days. Agnes had purchased a piece of land only a couple of miles from our farm. There was a small but adequate house on the property that was perfect for them. But this wasn't all the news. Agnes had also purchased land across from Peter and Beth's property and eventually George and Alice would build a house on that land. They were also planning to wed but hadn't set a date yet. The plan was for them to live with Peter and Beth while their house was being built.

I knew this would be a welcome change for my younger brothers and little Anna. Not only would they have more living space, but they'd also be close to their older siblings for visits. Marie wouldn't have to work as hard trying to keep all of them fed and in clean clothes, and nor would I, once I returned. It was all good news. I did have a little chuckle, thinking about stepsister Beth now being my sister-in-law, and stepbrother George soon to be my brother-in-law.

We said our goodbyes when we heard the announcement that visiting hours were over, and my father and Marie promised they would return when they could.

Chapter 25

———∘◦⬅️◦∘———

THE FOLLOWING MORNING, while I was eating breakfast, Dr. Bentley came in. He pulled up the gray chair alongside my bed and sat down. I couldn't help but notice those features Nurse Atti pointed out.

"Good morning, Stephanie. I hope you slept well," he said, pausing long enough for me to smile and nod. "Nurse Atti had mentioned that you were asking about how long you would be staying here . . . I cannot give you an honest answer right now." He paused again. "What I can say is that it won't be measured in weeks but rather in months."

"Months? Why that long?" I asked.

"You've had a serious operation. The healing will take time. New bone has to grow around the metal plate and screws. The cast will restrict your movements, so that's why you must stay in bed. The infected bone was removed, and I don't think tuberculosis will return, but we will x-ray and monitor the area. I'm afraid all this will take time."

I had to ask the question. "Will I be crippled?"

"I am not sure what you mean by crippled. You're young and not finished growing. The left leg will grow, but not as much as your right leg. You'll have a limp. Your mobility in that hip will be limited. It will be stiff. You'll need rehabilitation once the cast is removed." He took a deep breath. "I understand your concern, but you must focus on how fortunate you are. This operation saved your life even though it means an extended stay in the hospital."

"I know. I have to concentrate on how grateful I am and stop thinking about the negative. It won't get me anywhere," I said, feeling a little more

89

down then I let on. "Oh, I almost forgot. Dr. Huntley asked me to pass a hello to you," I said, changing the conversation.

"Thanks, Stephanie. Dr. Huntley is admired by many of his colleagues, including me. He's one of the best surgeons in the country. I must continue my rounds now, but I will hopefully have some spare time to share my latest horse adventures with you. The nurses will get you out of your room for a while. We have a nice sitting area that can accommodate your bed. I am sure you'll enjoy it. There are always people coming and going from there, so you will have company, and that should help your days go by more quickly. See you soon," and with that, he left.

That's when I realized uncontrollable tears were pouring down my cheeks. Nurse Atti appeared and without reservation came over and cradled me in her arms. "Oh, my poor girl. There, there, now. You've been through so much. Let it all out, Stephanie, and you'll feel better."

My head was resting on her shoulder with one of her hands on the back of my head, the other circling along my back. The emotions coming from the pit of my stomach made my whole body shake. I had so much piled up inside. Even though I wasn't close to pouring it all out, I started to feel more and more relieved.

It was me who first saw Dr. Bentley come back into the room. With concern, he asked, "What's going on here Nurse Atti? Is everything okay?"

"Yes, Doctor. Stephanie's having a difficult time working through her emotions, and I'm comforting her."

"I understand. Please take the time you need," he commented, as he left my room.

Our embrace had been broken when we heard Dr. Bentley come in. Nurse Atti could see my sorrowful, troubled eyes, as I could see hers. We both sat for a while before she broke the silence with her concerning question.

"Stephanie, why are you so sad?" She paused, but when I didn't respond, she asked again, "Stephanie, please talk to me. Are you afraid of what Dr. Bentley told you?"

"It's so difficult for me to accept what he told me. But that's only part of it. Someone at the university hospital tried to tell me what I'd be facing now, but I didn't believe him. I thought he was lying to hurt me. I acted out toward him in a cruel way. It felt good to unload on him at the time. But now I feel so horrible inside. Perhaps he was right," I said, looking down.

I never shared all my thoughts with Nurse Atti because I didn't know if she would understand, but I knew my rage toward Jackson was brought on by the master himself; the Devil had filled me with fear.

"Stephanie, I'm sure you didn't mean any harm. You were only protecting yourself, or so you thought at the time. Maybe you just have a tender heart. We all make mistakes. No one is perfect."

"Thanks, Nurse Atti," I replied in the most convincing voice I could muster. "I'll work on putting it behind me. What's done is done. I can't take it back."

Later that day, I went to the sitting room. A cloudless sky meant the winter sun was beating in through the windows, and I found it enjoyable sitting and looking at magazines. Up to this point in my life, I was satisfied being able to read enough simple words to get by, but looking at the intriguing pictures in the magazines got me starting to think that my level of reading wasn't going to be enough. I wished I could read and understand all the stories in these magazines, and a burning desire began to grow.

The night was upon us, and I was looking forward to sleep when Nurse Atti asked how I enjoyed my day. I expressed my feelings of regret about my reading level. When I explained that I only had a grade four level of education and was disappointed that I couldn't read every single word, she got excited and told me that she could teach me. It would have to be on her own time when she was off duty. Both of us got excited as she talked about the plan to bring in some books. A new challenge was what I needed. She helped me get ready for bed. Before she left, I asked if she would mind pulling the curtain to have it encircle my bed.

"Sure, Stephanie I will do that, but why do you want to hide behind the curtain?"

"What a way to look at it, Nurse Atti. I'm not hiding. I'll hear less of the noises outside my room. And yes, I guess I'm hoping that having it surround me makes it more cozy and private."

She glided the curtain along the one side of my bed around to the foot. Next, she pulled the second curtain down the other side to enclose the bed. They didn't quite meet so I could see the large mirror on the opposite side of the room through the crack in the curtain. The reflection in the mirror gave a full view into the room behind the partition.

Nurse Atti bid me goodnight, telling me to have a good rest and that she would see me the next day. She was correct in saying the other side of the partition was well lit up by the street lamp in the parking lot. I could see the nightstand, bed, and gray chair in the mirror. The amount of light coming through to my side of the room was perfect.

I looked at my surroundings more closely as I lay in my bed. It was then I realized the curtain that enclosed my bed was white. A sudden uncontrollable feeling of peacefulness descended upon me. My Matka was here reaching out to me from beyond the white curtain, and I suddenly felt empowered.

Chapter 26

DAYS HAD GONE by without any of my family coming to visit. My reading lessons had begun. One Sunday, Viviana and I were sitting in the sunroom working on my reading and writing skills. Nurse Atti requested that I use her first name when we were alone. It was proper since we had become friends and were growing closer to each other the more time we spent together.

When Viviana realized I had three visitors, she gathered the books and was going to leave. I stopped her, feeling it would be rude not to introduce her. "Nurse Atti, this is my second oldest sister Alice and her fiancé George. And," … with my eyebrows and shoulders raised in a quizzical way George took over introducing the stranger who was with them.

"This is Adam Panchyk. He has been a friend of mine for many, many years. We go to the same church. After the service today, we invited Adam along to meet you, Stephanie," said George. Adam shook Nurse Atti's hand and then mine.

Viviana wasn't in uniform as it was her day off, so of course, Alice questioned why she was with me, and what we were doing with the books. I explained that we had become friends and the books were some pictures from Italy where she grew up. It wasn't a total lie because Viviana did show me some photos of the beautiful place where she had been raised. When it came to Alice, the less information she knew about me, the better. I wasn't in the mood to be questioned to death by her. She liked to bully her way around, so I had learned to sit and listen, knowing better than to share my thoughts with her. Alice made it easy.

"How are you feeling, Stephanie?"

There was a two-second pause.

"You look terrific, well-rested, and color in your cheeks. How long will you be staying in here?"

A short pause, with no time to answer, even if I wanted, before she began again.

"I don't know why I asked you that. I heard from Marie it would be measured in months, with no precise timing yet."

Next came her third question; I was silently counting.

"When do you think you'll need your hair trimmed? I remember Marie saying she was going to cut your hair the next time she came to see you."

Poor George and funny little Adam didn't even try to get a word in. I suppose they knew Alice as well as I did. She rambled on for another hour or so. I can honestly say I'm not sure about what because I was off in another world, practicing the new spelling words Viviana had taught me.

"Stephanie, did you hear me? I said we must leave now. Our visit is over for today, but we'll be back another day... What is wrong with you? This is the second time I 'm telling you that we're leaving."

"I'm sorry, Alice. My mind must have wandered off for a few minutes," I lied.

Adam may have talked before then, but I wasn't sure. He got up from the chair and walked over to me.

"I enjoyed meeting you, Stephanie. I wonder if I can come back to visit another day?"

The softness in his voice gave me the feeling he was a kind-natured man. I could see the shyness in him when he looked at me.

The three of them were waiting in anticipation for my answer. Did anyone think I could say no at this point? Looking back, I wish I would have politely made up an excuse, any excuse, even a lame one as to why I didn't want visitors. I was trapped into seeing this new friend. Strange as it sounds, when thinking back, I often wondered how my life would have turned out had I answered plain and straightforward, *NO, I don't want visitors.*

It was early afternoon a few days later when I woke up from an afternoon nap. With my eyes still adjusting to the light, I caught a glimpse of movement in the mirror. I realized quickly there was someone on the other side of the closet, sitting on the chair by the bed, twiddling his thumbs. As I was getting ready to scream, I recognized Adam.

Not knowing what else to do, I coughed to get his attention. I watched him in the mirror as he looked up and I could see the eagerness in his eyes.

"Hello, Stephanie. I hope you don't mind I stopped by to visit. When I found you sleeping, I decided to sit and wait until you woke up."

"Hello, Adam. How long have you been here?" I questioned in a bit of an intentionally annoying tone. It didn't sit well with me, knowing he'd been in my room, watching me while I slept.

Looking down at his watch, he said, "Close to an hour, and at first, I sat there by you. But, I realized how frightened you might be when you woke up, so I moved to the other side of the partition."

I nodded my head, thinking Adam was too bold, and I didn't like it. "If you decide to revisit me and I'm asleep, I prefer you wake me up."

"Yes, Stephanie, if it happens again I'll wake you. Is now a good time to visit?"

I pointed at the chair for him to sit down. His voice was clear, light, and pleasant. Adam had appealing, large brown eyes with dark lashes that were overpowered by his thick, unkempt, bristly black eyebrows. His cheekbones were broad and prominent. I suppose he didn't need to go for a haircut often, as he hardly had any hair on the top of his oddly shaped head. I couldn't help picturing him with a hat on as it would be a welcoming change to his appearance. A lingering smile on his thin lips and the look in his eyes told me I was right about my first impression; he was a good person who needed a friend.

Adam was a talker, and I found myself astonished as I listened to his life story. His English was perfect, but at times, when he got excited about sharing a story with me, a touch of his Ukrainian heritage slang came through. It would happen when he talked quickly and wasn't self-conscious about his words. Even before I asked him if he could speak Ukrainian, I knew what his answer would be. Polish and Ukrainian were close, and I knew we would be able to have a conversation in either language or a combination of the two.

Adam had a small house on farmland located only two miles north of town. As my home was fifteen miles south, we didn't live far apart. His place was paid for because he'd had it for several years. He was fortunate, being employed on the rails doing maintenance.

Everything was in order. He was living a content life. Besides the shape of his head, there was another thing I found odd. He was thirty-two years old and had never married. Would his flattened head keep the ladies at bay? It was so noticeable that it could be a good reason for some women to run in the opposite direction. As I sat in my hospital room with Adam, I realized that my strongest connection with him was because of his far from perfect skull. I found myself looking past it, and hoped that people in my life would be able to accept me. The fact was that I'd become a cripple, and I hoped others would look past it too.

Chapter 27

MARCH 20TH, MY 15th birthday. I thought back to before Matka passed on and what a difference to how we, as a family, celebrated. Our family didn't have cake. We celebrated in a unique way. Matka and Tata would talk about how we came into the world. I could never figure out how they didn't mix us up. They remembered the arrival time, who cried the loudest or longest, and even who was the bluest. I knew I was born at 1:00 p.m. during a spring snowstorm, the wet and heavy kind that can happen in late March.

Matka talked several times about how much long black hair I had when I was born. At first, they didn't realize it because my hair was plastered down to my head. When I was cleaned up, the hair poked up and out making me look like a little old lady. I never understood how a newborn baby could look like an old lady. A birthday didn't go by without us hearing about these beautiful reminders. We were all reassured how much Matka and Tata felt each of us was their blessing. It all stopped after Matka passed. We continued to acknowledge each other's day of birth, but that was as far as it went.

I was hoping some of my family and friends would come by to see me, but I knew there was a good possibility that wouldn't happen. They were busy with life, and with me being in the hospital, I could understand it being forgotten. That was lingering in my mind when in came Nurse Atti. She was followed by other hospital staff, which included nurses, Dr. Bentley, and Dr. Owen. (Dr. Owen was a well-liked doctor who had recently come from the city to settle in our small town. His children were grown, and as he and his wife wanted the quiet life, they loved living in Mayley.) Nelly and Pete came in next, followed by Adam and all my family; they kept coming. I realized soon that Agnes wasn't part of the celebration. But why would she be? She'd wished death upon me. I bet she was at home sulking.

As everyone was finding a spot in my room, Viviana's Aunt Angela arrived, carrying the most beautifully decorated cake. It had chocolate icing with pieces of fruit around the base. I was touched to think they came to see me. Adam brought a box of chocolate-covered cherries. There was lots of laughter. Sharing stories made it a fun time in my otherwise dull day. The hospital staff stayed long enough to enjoy some of the delicious cake but then had to leave. My family stayed for a while longer, but then Father said that he had some errands to run.

"I'll be back soon. Happy birthday, my girl. You'll always be my little girl even though I see you are becoming the most beautiful woman. You are so much like your Matka." Father looked at Marie and told her to stay, that he would return for her a little later.

"That would be wonderful," Marie replied. Before she even started telling me what was going on at home, I had sensed there was a problem. Father looked like he lacked sleep and I could feel the tension.

"Oh, Stephanie, things aren't right at home," she began.

"What do you mean?"

"Well, something is wrong between Father and Agnes. He tries to hide it, but he can't fool me. During the day, he doesn't even look at her, let alone talk to her. It really gets bad after they go into their bedroom. First the whispering, then it gets louder. They can't control their anger.

"The one night I heard him asking Agnes why she would do such a cruel thing. She got all fired up and kept repeating that she hadn't done anything. Next, she accused him of making up lies to get rid of her. Almost every night, Agnes gets up and comes to the empty bed across the room from Anna and me. I don't know what has happened between them. I would have a difficult time believing that Father has discovered what a whore Agnes is."

"How would he have found out about Alex? Do you think either Alex or his wife would have told him?"

"It's hard to say. We'll never know. When I went to pay a visit to Alex and Grace, their landlord told me they'd moved, but he couldn't tell me where to."

"Really, they moved? I guess we shouldn't be surprised. Think about the trouble they had living there all because of that she-devil."

"I agree, and why would they stay around here? Father is extremely upset with Agnes, but it can't be because he knows about Alex. Remember how we both agreed that if he ever found out, there would be more than squabbling between them. We both know our father is as gentle as any man could ever be but equally as proud." Marie paused, chuckling, she added, "If he knew the truth about Agnes, he would throw her out the door, wearing that piss pot for the second time." The vivid memory was there for both of us, and we laughed hysterically.

Our conversation made me tense, and our laughter was a welcome relief. "What you are saying makes sense, Marie."

What if this is because of the note? The thought reeled around in my head. Perhaps my father had found it. I had the perfect opportunity to share Agnes's death wish for me with Marie, but I kept my mouth shut. I couldn't deal with that right then.

Chapter 28

———————$\rightarrow\circ\mathcal{LED}\circ\leftarrow$———————

WATCHING DR. BENTLEY and Nurse Atti together was great entertainment. Their relationship with each other was natural and comfortable. They were often teasing each other, and they brought me into their fun whenever they could.

One morning, when Nurse Atti came into my room, she asked if I would mind if she offered Dr. Bentley a chocolate from the box still sitting on the nightstand.

"Of course," I answered. "I'd love to share them." She smiled, popping one into her mouth.

Her opportunity came along later in the day. They were both in my room, and Dr. Bentley had gloves on while examining my foot, which appeared a little more swollen than usual.

Viviana went over and took a chocolate from the box. She turned, and when close enough to his mouth, said, in a teasing way, "Open."

It seemed as though he knew better than to hesitate. His mouth opened in time to barely catch the chocolate-covered cherry. As he bit into it, some of the sweet sticky syrup ran down his chin. He didn't have time to feel embarrassed.

"Oh here, I can help you with that." She put her finger on his dimpled chin, where the syrup rested. She wiped it up and put her syrup-covered finger in her mouth. "Mmm, thanks for sharing."

He never said a word, but his eyes were filled with lust for her and I could tell that she knew it.

It was the start of my realization that I was witnessing passion between them. They tried to pass off their physical attraction for each other as having fun, but I knew differently. What I didn't realize was how the two of them would be a vital part of awakening my sexual curiosity.

I was about to see more than I ever should have. My only experience of seeing how boys were built differently was catching a glimpse of my younger brothers naked. I was aware of my own body, and I did what came naturally to please myself. Until that day, I'd never known what it was like to create fantasies in my mind. Seeing for the first time two people together, doing it, changed me. It was a part of me that was gone. I realized my innocence had been taken away by Viviana and Dr. Bentley.

I never heard them come in, as I slept soundly. They knew this about me, which was why they chose my room. Then, again, maybe I was wrong; maybe they never thought about it at all. Once they were in my room, there was no turning back. They tried, but their desire for each other made it impossible.

It was getting close to morning, but not yet time for the sun to peek into my room. I woke, thinking my position was what made me come out of my deep sleep. I needed to change it up, so my hip would get some relief. That's when I saw movement in my mirror. I could see it was Viviana and Dr. Bentley. I had to strain my ears to hear what they were saying. Even though the curtains were encircling me in my bed, the crack was there, allowing a perfect view of the two of them in the mirror.

I could hear aggravation as he whispered, "I see how he looks at you . . . and you smiling at him and teasing him. You're giving him what he wants. You have been acting inappropriately. You need to stop."

Just as heatedly and with her hot Italian blood, she was ready to spit fire. "What I do is none of your business. He's told me that I'm attractive and smart. He loves me and would do anything for me. You're right. I do give him what he wants. He's the kindest man I have ever known."

"Look at me, Viviana, and tell me you love him." He waited, but she didn't answer.

"He's at least twice your age. He's a married man who's never going to leave his wife. He has children who are grown adults. Of course, you would be a prize for him. Doesn't it bother you what people will say when this comes out?"

He hit a nerve. I could tell she was thinking.

"I've already told you that what I do is none of your business. I don't have to guess about his feelings. He has said how much he wants me. He isn't all about boyish grins and game playing. He's a real man," she said sharply. "You've made it clear you don't want a lasting relationship, so why do you care? You're happy with the way things are between us. I need more."

As she turned to leave, and I was about to shut my eyes so I wouldn't be caught, I saw his hand grab her slender arm. I thought she was going to slap him.

I could only see the side of her face, but it was enough to make me understand how she had changed. Anger and tension were draining away. His eyes engaged hers; I knew he wasn't finished. His hand quickly cradled the back of her head. Close enough to feel each other's breathing; I was expecting them to kiss. Neither of them willing to make the first move, his hand dropped away from the back of her head. She turned to leave. I shut my eyes and kept them shut until I knew he had followed her out the door.

Only a half hour or so had passed. I didn't hear the door open, but I knew it had as I could see light from the hallway. I could see in the mirror they had returned. I wanted to watch.

He was sitting on the edge of the bed. His hands were on her waist while she was standing between his knees. With her hand on the nape of his neck, she pulled him closer. I'm sure he could hear her heart beating. Tenderly, he looked up at her, and with his hands still around her slender waist he stood up. Their eyes never left each other. She reached down to feel him, unzipping his trousers.

She gently pushed his chest. Silently, he sat back down again on the edge of the bed. I could see that she had exposed him.

As she kneeled between his legs, he reached for the pillow at the head of the bed and tossed it on the floor, so her knees could rest on it. Her hand was wrapped around his manhood. He was looking down into her eyes. Both were knowing what was coming.

She put her tongue on it. Her head tilted back just enough to watch him while her tongue moved slowly over the end of it. I heard him, "Viviana, take me farther."

She did, he watched her, and so did I. Her movements became faster until it happened. Only then did his eyes close. His head tilted back, off to one side. His back arched and his pelvis came forward. I heard him call out with a groan, then, "Oh Viviana." He'd lost all control. She never moved, except to lay her head on his thigh.

I needed to clear my throat, but I didn't dare. I thought they were done, but then I saw his hands move.

He reached down, removing the elastic from her hair. When he got it loose, she reached up before her hair could completely fall and brought it over her shoulder.

Looking up at him she whispered, "What are you doing?"

"I want to make it perfect for you." He used his hand to bring himself back for her. She watched him as he slipped her elastic over the top of it and worked it all the way down as far as it would go. I didn't understand what he was doing.

Looking down at his hardened manhood, giggling a bit, she asked him, "Why did you put my elastic on it?"

With a smile, he answered, "This is my second time. I didn't come prepared, but your elastic will do the job. It will keep me harder for longer, for as long as you need."

She stood up. He kicked away the pillow she had been kneeling on. Still sitting, he pulled her in close and lifted her uniform up to her waistline. His hands were cupping her rear. He kissed down between her thighs. She pulled away long enough to remove her panties. Then his tongue was on her until she pleaded, "I want you inside of me."

She knelt over him. I could see her hand guiding him in. Both of his hands still holding her rear until she reached around and brought one to the front of her.

"This is where I want your fingers. Yes … right there, don't stop."

His answer was quick, "I won't. Let yourself go."

With her hands on his shoulders, I could see it was her who had control. I saw her back arch, and her whole body stiffen as she let out a soft, musical sigh. She lifted herself enough to free him, and I could see he was still hard.

Her hands now in front were busy. I saw her use the elastic which she had removed from him to tie up her hair, so it was off her neck.

Even after they left, what I saw didn't leave me. I played their lovemaking over and over in my head until I fell asleep. Then I dreamed.

I was lying in a bed I didn't recognize, yet it seemed eerily familiar. A baby blue sheet, light and airy, covered my naked body. Something was pushing up against my arm. I heard a familiar voice asking me to feel his private parts with my hand. I couldn't see who it was, but I recognized the voice. Again, he told me to feel him, not where I could already feel it touching me but to take it into my hand. Without hesitation, I answered, "No."

His hand started coming under the sheet toward my closed legs but stopped when he sensed I didn't want him touching me there. He wanted to know why he couldn't touch me because he wanted to so badly.

"I don't even know you, and we shouldn't be doing this."

"Yes, you know me. Look at me now. I'm with you. It's Jackson."

When I woke, I couldn't deny what had happened. Never had I felt such intense pleasure without being touched. It was why I called my dream, "A gift from my brain."

But then came, the question—*Why him? Why was Jackson in my erotic dream?* I pushed the thought out of my head.

∾

I couldn't forget seeing Dr. Bentley and Viviana making love. The next few times they came around me, I felt squeamish. My guilt for watching them was the cause of how I felt for the first little while. I could tell things had changed between them. They weren't as close to each other. It surprised me. I was curious about what was going on between the two of them. At times, they ignored being in each other's presence.

I also couldn't push their argument out of my mind. Viviana, clearly, had another man. A much older man, of whom Dr. Bentley didn't approve. I would find out eventually, but I knew I'd have to wait until Viviana wanted to talk.

Three weeks after seeing them together, Viviana came into my room to help me with my reading. After we worked for an hour or so, she went over to the other bed and lay down. I could see her in the mirror and hoped she wouldn't figure out that I could watch her from my bed.

"Are you okay, Viviana?" I asked. "You don't seem yourself lately."

"I am feeling tired lately, and I have lots on my mind," she replied, with a troubled sigh. "Don't tell anyone, but I'm thinking of going back to Italy."

"Really? Viviana, I'm surprised. I thought you loved your life here. What about your job and your feelings for Dr. Bentley? I thought maybe you and he would ..."

Viviana cut me off. "Remember when I told you that my mother had married, and I was in their way? Well, there's more to it than that. You see, Stephanie, my stepfather did some horrible things to me." She closed her eyes. "When I told my mother, she refused to believe me. That's why they sent me away, and I ended up coming to live with my aunt. Regardless, I miss my home, and I want to go back."

"Are you telling me that your stepfather was abusive?" When I asked the question, I saw her put her hand on her forehead.

"Yes, he did some stuff to me, touching me in places he never should've. He's a sick man, but my mother doesn't see it. He is wealthy, and he buys her whatever she wants. She only believes what she wants to."

"What would be different now if you go back? Do you think he's changed?"

Her voice quivered. "Everything's changed with me, and that's all that matters. He won't want to touch me, now. I told my mother that I was coming home, but she didn't sound pleased. She even offered to send more money to keep me here, but I need to get back to my roots.

"As far as Dr. Bentley goes he's a free spirit who doesn't want to settle down. Have you noticed how he is flirting with Mary, the new nurse? It makes me sick to watch him carry on with her. She'll be his next one." She paused. "I've thought about warning her, but there's no use. She won't listen anyway. I feel sorry for her. Maybe I should warn her. He doesn't matter to me anymore. I have to accept my part. I was a fool to let him play with my head. I don't think I can trust a man ever again."

I could tell Viviana was done talking. She sat up on the bed and slowly got up to join me. She looked tired and drained, and I wondered if it was because of stress. What a difficult decision it would be for her as to whether to return home. Viviana sounded confident that if she went back home, her stepfather would no longer bother her.

Chapter 29

————⊸∘⊂⬤∘⊸————

THE FOLLOWING DAY, my father and Marie came for a visit. After Father stayed for a while, he usually went to do some errands, and this day was no different.

As soon as he left, Marie talked as fast as she could "Stephanie, I have so much to tell you. Things have gotten worse between the two of them. They don't even sleep together anymore."

"Have you figured out what the problem is? It's carried on for a couple of months now, so whatever it is, I would guess it's never going away."

As I talked, I thought about the note. Unless someone brought it up in conversation, I wasn't going to talk about it. I wasn't sure whether it was a right decision or not, but it seemed to me it was the best thing to do.

"I heard them in an argument a couple of days ago. They were both in the kitchen, and she said, "You should be ashamed of yourself.""

His reply came with a grunt, "What about you Agnes? Are you ashamed? I can't believe how you had me fooled. Not anymore. I see what you have in your heart. When are you going to get the hell out of my house?"

"She never answered him. I could see her from father's bedroom where I was putting away clean shirts. They didn't know I was in there. Usually, they control their tongues when anyone is within earshot. I waited until Agnes went into her bedroom before I came out. I could tell Father was surprised to see me.

"Right then and there I asked him, 'What's wrong between you two?'

"His answer was a short one, 'Stay out of it Marie.'

"It's best that we don't know. I already hate that woman so much. Honestly, I don't think they'll stay together much longer. The day she leaves will be a happy one. All she has done is make trouble, ever since she came into our lives."

Agnes's written message, "This will be your last ride," had been wishing my death so she wouldn't have to see me again. Maybe she would get her wish. Not because of my misfortune but her own. Whether it was because my father saw the note, or because of something else he found out about her, it was beginning to look like she would be out the door before I returned home. I never wanted to be the cause of anyone else's troubles. Not even Agnes's. But thinking of returning to the home I'd known before she came into our lives made me smile.

I changed the subject, and Marie's face went from rigid to soft when I asked about the others. She shared a few funny stories about the younger ones. I loved all the stories because it brought me close to them. My brothers and little Anna didn't come to see me often. Most of the time, they stayed back, over at Beth's and Peter's or Nelly and Pete's.

Nelly asked Marie to pass a hello to me. Both she and Pete were doing well. For as long as I could remember, our families helped each other with whatever was needed. Whether it was harvesting, lending equipment back and forth, or butchering our meat; they were there to help. We had shared tears and laughter that was so ear-splitting I knew the neighbors could hear us. Our bond with them was unbreakable. They were like family.

"How often does Adam come in to see you?" Marie's question caught me by surprise.

"It depends on his work schedule, but he's in at least four times a week. Some of his visits are short. Then there are times when I feel guilty because I wish he would leave already. Why are you asking?"

"Well, I was told by Alice that Adam is fond of you. He loves coming to see you." As Marie talked, I could tell she was trying to sense how I was feeling.

"No, fond of me? You mean as a friend?"

"He has special feelings for you, or so I've been told. We believe that Adam is a man of great makeup. He is kind, mild tempered, and has high morals. He has many qualities to be admired, Stephanie."

"Don't you think he is a bit odd? He's 32 years old, and he's never been married? At first, I thought it was because of shyness, but once he was around a few times, I came to realize he's far from shy. I don't know Marie. I find him a little strange."

"What makes you think that? Maybe he hasn't met the right one. You know, his soul mate, like Matka told us?"

Father walked into the room, so that was the end of our talk about Adam.

"I thought you would've been back for me an hour ago. What held you up?" questioned Marie.

"I was in the post office, and Viviana came in. We decided to go for coffee."

I was baffled, "Why would you two go for coffee? I didn't know you were friends with Viviana."

Chuckling, he answered, "You don't know every person that I talk to. How do you think I keep up on your well being?"

More seriously, he continued, "We've had coffee on occasion, but most our conversations have occurred right here in the hallway. From what Viviana has told me, leads me to believe she loves you like a sister. I'm grateful that you two have become so close."

I didn't say anything because I'd promised to keep Viviana's secret about returning to Italy, but I wondered if my father knew about her plan.

"Nelly is looking after the children, so we need to get back home, but I do want to talk to you about my conversation with Dr. Owen. He is your doctor from now on." He could see the shocked look on my face at his announcement.

"What's going on? Is Dr. Bentley leaving?"

"It has nothing to do with Dr. Bentley, Stephanie, and everything to do with you and the best doctor to help you going forward with your recovery. Dr. Owen has all of your records and will be reviewing your history."

"But why? Dr. Bentley is so kind, and he's a good doctor. I like him, and I don't want a different doctor."

He put his hand on my shoulder as he spoke firmly. "It has already been arranged. I am not going to change my mind. You need to concentrate on what will be happening next. Dr. Owen told me that your cast would be removed within the next couple of weeks and then therapy will start."

I sat there after they left, feeling abandoned. I was already afraid of losing Viviana. How come my father made this decision without giving me an explanation? I knew Viviana wasn't going to be at work for a few days, but there was a good chance she would come in to see me on her time off. I wanted to tell her about Dr. Owen.

Chapter 30

———◦◦◦◦———

WHEN I SAW Viviana and Adam come into my room later that week, looking troubled, I knew they had bad news. My heart pounded, and I prayed that nothing terrible had happened. "What's the matter? What's wrong?" I asked.

They stood on either side of my bed. Viviana took my hand and looked over at Adam, waiting for him to talk.

"Stephanie, I have some bad news. There is no easy way to say it." He swallowed hard and pushed the words out. "Agnes is dead." When Adam put his hand on my shoulder, I could feel his clamminess.

First, I felt shocked, then came undeniable relief. Then guilt. The fear that I had from the thought of losing someone I loved left me. Silently, I thanked God it wasn't my own family. Tears slid down my face.

"What happened to her? Where is my family?"

"Your father said to tell you they'll be in to see you within the next two days. They're okay but are dealing with a lot. Agnes was found this morning, at daybreak, on the railway tracks. The police are investigating."

"Why was she on the tracks? Who found her?" None of it made any sense.

"The crew on the speeder found her. We don't know anything more, but it looks like she may have committed suicide. They found her lying on the tracks. I am so sorry, Stephanie."

Viviana and Adam were looking at me, waiting for my grief to become apparent. It never did. My tears stopped falling as soon as Adam said my family was okay. I had guilt running through me, more than anything. In a quiet voice, I said what was expected of me. "That's so sad. Why would she do such thing?"

Viviana leaned forward, "We never know what another person is feeling. Sometimes there are the obvious signs, and sometimes it comes as a total surprise."

Silence filled the room. "When someone takes their own life," Viviana said, "They must have a feeling of helplessness. They see it as the only way out. I'm sorry for you and your family. It's hard for everyone, especially your father. It's not going to be easy for Beth and George either. They've lost their mother in such a horrible way."

I choked up and felt tears rolling down my cheeks. I knew what it felt like losing a mother. Her eyes on me, her last words, and watching her take her last breath. Those memories would stay with me until I went to her, in eternity. Until then, I had her beside me in spirit. Her presence was as strong as ever. My prayer for Beth and George was that they felt Agnes's spirit. She was a good mother to them. Many times, I heard them reminisce about their happy childhood, and how caring and nurturing Agnes was. They had no idea about the monster I knew lived within her.

Viviana noticed my tears, and put her arms around me, softly whispering, "I'm so sorry, Stephanie." She held me for a short time. When she pulled away, I saw tears in her eyes. Viviana was a blessing. My heart cherished her presence and thinking about her going back home was unbearable. Over the last few months, our friendship had developed into a strong bond. I knew that even physical distance between us wouldn't break it.

Before Adam and Viviana left, she reassured me she would see me during her lunch break the next day. Adam gave me a quick hug and said that he didn't know when he would be back. He had offered to help my father with chores, funeral arrangements, or whatever was needed. It would depend on my father's acceptance of his offer. He was scheduled to work but would try and switch days with another worker.

I closed my eyes and tried to make sense of what was going on inside me. Even with how I felt about Agnes and how well she served the Devil, my feelings were not straightforward. I had feelings of sorrow, but my nagging gut trumped all my other emotions. The torment was powerful. It was filling me with fear. I wanted to talk to Marie.

The next day, while Viviana and I were together eating lunch in my room, my father and Marie arrived. One look showed me they were suffering.

My father spoke, "Stephanie, I'm so sorry we couldn't come in yesterday. How are you doing?" He gently rubbed my head.

"I'm alright. How are you?"

"Shocked and heartbroken. Beth and George are having a very tough time, but having God and each other will help us all get through this."

My father's voice broke as he fought back the tears. He didn't believe his own words. He was trying to be strong. That's when I broke down and cried the hardest. It was unbearable seeing him like that. The three of us hugged each other. It must have been then that Viviana left the room, as she was gone when we finished our embrace.

Marie stayed with me while my father went to deal with some of the arrangements for Agnes's burial. Marie shut the door, then sat down by my bed.

"What happened? Adam told me she had lain down on the railway tracks. Why would she do such a thing?"

"Nothing happened out of the ordinary that day. I told the policeman that Father and Agnes hadn't been getting along, but their arguments were never serious. That day was no different. I heard them bickering off and on before she left that afternoon. Nelly was coming to visit and saw Agnes heading north through the field. The kids were over at Beth and Peter's, and they stayed until after supper.

"Father was worried when he discovered Agnes wasn't in her bed the next morning, so he went to report her missing. That's when the police told him there was a badly mangled body found on the tracks. They took him to the spot, and he identified the body. It was horrible for him."

Marie stared down at her hands, which were locked together in her lap.

"Where was she on the tracks? How far from our house?" I waited to see if Marie would look at me. Her eyes met mine.

"They said the body was found about two miles away from our house, but the train dragged her a fair distance. We couldn't come here yesterday because the police spent most of the day at our house and on the property. They talked to Nelly to confirm she saw Agnes walking in the field heading north."

"Why were the police at our house?" I asked.

"Agnes wasn't wearing her wedding ring, and they asked if it was in the house. We searched for it, but we never did find it."

"Did you tell them about Agnes and how she was? Do you think the police will be in to talk to me?" I asked.

"No, they have no reason to talk to you. You and I are the only ones who knew about Agnes's mean streak. It needs to stay like that, Stephanie. The police will think they need to poke around if they have even the smallest reason. The police are puzzled by the way she took her own life."

"Puzzled why?"

"Men are more likely to commit suicide in a violent way. Women usually don't. "

"What about her ring? We know she never took it off."

"When we couldn't find it, we assumed one of two possibilities. Agnes either threw it away, or it came off her finger upon impact and is close to where she was found."

"This doesn't seem real to me, Marie. I still can't believe Agnes would do this to herself."

"I can. Remember when I told you how her life might as well be over if the Devil leaves her alone, and she doesn't replace him with God? It happened, and with the Devil not guiding her and protecting her she couldn't deal with herself."

Marie's words were strong the first time she said them to me, and now they were spoken in a matter of fact tone.

"Doesn't it make you sad to think about how desperate she must have felt?"

"I can't think that way, Stephanie. Why would I feel sorry for her? Why would you? She was put into our lives for two reasons. To teach us what can happen when we let the Devil in, and how dangerous the Devil's workers can be. I knew that when he left her, she wouldn't be able to go on. What we need to pray for now is that Agnes accepted God when she was in transition. She is either singing in heaven or burning in hell, and it's that simple. All you and I can do is pray for her.

"Now we're blessed with Beth and George. It'll be the hardest on the two of them. But don't compare it to what we went through when Matka died. We were younger and didn't have a life outside her world. She was our world and was taken from us way too soon."

Marie spoke lovingly when talking about Matka. "You're so much like her Stephanie, not a mean bone in your body. Always ready to forgive."

"I'll always remember her words to us, Marie, and how she wanted us to live our lives. Matka made sure we knew that if we put God first, all else would fall into place. I ask for signs from her, daily, and I always get one. She's right here with us and will be for eternity." As I spoke, I saw Marie gently nodding her head in agreement.

We heard my father and Viviana talking as they came through the door. Viviana said, "I was telling your father that Dr. Owen says your cast will be coming off the day after tomorrow."

I still hadn't asked Viviana why Dr. Bentley wasn't looking after me anymore, but I couldn't do it in front of my father. We all smiled and shared excitement at the thought of my cast finally coming off.

Our moods changed when my father started talking about the arrangements for Agnes's burial. She would be laid to rest alongside her first husband the day after next. I didn't have to ask which cemetery. The only one around for miles was the one where Matka lay. It would be a graveside service with the minister, family members, a few close friends, and Pete and Nelly expected to attend.

Chapter 31

———◦◦⊱⊰◦◦———

THE DAY ARRIVED, and my cast was finally removed. It happened on the same day as Agnes's funeral. The timing was perfect. My day was so emotional that I didn't want anyone around, not even Marie.

I flipped the sheet back to get a good look at the lower part of my body. The cast had deceived me over the last six months. They had removed the cast and x-rayed at various times, but I'd never really got a good look at my leg. Concentration was always on the surgery site. Each time the cast was removed, my hip was x-rayed, and because it was essential to keep it immobilized, a new cast was put on quickly.

I expected to see a fair-size scar, but nothing could prepare me for what I saw. I trembled with shock when I compared my good leg to my bad one. It was so deformed that when I looked at it, I questioned if it was what the doctors expected. It sure wasn't what I had. My bad leg was so skinny, and my feet didn't end at the same spot on the bed. The bottom of my foot attached to my matchstick leg could rest on the top of my other foot because it was at least one or two inches shorter. Staring down, I could see the varied size of my legs. My hip bulged out way more than the other one. I felt ashamed. The scar from surgery was there, but it was only a small part of how self-conscious I felt about my new body.

A few days later, I was reading in the sitting room, and I heard Dr. Bentley's voice.

"There you are, Stephanie. I just peeked into your room and thought perhaps you might be in here. You're looking well. How does it feel to have the cast off?"

He was standing in front of me, wearing trousers and a blue shirt, blocking the warm sun that had been blanketing me. It was clear he wasn't working that day, and that was confirmed when he said it was his day off. He'd come into town for supplies for the horses.

"Hello, Dr. Bentley." I smiled. "At first, it felt strange, but now that it's off I don't know how I endured having it on for so many months. It feels darn good, but my leg is so different now and not at all what I expected."

This was the first time we'd seen each other since he was removed from looking after me and I wondered if he felt as awkward as I did.

"Your description of how it feels is understandable. You'll have to discuss it with Dr. Owen. I am not at liberty to give you any medical advice. I enjoyed being your doctor, so I was surprised and disappointed when your father decided to have Dr. Owen take care of you. Do you know why he made that decision? The reason was never given to me."

I could feel the heat come into my face, and since I didn't know how to answer him, I hunched up my shoulders, showing I knew nothing.

"I guess it'll remain a mystery," he said with a smile. "I was told I could visit you on occasion, but I'm not allowed to discuss any of your medical information with you. It's good to see you doing so well. I know Dr. Owen will do an excellent job seeing you through your therapy."

"It was good to see you too, Dr. Bentley. Thank you for coming." As I spoke, it occurred to me he was as curious as I was about my father having him removed from my care.

"I'll be going on vacation the week after next, but if I have time before then, I'll stop back to see you. It's best I visit you when I am off duty."

Then, he was gone.

My gut told me he would never be back to visit, and it made me sad because he was a good doctor. I found myself thinking back to the start of my journey. The first time I'd come in here, within days, Dr. Bentley got me into the city hospital. All the tests I went through, the surgery itself, and the painful days following, were all behind me.

My thoughts were interrupted when I saw Viviana hurrying toward me.

"Stephanie, was he in here? Was Dr. Bentley in here to see you?" Viviana sounded annoyed.

"Yes, he stopped by for a short visit. Why?"

"What did he talk about?" She asked.

"Not much really, he didn't stay long. It was the first time I had seen him since he isn't my doctor anymore. Do you know why my father has Dr. Owen looking after me now?" I watched her face to see if I could pick up on what her answer might be.

"No, I know nothing about it. But even if I did, I wouldn't be able to tell you. What I do know is that your father will always do what is in your best interest. Remember that and let it go." Viviana's voice was stern.

"Dr. Owen has a lot of experience. He has been practicing medicine for forty some years. He's an individual who can be trusted, and he's a well-respected doctor."

I took a chance. "Do you not like Dr. Bentley anymore?"

"As I said before, he had me fooled, and that's as much my fault as his. He's charming and seems to get what he wants. There was a time when I had nothing but kind words to say about him. But now I realize he has many issues, and my world has turned upside down." She was starting to tear up.

"Remember how he was carrying on with Nurse Mary? Shortly after that, I saw the two of them out horseback riding. I tried to talk to her, to warn her about him, but she told me to mind my own business."

Viviana's demeanor changed, and she sounded resentful. "What did you two talk about?" She wasn't letting up. "Did my name come into the conversation?"

"No, it didn't. He wasn't here more than a few minutes. Nothing was said about you. He asked if I knew why my father removed him from my care and I told him I had no idea. I'm not happy about my father's decision, but I have no choice. I was hoping you'd be able to explain why he wants Dr. Owen caring for me now. But it's best that I let it go as you suggested." As I said what Viviana wanted to hear, it became less important to me.

Thinking about Viviana, and how she was coping with knowing Dr. Bentley was focusing on another woman, was tugging at my heart. She was a pure soul and what I saw between the two of them was love on her part. I wasn't sure about him. I felt her pain from his betrayal. I wanted to tell her that I'd seen them in the mirror, but I knew how embarrassed she would be.

Chapter 32

∞◦⌾◦∞

PHYSICAL THERAPY WAS a slow-moving process. For weeks, all my exercises were done as I lay flat on my back. Muscle pain and spasms were recurrent. At times, I wondered if I'd ever walk again. Dr. Owen reassured me my recovery was coming along nicely. I had to strengthen the muscles in my hip and leg.

Most of my family had been in to see me several times since Agnes's funeral. The first few times Beth and George came in, I could tell they were trying hard to be positive. But I could feel their sadness.

Everyone seemed to move on with life except my father. I wasn't sure about him. Quite often, he would stay back from visiting me, and when I asked Marie why he didn't come in, her response was either, "He was tired and needed to rest," or "He had so much work to do he couldn't take the time." No matter which excuse she gave, it always ended the same: "He sends his love and will be here to see you soon."

"Well, I hope he's alright and not sick."

"Oh, no, he's okay. He isn't as worried about you now. He knows the rest of us are in here often. You're getting so close to walking, Stephanie. Can you believe you'll soon be up and about?" Marie's voice was happy and filled with excitement.

"I know. Soon I'll be back home, and I can't wait. Would you like to see my leg?" I asked, knowing very well she would.

"Oh, can I?" she responded. "Let me help you get the blanket off so you can roll over. I'll push your nightgown up." Marie followed through gently, careful not to hurt me.

With my leg out in the open, I looked up at her and saw her face. I wanted to cover it up again. She gasped. I could see sorrowfulness in her eyes. I started to cry as she stood beside my bed, rubbing her eyes trying to mask her own tears.

"I'm so deformed. See how much shorter this leg is? It looks and feels so skinny. I hate it, Marie," I said tearfully. I laid my head back on my pillow and closed my eyes so I wouldn't have to look at it. Marie's arms were around me, and we sobbed together.

"I know this is painful for you, but you'll have to accept your body for now. It'll change for the better once you're up and walking. Think of how much worse this could've been. You might have lost your whole leg. Or worse, you could've died. I know it's not easy, but try to look at this as a blessing." Marie always had the best words when I needed them.

"You're right, it is a blessing," I replied, "I should focus on getting up and walking. You can't blame me for feeling sorry for myself, though."

"I expect you to grieve. But I know how strong you are. I know that you'll make the best of it." Marie was convinced of her own words, and I could tell she meant it.

I heard Viviana's voice, and when I glanced up, she was entering my room.

"How's my favorite patient doing?" She was chuckling, and it made us smile through our tears.

Viviana's concern showed when she looked at the two of us. "How are you feeling, Stephanie? It's good to see you, Marie."

"I'm a little tired." More than anything, I wanted to be alone, to rest my mind.

Marie stood up. "It's good to see you too, Viviana. I have to leave now, Stephanie, but I'll see you again soon. Get lots of rest. The exercises must be taking a lot out of you. Bye for now."

As she headed out the door, Viviana asked, "Oh, Marie, I haven't seen your father for a while, now. Is he doing alright, I mean since the funeral?"

I could tell Marie wanted to leave without answering. She barely turned her body back toward Viviana, "He's doing as well as expected. Thank you for asking." And she was gone.

Chapter 33

—◦◦⟨⟨⟩⟩◦◦—

AT THE START of my second phase of therapy, I never took a step, instead only practicing my balance and putting weight on my legs. Then came my first unsteady steps. Thankfully, I had a physical therapist on one side and a helper on the other. My bad leg did change in appearance. Nothing very dramatic, but I could see it was increasing in size. My limp was noticeable due to my bad leg being so much shorter. It had been about nine months since I'd walked. Now that I had a different hip, I had to learn all over again, but I was thankful there was progress.

They referred to my condition as a stiff hip. I soon realized it was a perfect definition. While sitting, I couldn't reach down or bring my foot up to put on my socks. My leg would bend at the knee, but my foot had to extend out behind me. So, I stood on my good leg, bent the knee on my bad leg, so my foot was behind me, and that would allow me to reach behind and put on my sock or my underwear. No more wearing slacks, but that didn't bother me. Not as much as knowing I would never ride a horse again, which saddened me to no end.

Dr. Owen came in and gave me the news that he felt I was doing so well with my recovery that my release date was getting near. He expected if I kept progressing without any unlikely complications, I would be released within two weeks.

My excitement and feelings of relief were short-lived. Alice, George, Beth, and Peter were the first ones to spoil it. Of course, Alice was the leader, always the one talking.

"We're all grateful you're getting released soon," she said, grabbing my hand. "We have some news for you. Adam came to us, well to George first, then to all of the family to let us know he plans on asking you to marry him." Alice's voice went squeaky with joy.

"What? Is this a joke?" I gasped. I started laughing uncontrollably. I looked up at Alice first, and then the others and saw they weren't smiling. Alice was serious.

"Stephanie, why are you so surprised? He's been coming in to see you and showering you with gifts for some time now. How could you not know that he wants you?"

"Don't you turn this on me. I think of Adam as a friend. The thought of marrying him is laughable." My jaw clenched as I stared at them.

Now it was Peter's turn. He was usually quiet in such intense situations, but I suspect Alice had put him up to it.

"Stephanie, give it some thought. All of us feel it would be the best for you."

"I've known Adam for years, and he's a good man. Everyone likes him," said George.

"What about you, Beth? Would you also like to convince me I should marry a man more than twice my age?" I glared at her. She shook her head and looked down at the floor. The others' eyes were on me with self-righteous intent. I needed alone time, to let my anger dissipate.

"All of you leave, now. Get out."

They turned to leave but not before Alice's big mouth went off again.

"I'll tell Father and Marie to come and see you, but they also think you should marry Adam."

Of course, it wouldn't be natural if Alice didn't get the last word.

I should've told them to tell Adam to come here. Now it made sense to me why the little weasel hadn't been around for a few days.

The next day, Marie came. My father wasn't with her.

"I'm not surprised after hearing the news yesterday that you wanted to see me. I should've been the first one to tell you about Adam and his intention to propose," she said, sorrowfully. "I'm sorry, Stephanie. I've had my hands full at home, and I have to confess, I haven't been honest with you about what's been going on with Father."

"Is he alright?" I asked.

Marie looked sad as she spoke. "Ever since Father and Agnes started fighting, we saw a change in him. He began drinking, and the more it gets hold of him, the more cantankerous he gets. It started with a couple of shots a day, and now it has progressed to much more than that. It's like our father has disappeared and been replaced with a person whose heart is numb.

"His rage comes out in words he uses as weapons to defend himself when he drinks. He tries to make us think we're the problem, and the cycle repeats itself. It's been horrible lately. The children have been staying over at Peter and Beth's."

I was shocked to hear this about my father. "I'm upset that all of you have kept this from me."

"I couldn't come in here with what you've been through, to tell you such worrisome news. What would've been the point?" Marie paused, looking down. "Please forgive me. Understand, I couldn't tell you."

Marie put both hands up to her face. With her eyes closed, she massaged her forehead with her fingertips.

Even though I was upset, things made sense. That was why my father hadn't been in to see me.

"Have you tried to talk to him about this, Marie?"

"You can't speak to him, Stephanie. I don't think you understand how bad it is. When he gets up in the morning, he has his coffee and breakfast, and sometimes the bottle will come out even before dinner. If he doesn't start drinking by noon, for sure he is into it by mid-afternoon. Supper is hit and miss, depending on how much booze he has in his belly. Asking him to sit down and eat his meals when he is drunk turns into an argument, ending with Father yelling and me crying."

"He never had a drop of alcohol in his life, so why now?" I asked. "Do you think he loved Agnes, and now he can't cope with living without her?"

Marie scowled. "No, he started drinking before she died, when all their fighting was going on, but it's gotten way worse now. Father never had money to squander on booze, but now he does. Agnes left him with enough that he doesn't have to worry about where the next dollar is coming from." Marie was shaking her head. "Do you understand now why returning home would be a terrible idea, Stephanie?"

"So that's why you all think I should marry Adam. I'd have a place to go, and he could look after me. I get it now."

"We're only trying to help and do what's best for you. It's not easy for you now that you're crippled. Adam is a good man and has strong feelings for you."

I never said a word. Now I knew what they were thinking. *I was disabled, so they felt I should take whatever man I could get. Who would want a burden to look after for the rest of their life?*

Before Marie left, I asked her to let Adam know I wanted to see him.

Chapter 34

————⊸∘⟨⟩∘⊷————

WHEN ADAM CAME in the next day after work, I was ready for him and knew what I was going to do.

"You know that all of them came in to tell me what your intentions are. Why didn't you talk to me?"

He hung his head and mumbled, "I know I should have come in first, but I told George what my intentions were, and he suggested they come and talk to you first. I'm sorry if that upset you, but I am here now. Stephanie, will you marry me?"

His eyes were pleading as he waited for my answer.

"Why do you think we should get married? I've always thought of you as a friend."

"I'm fond of you, and we get along so well. We'll be good for each other."

Adam sounded as though he was trying to convince himself, along with me, that marrying him was a good idea.

"I've never thought of you becoming my husband. Has George told you about my father?"

"Yes, I've known for a while now."

"So, is this why you're proposing? Because you know I have nowhere to go once I'm released?"

"Oh no, Stephanie. As I said, it would be good for both of us. I do get lonely, you know."

"Well, I could move into your place, and we could live together like roommates," I suggested. I could tell he didn't like my idea. He was set in his thinking.

"I've been a member of the Catholic Church for years, and my faith will not allow that type of arrangement. We must be married, in the church, with Father Paul doing the ceremony."

"I'm only fifteen years old. I don't even think I can legally get married."

"I took the liberty of talking to Father Paul and explained your situation of being in the hospital for such a long time. When I said I was going to ask for your hand in marriage, he told me that he would be glad to officiate the ceremony in the church." Adam replied, ignoring my comment about being underage.

Regardless of what he was feeling or saying, I knew what I needed, and I wasn't afraid to lay it on the line.

"If I agree to this, you must understand it will be under my conditions. Do you want to hear them?"

He reluctantly replied, "Yes, I do."

"I'll never sleep in the same bed as you. You are not allowed to touch me. Don't even look at me romantically. Your bedroom is yours, and you'll get a bed and set it up in the spare room for me. You told me you use that room for storage. You need to get your stuff out of there.

"If you need to marry in the church, it's all right with me, but there will only be us, two witnesses, and the priest. There will be no celebration.

"Never fool yourself into thinking my feelings toward you will eventually change. I don't love you Adam, and I won't pretend to. Our relationship will be caring for each other as friends do, and if you can agree to all of this, I will think about marrying you."

When I finished, I watched to see his reaction, hoping he wasn't too hurt.

"I can tell you now, that I'm ok with all your conditions. I don't need to think about it. You'll never regret this, Stephanie," he replied, with a reassuring smile on his face.

"Come back in a couple of days, and I'll let you know my decision."

I was feeling better about the idea of marriage after having let Adam know I'd never be a wife to him in the real sense. He seemed to accept it, and I hoped he was true to himself. What if he was trying to deceive me, or if he'd convinced himself that I would develop romantic feelings for him in time? That would create a huge problem, so I decided to reinforce my conditions in an agreement for Adam to sign.

I went to work, and since I wanted to keep it short and to the point, it didn't take long to complete. It read,

> *I, Adam Panchyk, agree to the following:*
>
> *My marriage to Stephanie Sadowski is an agreement for practical reasons and not out of love for each other, and for that reason, I will never expect her to share my bed.*
>
> *My property and assets will remain mine.*
>
> *Any current or future debts I have will not be Stephanie's responsibility to pay.*
>
> *I will provide money for food and household expenses.*
>
> *I will provide money for Stephanie's clothing and personal items.*
>
> *I will pay for all of Stephanie's necessary medical expenses.*

As I was finishing writing the agreement, Viviana entered my room and asked what I was doing. Up until then, I hadn't shared any of my family's plans for me to marry Adam with anyone, not even her. But now I was ready to tell her. I got most of it out, and I could tell by her squinting eyes she was disgusted and in disbelief. I handed her the agreement to read, and I asked her if she could think of anything else I should add to it, or if I had made any mistakes.

Solemnly, she looked over at me and said, "Yes, I can think of something to add right down at the bottom. How about you write ... If you ever try to touch me, I will cut off your nuts and throw them in the ditch for the crows to feed on."

She kept a straight face until I burst into laughter. She was unable to contain herself any longer. Both of us laughed so hard we had tears running down our cheeks. Quickly though, my tears became the result of my feelings of helplessness, and I knew Viviana's were now meant for me and my dilemma.

"I shouldn't have said anything so harsh. But I'm angry with the whole idea of you marrying Adam. I know it's against your will. Does your family want this for you?"

"Yes, they all came in, including Marie, and said they agreed it would be best for me. My father hasn't been in because of health reasons." I didn't see the need to explain any further.

Viviana surprised me when she confided that she knew about my father's overindulgence.

"How do you know about it?" I asked her.

"I've seen your father in town. No matter what the time of day, he has the smell of alcohol on his breath, so it wasn't difficult for me to figure it out. He doesn't seem himself. He wasn't in the conversation when we talked.

"I want to share something with you Stephanie, but you mustn't tell a soul. Remember I told you I wanted to go back home?"

"Yes." I already knew by the tone of her voice that she was going to tell me she was leaving.

"I've started making the arrangements to get back home. I have something I need to tend to here, and then I want to leave immediately. No one except you and my mother knows."

"How soon will you be going?"

"I know you'll be released from the hospital this week, and I plan to wait until then. I want to stay until you're released. If there were any way possible, I would take you with me. Who knows … perhaps one day you will visit me in Italy," she said, quietly smiling. "Leaving you behind breaks my heart, but I can't stay. We'll keep in touch, writing letters, and one day, I will share with you all my reasons for leaving."

I was starting to tear up again.

"Don't be sad, Stephanie. We'll always be connected. Distance will never interfere with the friendship we share."

We hugged each other, and I found myself not wanting to let go.

After she left, I went for a walk down the hallway, looking into rooms and waving at some of the patients I had gotten to know. I wasn't in the mood for conversation. The sunroom was empty, so I sat in my favorite chair and remembered back to when I left my home and traveled to the city for surgery. How afraid I'd been, especially when I read Agnes's note about it being my last ride. Once my surgery was over, and I realized I wasn't going to die, my fear of going back to Agnes's abuse had consumed me. I realized my worry was all for nothing. I was changed, but alive, Agnes was no more, and I had peace of mind knowing she would never hurt me again.

Chapter 35

————⊸⊙⟨⟨⟨⟨⊙⊶————

THREE DAYS LATER, when I came out of the bathroom, there were two policemen with Marie, waiting for me. My instincts told me to start preparing for sad news when they told me to sit down.

The tall, thin policeman was first to speak. "Hello, Stephanie. My name is Officer Murray, and this is Officer Bradley."

"Hello," I said apprehensively.

"I'm afraid I have some bad news." He paused, giving Marie time to come over to hold my hand.

"A nurse, with whom I understand you have a close relationship, has died. Her name is Viviana Gatti."

They knew I would go into shock, but none of them realized how bad it would be. At first, I was silent, while voices played over and over in my head, telling me, "Viviana is dead. Viviana is gone." *Please, dear God, I need you.* I rocked back and forth. When my mouth opened, I couldn't stop screaming.

Dr. Owen rushed in and gave me a tiny pill to swallow. I was oblivious to how much time passed before it worked to make me calmer. At some point, the policemen left. Marie climbed into bed with me and held my shaking body. I fell asleep, curled up in the fetal position, still sobbing.

When I woke, I noticed it was still daylight and Marie was in bed with me. I could see her pain when our eyes met. I felt the familiar feeling she always gave me that everything was okay. Marie's presence gave me the strength to hear more.

"What happened to her?"

"Late last night, when her aunt and uncle came home from the city, they found her drowned in the bathtub."

"Oh no, my dear God. I don't understand how that could happen." I cried.

"I don't know, and the police aren't saying much. They came out to the farm to tell us, and to have us come in to be with you. All they said was Viviana had died in the bathtub. Her aunt told them you were close to her, so they wanted to ask you some questions. I expect they'll want to come back and speak with you."

"Speak to me about what?"

"I asked them the same question. When someone dies, there must be an investigation, even if it appears to be an accident or possible suicide. Like when Agnes died on the tracks, questions were asked. It's part of what they have to do." Marie's words made sense to me.

"Do they think Viviana might have killed herself?" Even though I knew more than anyone about her troubles and heartbreak, the thought of suicide was unbelievable.

"I don't know, Stephanie. The police didn't say anything about how she died. I tried to ask more questions, but they told me no information would be released until they conducted a thorough investigation."

The sorrowful look on Marie's face told me I should stop asking her questions she couldn't answer.

Adam came in the next day to see how I was doing. Before long, the same two policemen showed up. I hadn't given much thought as to what I was going to say to them. I needed to answer their questions honestly, regardless of my sworn secrecy to Viviana. It didn't matter anymore who knew about her plans to leave.

"Hi, Stephanie. How are you doing today?" asked Officer Murray.

"I'm doing better, but still having a tough time believing she is gone."

Looking toward the other, heavier set policeman, Officer Murray said, "Officer Bradley will be taking notes as I ask you some questions."

I shot a half smile his way, then politely asked Adam to leave the room and close the door on his way out.

"How well did you know Viviana, or maybe I should ask for how long have you known her?" started Officer Murray.

"I met her for the first time last winter when I came into this hospital. I went to the city for hip surgery, and I was transferred back here to recover, so I have been in here for months. I got to know Viviana well, and considered her a dear and close friend."

"When was the last time you spoke to her?"

"It was three days ago. No, it was three days before yesterday, so four days ago."

"What did you talk about that day?"

"She shared her plans with me. She was going back to Italy, and her mother and I were the only two people who knew about it." The two policemen exchanged looks. "She didn't want me telling anyone, but it doesn't matter now."

"No, it doesn't. Don't think of this as a betrayal to Viviana. You're being a good friend in helping us determine why she died by telling us all you know."

"Yes, I understand." My eyes were sore from weeping, and when they started to fill up with tears once again, the burning was unbearable. I closed them, holding up a Kleenex to wipe the tears.

"Are you alright, Stephanie? I understand this is difficult for you, and we can come back tomorrow, but I only have a few more questions."

They waited for me to answer.

"Let's continue. Waiting until tomorrow isn't going to make it any easier."

"Alright, only a few more questions. Did Viviana tell you why she didn't want anyone else knowing about her plans to leave?"

"No, she didn't. All she said was that she had started making her plans. She knew that I'd be released from here within a week and she wouldn't go until after that happened. She hoped to leave shortly after she tended to something."

"Did Viviana tell you what she had to do before she left, or do you have any guess as to what she was talking about?"

"No, I have no idea. Before saying goodbye, she did say that we would keep in touch, and one day she would tell me her reasons for wanting to go back home."

"She used the word 'reasons'?"

"I remember her saying she had many reasons for leaving. I puzzled over what those reasons were after we said goodbye."

"Do you know any of her other friends? Or if she had a boyfriend?"

"We never talked about stuff like that. She taught me how to read and write on her days off, and this took up a lot of our time together. I don't think she had a boyfriend. When I first came here, she talked highly of Dr. Bentley, and I could tell she liked him a lot, but recently her feelings for him changed. I think it was because a nurse by the name of Mary started working here and she took up with him."

"Did Viviana tell you this? Was she jealous of Mary and Dr. Bentley's relationship?"

"Not in so many words. I noticed she was upset, and I asked her what was wrong. She said Dr. Bentley had her fooled, and he wasn't the person she thought he was. When she saw Mary and him riding horses one day, she went to Mary and tried to warn her about him. Viviana told her how he had a habit of playing with a woman's heart but would never settle down. Mary didn't want to hear it and told Viviana to mind her own business."

Finally, Officer Murray asked his last question. "Did Viviana ever talk to you about wanting to have a baby?"

"Never, she was dedicated to her job. She was an excellent nurse, always trying to help anyone in need."

"Thank you, Stephanie. We might have to speak to you again. If you think of anything else, please get in touch with us. You can call the station at any time and ask for Officer Bradley, or myself."

After they left, my mind was stuck on the question about the baby. What did that have to do with anything?

Chapter 36

—◦◦◦◦◦—

ADAM WAS READING the agreement the following day when Dr. Owen came in and announced I would be released the day after next. Even though the news made me smile, I was anxious. Adam had agreed to all my conditions and said he would get the paperwork we needed for our so-called marriage. Hopefully, Father Paul would be able to perform the ceremony the day I was released. I asked what we would do if that weren't possible, but Adam seemed convinced there wouldn't be a problem.

Later, Marie came in, and I tried one last time to convince her to let me come back home to help with my father. "With both of us, we can make him see how he's destroying his life."

"No, he's fallen too far into the bottle. You don't understand the situation at home. Believe me when I say there's no changing him now. I know what I'm talking about." Marie was agitated, but I wasn't ready to give in.

"Marie, remember what Matka said to us before she died?"

"Yes, I do," she answered. "If you're talking about waiting to find your soul mate, I think Matka wanted a fairy tale for all of us, but she didn't know what was going to happen and how life would change."

"I took what she said to heart, and I believe she meant every single word. Getting married to Adam makes me feel as though I'm going against Matka's wishes. Marie, maybe you should've married George, remember how fond he was of you?" If this didn't change her mind, I knew nothing would.

"Stop thinking that way. I'm sure if Matka were here now, with how life has changed for you and all of us, she would agree marrying Adam is the right thing to do." Massaging her temples, she continued, "George told me that Adam asked if he and Alice would go with you to the ceremony, and of course, they agreed. I'll bring some of your personal belongings either tomorrow afternoon or the next morning, for sure." Bending down, with arms reached out for a hug, she said, "Sleep well, Stephanie. You only have two more nights in here."

I looked away from her. She put her hand under my chin, turning my head, so I had to look at her. "Come on, don't be like this. I want a hug." Reluctantly, I let her hug me.

It was my second last night in the hospital. It had become my part-time home, and I was leaving soon. I should have been filled with joy, but instead, I cried most of the night thinking about Viviana. I never forgot about witnessing her argument with Dr. Bentley, and what he said to her about having an older man giving her attention. I didn't think it was necessary to tell the police about it, and there was no way I would ever talk to them about watching Dr. Bentley and Viviana make love. Their rendezvous wasn't meant for my eyes or ears, and I would never betray Viviana.

Chapter 37

———◦◦✐◦◦———

SIGNING MY NAME Stephanie Panchyk still seemed foreign, even though it had been a couple of months since our marriage, but I didn't have to do it often. I only had to sign on days when I was shopping at the general store. Adam would go in and pay our bill at the end of each month. Our living arrangement was working quite well so far. Adam never made any romantic moves toward me, and that was perfect. I laughed to myself when I thought about my last time with Viviana, and how she joked about his nuts.

Our only significant disagreement happened on the first Sunday after we were married. Adam dressed for church and assumed I would join him. His behavior was out of line when I told him I wouldn't ever be stepping foot in the church again.

"Why won't you come with me, Stephanie? I know you're with God. I hear you talking to him at night before you go to sleep. Father Paul will be disappointed, and I know your mother would've wanted you to join me. She attended church every Sunday." Adam tried so hard to convince me.

"I never once told you I would go to church with you Adam. Regarding Father Paul, I don't give two hoots about what he thinks or wants. He only married us because you gave him a generous sum of money. I'm questioning how he even pulled it off, me being only fifteen years old. It doesn't matter now. What is important to me is that God lives in my heart. His presence feeds me.

"And you're right, Adam. I do pray to God and Matka every night. When I'm not praying out loud, I know they are listening to my heart."

Adam heard and never again pushed me to join him in church. He would occasionally tell me Father Paul passed a hello to me, but I never responded.

Adam worked hard at his job on the rails. I kept busy preparing the meals, doing laundry and the house cleaning. I loved to read when I relaxed. My book collection was growing as Adam always made sure I had money to buy the books I wanted. I often read after our supper, right up until bedtime. I thought about Viviana daily and silently thanked her for giving me the gift of literacy. News of her tragic death had quietened down, but one evening I overheard George and Adam talking about it. They were sitting outside visiting, as they did at least three times a week, and with the window open, I could hear their whole conversation.

"I wonder why they still haven't announced a cause of death."

"I suppose the investigation takes time," Adam replied.

George and Adam spent hours and hours together. If they weren't at our house, they were over at George's, traveling the countryside, or in town. When I asked Adam where they had gone or what they were doing, he would say they were out driving, looking at the crops. Alice and I only saw each other on special family occasions, and I never had much to say to her. I assumed she was alright with her husband having such a close friendship with Adam.

Peter was never included in their "man sharing times," but I had a feeling it never bothered him. His marriage to Beth was blissful, and I could tell how much they loved each other. I smiled at the thought they might one day soon make me an auntie.

On my last visit to Dr. Owen, I suppose because I was married, he mentioned how my body had been through so much that it would be questionable as to if I would be able to carry a baby. With my hip being stiff, even if I carried a baby to term, the delivery would be difficult. I never told Dr. Owen about my arrangement with Adam, and at that point in my life, having babies wasn't even a possibility.

My bad leg was as functional as it was ever going to be. When I got tired during the day, I took breaks. I noticed the tiredness came along with pain when I walked or stood too long. Even my lower back gave me grief, and when I asked Dr. Owen about it, he reassured me it was expected. Rest was needed when the pain became overwhelming. He explained I was still growing, and since my leg was stunted, it wouldn't grow the same amount as my other leg. There was already a very noticeable difference in the length, and his words told me to expect that my body would be even more lopsided in time.

Between my physical disability and Father's drinking, I understood why my family had pushed me to marry Adam. I'd been through so much. Losing Matka, Agnes's abuse, the loss of Viviana, and even though my father was alive, I felt like he'd been taken from me too. My feeling of gratefulness was because I kept God and my Matka close to me.

Chapter 38

—————◦◦◦—————

I RECOGNIZED VIVIANA'S Aunt Angela before she got out of her new gray Ford Coupe, and I went out to greet her. When she got out of her car, I noticed Viviana's navy-blue leather bag in her right hand. I was reminded of times when we needed a bobby pin, notebook, or a pen, Viviana would laughingly say, "Let me look in my bag. You never know what I have stashed in here."

Often, whether it was a hankie, a pen, or buttons, she would pull it out and yell, "Look, Stephanie, it's magic. My bag produced it again."

"Hi, Stephanie," Angela said in a soft voice. "I hope I came at an appropriate time for us to have a visit."

"Yes, I have water on the stove to make tea, and I would love for you to join me." I opened the door and let her go in first. I invited her to sit at the table. She put the bag beside her on the floor.

"I want to talk to you about the investigation." Her eyes focused on the teapot in my hands. "It's been completed now, and I know you must be wondering what took place." She looked up at me with teary eyes.

"Yes, I want to hear it."

As I set the steaming pot on the table and sat down, she picked up the bag. "I brought this because I'd like you to have it and some of her favorite things as a keepsake. I know she would've loved for you to have it."

"I would love that. Viviana used to joke about her bag being magic because it contained whatever we were looking for on so many occasions." Remembering brought tears to my eyes. "Thank you so much for thinking of me. I appreciate your thoughtfulness."

"I know how much Viviana cared about you, Stephanie. She talked about you often, telling us how smart you are and how she enjoyed teaching you. When she asked me to make your birthday cake, her exact words were, 'Auntie, would you please make a cake for Stephanie? I don't think she'll expect us even to know it's her birthday. When she sees all of us, and a delicious cake made for her, she'll light up the room with her smile and words of gratitude.' I remember you did just that."

Angela's kind words made me smile.

"Finally, this can be put behind us, and we can move on with healing. Losing Viviana has been difficult as she was loved by so many."

"Yes, she was. We spent a lot of time together, and I'm sure you know how dedicated she was to help me learn to read and write. Viviana was always looking after others. She was a real blessing, and I can't imagine how difficult my time in the hospital would've been without her. What really happened to her?"

"It was complicated, and the police needed to rule out any foul play, mostly because of your father coming forth and sharing a conversation he'd had with Viviana."

"My father?" I could feel my heart beating.

"Yes, your father went to the police within days of Viviana's death and told them what he knew. She'd asked him to consider removing you from Dr. Bentley's care. Your father's immediate response was that he wasn't sure it was wise to 'change horses in midstream.'

"Viviana put all her trust in him and made him swear not to repeat what she had to say ... she'd suspected Dr. Bentley was taking drugs that weren't prescribed. She wanted to confront him, but would only do that after you were removed from his care."

"Oh, my dear God. So that's why my father did it. Viviana not only knew about it, but she was behind it." It all made sense to me then.

"Viviana didn't want you to know anything about it. She and your father wanted to protect you. Dr. Bentley knew how close the two of you were. Viviana feared that once she confronted him, he'd drag you into it."

I thought back to the day Dr. Bentley came to see me in the sitting room. "He'd asked me if I knew why he wasn't my doctor anymore. When Viviana saw him talking to me that day, she seemed anxious and asked what he wanted."

"It was hard on Viviana to report him since she loved him with all her heart. It wasn't easy for her. But she wanted to do the right thing.

"Even though Viviana's death appeared to be an accident, your father's visit to the police is what triggered the investigation. It was a tender love story that never got a chance to play out."

"I want to know everything, Angela, but if it's too hard for you right now, we can talk another day." I didn't want her to share unless she was ready.

"No, I'm alright. It's time you knew the truth.

"The police questioned everyone who was part of Viviana's life. Nurse Mary was interviewed. She told the police that Viviana had suggested she stay away from Dr. Bentley, but she ignored the warning, thinking it was due to Viviana's jealousy. Eventually, she decided to end the relationship. It became apparent she was a pawn between two people who were very much in love, but had obstacles to overcome."

I had to ask. "Did Dr. Bentley tell Mary that he loved Viviana?"

"Not in so many words, but everyone at the hospital knew his heart was with Viviana. The gossip was that they were going through a rough time. Their colleagues felt it would be resolved, and they would be together in the end.

"When the police asked Dr. Bentley if he had a drug problem, he didn't admit to it at first. A few days before they got the autopsy report back, they called him in for the second time. It was then that he shared they were in a

146

relationship, and even though they were so much in love, he'd made it clear to Viviana that settling down wasn't in his plan.

"This is what he always told Viviana. Now, we realize he was only trying to protect her from his dark side. He was addicted to morphine. He cried like a baby when he confessed to the police. Viviana found out about his problem and insisted he get help or she would go to the Medical Association. Even though he fought her, she wouldn't give up on him.

"Viviana told him a secret when she saw him the night she died. Dr. Bentley broke down and told the police what they were soon going to confirm from the autopsy report. Viviana was carrying his baby." Angela's voice was cracking.

I shook my head in disbelief. "I remember she wasn't feeling well and talked about being tired. So, this was the reason she planned to go back home to her mother and stepfather."

That was why Viviana thought her stepfather would leave her alone. I wondered if Angela knew about his abuse.

"Yes, it appears she intended to report Dr. Bentley, then leave the country," continued Angela.

"After Viviana told him about the baby, she left him to think about it. He told the police he realized how much he needed her and his child, so he made a phone call to a colleague for help. He went over to her house later that night and asked Viviana to forgive him. He explained that he had contacted a colleague for help, and he was ready to be together, whatever it took.

"The next day, however, the start of what could've been a perfect life together ended. He found out about Viviana's death, and even in his remorseful state knew very well if anyone else knew about their relationship, he could be on a list of suspects for her murder. He kept quiet at first, but he couldn't go on with the lies.

"Finally, the autopsy report came back, and the cause of death was determined accidental due to a pre-determined medical issue. Even though Viviana had never had a seizure in her life, she got into a hot bath and had one. We couldn't understand why this would happen, but according to the professionals, hormonal changes are a common cause of seizures."

Both of us sat in silence. I was drained. I could tell Angela was too. There didn't seem to be anything more to say. We went outside, said our goodbyes, and promised to keep in touch.

I came back into the house, picked up the bag, and without looking inside put it in my bedroom closet. It stayed there, out of sight, until one day, weeks later.

What I found couldn't have been more precious. All the possessions Viviana loved. Some of her most treasured books. A gold-framed picture of Viviana that I knew was relatively recent because I recognized the light pink blouse she wore. There was a tiny pink box, and when I opened it, I found her silver chain with the cross pendant she always wore. The first time I'd admired it and complimented her, she'd held it out to show me how the cross had a tiny diamond in the middle. I remembered her words.

"Look carefully, see the diamond in the middle of the cross? It's the only diamond I own, and it's the only one I'll ever need. My father gave me the pendant before he died. He told me to save it until I was old enough to wear it on a silver chain. I never take it off."

Chapter 39

FALL, TWO YEARS later, 1941

I was in the general store and stopped shopping when I heard the torrential rain hitting the roof. With little Emma in my arms, I headed toward the window, which looked onto the street. "Oh dear, look, baby. Look at the big raindrops." I pointed outside so baby Emma would see how hard it was coming down, and when I saw her quizzical expression, I was lost in the moment. She had a way of capturing all my attention.

I jumped when I heard a woman's voice alongside me. "Stephanie?" Laughingly, she spoke again with a caring tone, "Oh, I didn't mean to startle you. I'm sorry."

I smiled back at her. "Yes, I'm Stephanie. It's alright. I was showing little Emma the rain, and I was so taken by her reaction, I didn't notice you beside us."

"My name is Ava Hoffmann. You don't know me, but I've seen you around town. I've been inquiring around for a woman to help on our farm, and someone mentioned you're a great cook and a hard worker. I hope approaching you in this manner isn't making it awkward for you, but I need to find someone. It wasn't mentioned to me that you have a baby," she said, smiling at Emma.

"No, no, she's not mine. She's my one and only niece. I steal her away from my brother and sister-in-law whenever I can." I looked at Emma, who had lost interest in the rain, and our conversation. Her eyes were on my necklace, and she gently tugged on the chain until the tiny cross was between her thumb and index finger. Emma was an expert at finding the cross whenever I held her.

"She's a sweet baby, and that's a beautiful necklace. Where did you buy it?"

"Thank you. It was given to me in remembrance of a friend who passed away about two years ago. I never take it off. Baby Emma knows she can hold onto it, and she never seems to get tired of looking at the tiny diamond in the middle of the cross."

"I am sorry to hear about your loss." Next, Ava asked, "How'd she pass?"

"Her name was Viviana, and it was an accident. She had a seizure while in the bathtub, and she drowned." I never mentioned Viviana was pregnant when she drowned because I knew the more information I gave, the more I would have to explain. My heart still ached when I thought about it.

"How tragic. I'm sorry." She looked down at the floor and shook her head. I didn't want to continue talking about Viviana, and I hoped she could tell.

"I don't expect you to make a decision right this minute. But is there a possibility you could come and help us through our busy harvesting time? Would it be possible for you to let me know before the week is up?" Ava watched me with hopefulness in her eyes.

"I most certainly will think about it. Where is your farm from here?"

"We have three sections of farmland 17 miles north of town. Each year, we seed around 1500 acres."

"Oh, I've heard about a huge farm north of us. It's probably yours. We're fifteen miles apart though, and I wouldn't be able to drive to you every day. Adam, my husband, uses our only vehicle to get to his job." I was interested in going to work, but could already see obstacles that wouldn't make it feasible.

Ava replied, "When the weather allows us to work in the fields, we go nonstop, and sometimes work until after dark. There would be early mornings, and late nights for you, so you'd need to stay with us. It depends on the weather, and when it rains, I could take you home, until we're able to get back into the field."

Ava was trying to be as honest as she could be, but I could tell what she was thinking even before she asked me. "Would it be a problem for you—staying with us? You'd have your own room. It'll be demanding work, but I'd pay you well." She sounded desperate.

"Staying at your house wouldn't be a problem for me. I do have to tell you though, or I guess, you've probably already noticed, I'm crippled. My body won't allow me to work for hours on end. I need to have rest during the day."

Ava rolled her eyes and let out a friendly laugh. "Oh, dear, I wouldn't work you so hard that you couldn't take breaks. With the war going on, we've had to hire women to work in the fields, as well as older men. We've accepted that the job will take longer. Of course, you'll have time to yourself once the workers are fed, and the cleanup is done."

"How soon do you need me?" I had already made up my mind. I wanted to do it.

"Sunday would be a good day for my son or myself to pick you up. How does that sound?"

"I want to try and help you. So, I will say yes to your offer, and Sunday would be okay for me." I barely got the words out, and I questioned what I was in for, but I was being pulled toward Ava and her kind offer.

That evening, while eating our supper, I told Adam about Ava, my plan to go to work for her, and that she would come and pick me up if the rain stopped. He seemed disconnected. In between taking bites and giving me the occasional nod, he got up from the table to peer out the window. Annoyed by his lack of attention, I asked, "What are you looking at?"

"Oh, George is coming over. I'm checking to see if he's outside waiting for me. We're going to check the crops to see if they're ready to harvest." He came back to the table. "He should be here anytime now."

I thought about telling Marie about my new job but reconsidered. I knew her opinion wasn't going to change my mind. Ever since my marriage to Adam, it seemed we were becoming more and more distant. She had her hands full, looking after the farm, and the kids. My father was still drinking. When we did get together, he joined us, but it wasn't the same. His health wasn't good, and he hadn't made any changes to better himself.

We usually included Nelly and Pete in our family gatherings. They were finding it harder to stay on their farm. Pete's health was good, but age was starting to slow him down. Peter, George, and Marie helped them out whenever they could.

I'd helped them with the canning last fall, but with the job I was taking on, it wouldn't be possible for me to pitch in. All of us—Alice, Beth, Marie, Nelly, and even Anna—had a part in harvesting the huge garden. We all got along, and even though it was demanding work, it was fun. It was so rewarding when we worked together. All the vegetables we grew in the garden that could be canned, were. If one household ran out of a particular canned vegetable, we would share what we had. Even though I wouldn't be able to help with the canning, I knew my family would share with me.

Chapter 40

I WAS ALMOST packed, except for a few pairs of shoes. As I went out to get them, I noticed Adam looking at the suitcase laying on my bed.

"What's the suitcase for, Stephanie?"

My mouth froze wide open, with an expression of stunned surprise. Still eyeing him, I asked, "Adam, don't you remember me telling you I accepted a job on a farm north of us, and that they'd pick me up today as long as the weather held out?"

"Oh yes, sorry. I forgot all about it. What time are they coming?"

"Ava said she'd either come or send someone to get me right after dinner, so I want to be sure that I'm ready." I turned and walked out to the clothesline. I felt his eyes on my back, following my steps. He wasn't finished talking.

Afterward, when we sat down to eat our dinner, Adam, caringly asked, "Are you sure you can handle this, Stephanie? I mean, with your bad leg? You know that whenever you overdo it, you suffer."

"I think I can do it. All I can do is try."

With a concerned look, he continued, "Promise me, Stephanie, if you're uncomfortable in any way over there you'll tell them to take you home. Do you want me to come and check on you in a few days?"

I chuckled. "No, if it isn't working out, you know me. I'll have no problem letting them know. Thank you for caring though."

We both stood, and as we hugged each other, Adam said, "Stephanie, I know you won't have any problem leaving there if it isn't right for you. I'm willing to bet, that if you aren't content with the situation, they'll be glad to get rid of you." We both chuckled.

The front window was wide open, and when we heard a vehicle, we saw Ava driving up. Adam helped me carry my suitcase out to her black sedan. Ava watched us, and when we reached the vehicle, Adam and I said our goodbyes. Through her open window, I introduced Adam to Ava. He smiled, "Hello, Ava. Pleased to meet you. Where would you like me to put Stephanie's bag?"

"You can place it on the rear seat. Pleased to meet you too."

Adam opened the back door and put my suitcase on the seat. He gave me another brief hug and stepped back.

I crawled into the front seat next to Ava. We backed out of the driveway, and I gave Adam one last wave, but he had already turned to head back to the house.

As we started down the gravel road, Ava turned toward me. "Thank you so much for coming to work for us, Stephanie. I can't tell you how much of a relief it is to have some help finally. I'll do all I can to make your stay comfortable. I hope Adam isn't upset."

"No, not all. As a matter of fact, he'd forgotten I was being picked up today." I chuckled. "He'll be fine on his own."

While Ava drove, we chatted about the weather, the crops, and what would be expected of me in the following days. Ava seemed organized, and I already appreciated that about her. She was direct and full of advice on how I should use my time when it came to prepping meals. The ride seemed short, maybe because listening to her was so informative.

When we approached the farm, I couldn't help but notice the large, white two-story farmhouse that stood to the right of the driveway. How glamorous it would be to live here. The sun was shining on the green roof, which matched the color of the spruce trees growing all along the back side of the house. A porch enclosed by a wooden railing led to the front door. A large old barn and two small sheds stood on the far left side of the farmyard. I could see a fenced-off area where the pigs were mucking about, and next to it, what I assumed was the chicken coop. Two more small buildings were just past the main house. Ava told me they were bunkhouses for the hired hands. In between the house and the two bunkhouses was an outhouse.

We parked next to two other vehicles. Both were trucks, one much older than the other. I noticed a yellow lab approaching us.

"His name is Hank," said Ava. He never misses a thing around here. He's an excellent watchdog and so smart. The only time he barks is when a vehicle he doesn't recognize pulls into the yard. Don't be afraid of him. He's friendly to everyone, but he seems to prefer the women over the men. Except for my son, Walter. Hank's his dog."

I opened the door. Hank stood there, waiting with his tail wagging. I reached down, and patted him on the head, "Hi, Hank. You're a sweet boy."

He followed us right up to the porch. Ava pointed at a blanket laying on the porch, "Go and lie down, Hank." He instantly obeyed.

Before we opened the door, I could hear some commotion going on inside. Ava shoved the door wide open, and yelled, "Good Lord, what are you two fighting about now?"

Two young men stood with their noses only inches away from each other. The dark-haired one had hold of the other by his shirt collar. "You dumb ass. What the hell were you thinking? I should knock your lights out right now." As he yelled, his grip tightened on the other's shirt.

The other, who had curly light blond hair, laughed out loud while staring into the eyes of his opponent, "Try it," he hissed out through clenched teeth. "I'll set you back on your ass so fast you won't know what hit you."

From the top of the stairs came a female voice, "Mama, those two have been at it for the last 5 minutes. What a pair of heathens."

"Never mind, Lotte. Come down here and meet Stephanie, our new helper." The two finally noticed us. I could tell both were feeling a little sheepish.

"Let's all go into the kitchen, where I can introduce you. Stephanie, this is my daughter, Lotte, and her two older brothers, Walter and Karl.

"I must say, with the show you two put on, I'm sure Stephanie thinks that the dog is the nicest creature around here." Shaking her head, she continued, "I don't know what gets into the two of you."

The dark-haired one interrupted her, "He's always egging me on."

"Enough. I don't want to hear any more, and neither does Stephanie." She turned to Lotte and asked if she could bring a pitcher of lemonade from the fridge.

I sat at the table and watched the four of them, all moving in different directions. Lotte was at the refrigerator, searching for lemonade. Ava went to get some glasses. Karl was trying to tune in the radio. Walter sat across from me, and I figured he'd be a talker. I could tell from the way he was studying me.

There was no doubt that Lotte and Karl were brother and sister. They had the same dark hair, brown eyes, round faces, but there was no resemblance to their mother. Walter was a different story. Curly blond hair, blue eyes, and his face was heart shaped. He had his mother's blue eyes. But that's where the resemblance stopped. Lotte appeared to be around my age, seventeen or eighteen. Karl, I guessed, was in his early twenties. I suspected Walter was the older of the two boys.

We got to know a little about each other over a glass of lemonade and some homemade oatmeal cookies. In the first hour, I knew this family was different than mine. They teased one another sarcastically and laughed about it. The fighting between Karl and Walter was unusual. My brothers never fought unless in fun.

Lotte and Karl went outside to do some chores, and Ava went down the hall into her bedroom to change clothes. Before Ava left the kitchen, she told me to get settled in my room upstairs. I would know which room because Lotte had set my suitcase inside the door. Walter and I were alone in the kitchen.

When I got up and started gathering the dirty glasses to take to the sink, he joined in to help. Hands full of glasses, he followed behind me. "What happened to you? Why are you limping?"

I had become used to the question, and it usually didn't bother me, but coming from him, I cared. "I had to have surgery. I had tuberculosis in my hip, so they removed it and put in a metal plate. With tuberculosis and the surgery, my leg didn't grow the same as the other one."

Looking down at me, with his soft blue eyes and the most charming smile, he said, "I'm happy you have a bummed-up leg."

I started to tell him he was mean, but he put his finger to my lips, to silence me.

"I'm happy because someone like you, so beautiful, would never settle for someone like me. If you tried to run away from me, I'd be able to catch you." He slowly took his finger away from my lips.

No one had ever said anything like that to me. I stood in stunned silence, not knowing what to say. He was still watching me, anticipating my reaction. My face was flushed.

"What are you going to say, Stephanie?" His eyes filled with amusement.

I felt silly standing there, looking up at him, trying to think of what I was going to say.

"Hmm, I've already had my first fight over you, and you won't even talk to me?"

"Your first fight? What are you talking about?"

"Karl and I were upstairs, watching out the window when you drove in, and as you got out of the vehicle, I saw you. I looked at my little brother and told him you were my gal. His cheeky reply was, 'Someone like her? You're fooling yourself. She won't give you the time of day.' He took off down the stairs, and I followed him and used a few words on him that I won't repeat. Then you and Mama walked in on us."

"I heard him tell your mama you egged him on."

Walter laughed, "Karl always says that I start the fight, but believe me, it's him."

I turned away from him, but not before Ava saw us, having returned from changing her clothes.

"Why are you still in here, Walter? The grass needs cutting. If you get at it, you might get it finished before supper." Ava was looking at him, and I could feel how annoyed she was.

"Yes, Mother. I was helping Stephanie clear the table. I'm heading outside right now."

"See you at supper, Stephanie." He threw me a sideways grin before leaving.

I didn't reply.

Ava asked, "Have you gone upstairs to unpack?"

"No," I replied, "but I'll go now. I won't take long."

"Alright, I'll start peeling potatoes, and when you come down, you can make a green salad."

I nodded.

I stood at the top of the stairs, looking down the long hallway. The first two open rooms, across from each other, belonged to Lotte and the brothers. The second door on the left was tightly closed. When I glanced into the second room to the right, I saw my suitcase.

My room faced the backyard, and I could see the large trees I'd noticed when we drove in. The dark wood dresser had ample room for my clothes. It only took me a few minutes to unpack, and I headed back down the hallway. My foot was on the first stair, but I stopped and turned back. Noises were coming from the room across from mine. It sounded like someone clearing their throat. I waited to see if I would hear it again, but I didn't, so I continued down the stairs. Ava's voice drifted up toward me from the kitchen, talking to someone.

When I reached the bottom, I saw a man beside her, watching her peel the potatoes. "Stephanie, this is my husband, Arnold," Ava said.

He put his hand out to shake mine, "Pleased to meet you, Stephanie. We're glad you can help us out through harvest time."

He turned to Ava. "I'm going to wash up and then relax before supper is ready. Is the pail of water hot?" He was heading toward the wood burning stove, where there were two pails of water.

"Yes, the front one should be warm now," Ava replied.

Ava and I worked away, preparing a hearty supper. She explained they had three big meals a day. When the workers were in the field, their dinner, supper, and coffee with snacks were packed up, and we took it out to them. Breakfast was eaten at the house because the time allowed it. Often, the crops were covered in the morning dew, so they needed the sun for a couple of hours before harvesting could begin.

The six of us sat at the table, and I realized it would be ample for fourteen people. I had never sat at a table that size. We passed the food around and started to dig in when the eeriest of noises started echoing throughout the house. It scared me, and when I looked up, from one to the other, they could tell I was frightened.

Lotte, Karl, and Walter were laughing at me when Ava cut in with the explanation. "Those noises are nothing to worry about Stephanie. It's Gross-mutter—she stays upstairs because she's bedridden. What time did you feed her dinner, Lotte?"

Lotte didn't answer.

"Lotte, when did you take Oma her dinner?" Ava's voice was stronger this time.

"It was a little earlier than usual, but not a lot. I stayed with her, and she cleaned up all her food." As Lotte spoke, she crossed her arms in front of her chest. "Why are you asking me about it?"

Ava ignored her question. Instead, in a flat tone, she said, "Okay, I'll get her supper plate ready. Lotte, you take it to her."

Walter spoke up, "Mama, I'll take it to her this time."

"She only wants to see you anyway, so you should be the one waiting on her." Lotte spoke to Walter, but she was looking at me.

"That's enough, Lotte," shouted Ava. An awkward silence passed. Then, in a much calmer tone, she answered Walter. "Thank you. Eat until I get the plate ready."

As she dished another plate, she finally realized I was still in the dark, and that she needed to explain the noises still emanating from upstairs.

"Grossmutter means Grandmother in German. Most of the time, we call her Oma. She's my mother and is 82 years old. She has lived with us for over seven years—ever since my father died. It's only been in the last year or so that she can't walk, and judging from the noises coming from her right now, we question if her mind is right. She goes on like this until we go to her. If we don't get her meals to her when she's hungry, or if she has soiled her bed, or if she's thirsty—and the list goes on—she will let us know with her loud, disturbing noises.

"Here you go, Walter." Ava handed him the filled metal plate and a metal cup full of water. "Soon as she sees Walter, the noises will stop."

Lotte piped up, "That's a certainty because Oma only loves Walter."

"That is not true Lotte, and you know it." Ava was exasperated.

I watched Lotte flip her head back and snort. She obviously didn't agree with her mama. If Ava had noticed, she never challenged her daughter.

Chapter 41

—◦◦⟿◦◦—

IT WAS A miserable, wet day. A week had passed, and a lot of time had been put into harvesting. It was a productive week, and that was good because, with the rain, it would be a couple of days before they could get back into the fields. My days had been hectic, but yet so rewarding. Ava worked alongside me for the first few days, and I could tell from her comments that she knew I was handling my duties exceptionally well.

The rain was to stop by the end of the day, so when Ava asked me if I could stay and help with some baking, I decided I would. They expected to be back in the fields within two days if their weather predictions were correct.

Lotte and I had finished making a double batch of oatmeal cookies, and the kitchen smelled heavenly. It was getting close to dinner, so we decided to bake more goodies after everyone was fed and gone from the kitchen.

Lotte dished up some beef soup and egg salad buns and headed up the stairs to Oma. She wasn't gone long enough to have fed her, so when she returned, I asked, "You don't have to feed her?"

"Oh no, she can feed herself. We sometimes stay with her so that she has company while eating. When I go back up to get the empty dishes, I'll take time to visit with her. I didn't want to leave you down here doing all the work. I'll get the table set, so you can continue filling the buns."

"Alright then," I replied.

We were finishing up our dinner with a piece of chocolate cake I had made the day before when we heard Hank barking. Arnold got up from the table and headed out of the kitchen down the hall to the front door.

Soon, I heard a familiar voice, but I wanted to be wrong. I said to myself, *Please, don't let it be him.* I rose from the table and went to the door. There stood Adam and Marie. I let out a little gasp. "What are you doing here?" I asked.

"I thought we should come for a visit when you never came back home this morning as expected." Adam sounded like my father checking up on me. I felt embarrassed.

"Ava asked me to stay and help do some baking so when we got busy again, we would find it easier. It's only a couple of days, and the fields will be dry. I didn't see the point of coming home when I could be kept busy here."

Neither Adam nor Marie replied.

Arnold invited them in and pulled two chairs up so they could join us at the table. I introduced Adam and Marie to Ava, Lotte, and the boys. Being so nervous, I'd forgotten Adam had already met Ava when she picked me up. I glanced over at the boys and saw Walter staring at me with a look of shocked disbelief.

"Please join us. I'll cut a couple more pieces of the delicious cake Stephanie made." Ava waited for Marie and Adam to reply.

Adam spoke first. "Yes, I'll have a piece. I could never refuse Stephanie's chocolate cake. She makes the best one I have ever tasted."

"No, thanks," replied Marie. "I had a big dinner before we left, which included white cake and berries for our dessert."

Walter got right to the point. "Adam, how long have you two been married?" There were a few seconds of awkward silence.

Adam looked over at me as if I should be the one to answer. Maybe the look he was giving me had more to do with the nature of Walter's question than who should answer.

"We've been married for a little more than two years." Adam was looking directly at Walter. "It's been the best years of my life."

Arnold looked at Walter, catching the pained gaze he directed at Adam. The tension between them was obvious. It needed to stop.

Nervously, Arnold puffed out his cheeks then exhaled before asking Adam, "Have you started harvesting?"

"Yes," replied Marie and Adam, at the same time.

The rest of the visit involved talking amongst Ava, Arnold, and Adam about the war. The rest of us sat and listened. Walter would stare at me and the floor. I could tell he was upset.

Just before they got up to leave, Adam asked Ava if he could use the outhouse. She responded by telling him to use the inside bathroom, which was to the right of the kitchen doorway. It was expected, that we would use the outhouse whenever we could to save the inside bathroom for during the night, but guests were invited to use it. There was a toilet, a sink, and a tub, with only cold water. So, when we bathed, we warmed water on the stove and added it to the tub. The same if we had a sponge bath.

While Adam was in the bathroom, Marie asked if she could speak to me alone. She timed it, so no one else heard her. I walked outside with her, and we stood on the front porch.

"Stephanie, we're pretty busy at home with all the canning and taking our crops off. Nelly and Pete are helping as much as they can, but neither of them can put in more than four hours of work a day. I don't blame them. They're aging."

"How's Father doing?" I had to ask but didn't want to hear the answer, as it never changed.

"Some days are better than others. When he's pushed his body to the limit, he pulls back on the drinking, but it never lasts. As soon as he starts to feel better, comes out the bottle. On his good days, he helps the boys in the field, but he can't be relied on." Marie continued, with what I suspect was the reason for Adam and her visit.

"Would you reconsider, and come help us, Stephanie? This will be Nelly's last year of pitching in. We all miss having you working alongside us."

"I can't, Marie. I've made a commitment to Ava, and would never live with myself if I up and left. Besides, I'm enjoying the work and their company. They pay me well." As I spoke, the look on Marie's face told me she was still aiming to get her way.

"What do you mean, you enjoy their company? Are you talking about all of them? Or is there one in particular?"

"They're all good to me, and I am referring to all of them. I am not sure yet about Oma because she's their bedridden grandmother. I haven't met her yet. She stays upstairs in the bedroom across from mine."

"I couldn't help but notice the blonde-haired boy, Walter. How he was watching you. Does he know you are a married woman, Stephanie?"

"Well, he does now, Marie. What does that matter anyway?"

"It matters because it would be improper to lead him on when your heart belongs to someone else. Adam that is. Remember him?"

"Oh no. Don't you dare tell me who my heart belongs to. I was pushed into marrying Adam because I was a cripple. My family—and yes that includes you, Marie—decided I wouldn't be able to find anyone else. It was a horrible mistake on my part, and I accept that. From this point forward, I'll make my own decisions regarding my life."

Adam was putting his shoes on just inside of the door, and we both knew he could hear us. We stopped talking.

I waited until he joined us on the porch, before I spoke, "I promise, I'll return home the next chance I get. Hopefully, I'll be able to help with the canning." Adam smiled, and then reached out for me to hug him. Our embrace lasted a few seconds. I turned to hug Marie, but she was already off the porch, quickly stomping toward the vehicle.

Adam followed her, and as they drove away, Marie glared at me. If she chose to share our conversation with Adam, I didn't care. What I didn't want was him to come back to check on me.

Chapter 42

———◦◦⟨⟩◦◦———

THE RAIN STAYED away, and the crews were back in the fields two days later. Everyone was relaxing inside after a long day. It was already dark, and I decided to sit outside on the porch and listen to the sounds of nature. Hank always looked forward to our visit because I brushed him and gave him lots of attention. He had a place in my heart.

Walter and I hadn't had a chance to talk after Adam and Marie's visit. Part of me knew he would come outside, or perhaps it was a wish.

"Can I join you, Stephanie?" Walter didn't wait for my answer; he sat down next to me.

"We had a wonderful day, didn't we?" I asked. No answer, so I continued.

"Especially when we put in a full day with no break downs, injuries, or weather interruptions."

Walter turned toward me. "Stephanie, I want to talk to you about Adam. I had no idea you were a married woman ... not that it changes the way I feel about you."

"Walter, my life is complicated. At times, I look back at all the sadness, and I ask myself, what now? What is God preparing me for?"

"I'm going to share with you what my Grossvater ..."

I cut in, "Grossvater?"

"Ah, yes, Grossvater, means grandfather in German. He's been gone now for several years. Anyway, he once told me what I thought was a tall tale, up until I saw you." Walter stopped, "Did you hear it?" I shook my head, no. "Listen, it's a barred owl, and he will..." We heard it again. "Did you hear him?" Walter asked excitedly.

"Yes, I did," I answered.

"Listen carefully, to his hooting call. It sounds like, 'Who cooks for you? Who cooks for you-all?'" Within seconds, we heard it. Looking at each other, we agreed, that's exactly what it sounded like. "My Grossvater was who told me about it. I think it's a sign from him."

I looked over at Walter and studied him closely. His hair was a mass of loose, dirty blond curls that hung down to past his ears. He had tanned skin, where it was exposed, but I knew his natural skin was fair. With his slenderness, tall stature, and broad shoulders, his body was perfect. His voice was deep and full of calmness. It brought butterflies to my stomach.

"Grossvater and I spent a lot of time together in his last couple of years. I already knew about the birds and bees, but I wondered how I would ever find someone to love, have babies with, and spend the rest of my life with. I asked, 'Opa, how did you meet Oma, and how did you know she was the one for you?'

"Opa replied, 'Son, you will know when you see her. It's magical.'

"I told him, 'Opa, I don't believe in magic.'

"My Opa smiled at me and said, 'You will when you see her.'"

Walter was looking at me with his soft eyes as he reached down to hold my hand.

"Stephanie, he was right. From the moment I saw you, I knew." With a little chuckle, he continued, "I'm a believer now."

He looked away. "Do you think that sounds silly?"

My feelings were muddled, and even though I knew how I felt about him, I couldn't tell him. I thought about Adam, and how he and my family would look down on me.

I answered him, "No, I don't think you sound silly. My Matka, that's Mama in Polish, told me the same before she died. She had a different way of saying it than your Opa."

I needed to change the conversation before words came that I couldn't take back. I needed some time to sort out my feelings. "Walter, could I meet your Oma one day?"

"Of course, you have to meet her, and now would be a perfect time."

"What? Won't she be sleeping?" I was surprised and not prepared to meet her at that moment.

"Hard to say, she might be, but most likely she isn't. Seems like she sleeps more in the daytime, and off and on at night." He stood up. "Come on. Everyone has gone to bed now, so let's go spy on Oma." We shared some contained laughter as we headed in and up the stairs.

Lotte's door was shut, and so was Walter and Karl's. We knew Karl was in bed. We tiptoed down the hall, and when we got to Oma's room, Walter slowly opened the door. I could see there was a small lit lamp on a tall dresser in the corner of the room. Quietly, we started into the room, Walter first.

She was lying on her back with the sheet pulled up to her neck. Her eyes were shut and sunken. Her cheekbones stood out on her hollowed, lined face. It seemed that her mouth was the biggest part of her face. It was an empty, wide oval opening. Her witch-like chin was pointing straight up at the ceiling, and it gave me goosebumps. She looked frightening.

Walter bent down close to her ear, whispering, "Oma, are you awake?"

With my nerves rattled, I laughed to myself, as I thought a better question might have been; *Oma are you dead?* If she was breathing, it was very lightly from what I could make out.

"Oma, I brought someone for you to meet." Walter's hand gently swept the hair back from her forehead.

Her eyes opened, and she looked up at Walter, then at me, and that's where they rested. Walter helped her sit up and stacked pillows behind her back for support. With her mouth closed, she was puckering up her lips, and then relaxing them, repeatedly. I could tell it was her tongue moving inside her mouth that was causing her cheeks to suck in even more. Her lips curved and stuck out as if she was getting ready to whistle.

Walter must have known why Oma was twisting her mouth and lips. He reached down under the bed and brought up a container holding her teeth. "Oma, here you go." He helped put her teeth in, and her mouth relaxed.

"We keep Oma's teeth in here under the bed for the night. There's no nightstand by her bed because she has a habit of picking up whatever is within her reach and winging it onto the floor." Walter was bending down, putting the container back under the bed, when Oma winked at me. Next, a sly little smirk came across her lips.

Walter reached for my hand as he spoke. "Oma, I want you to meet Stephanie. She has come to help us during harvest time." Oma was doing an excellent job of sizing me up. I couldn't help but wonder what she was thinking.

"She's important to me, Oma. That's why I brought her to meet you. I'm smitten with her. How could I not be? Isn't she beautiful?" I wasn't sure if Walter expected her to reply or not. All she did was stare at me with a blank look.

"Oma, Stephanie doesn't know it yet, but one day we will marry. Our babies will be beautiful like her. We have a minor problem right now because Stephanie is married. But I am not worried because I know her heart doesn't belong to him," Walter told Oma with a coy smile on his face.

"We'd better get going to bed. You'll see Stephanie again. She'll bring you a meal or two." Walter looked at me, and I nodded my head to show Oma I would be back to see her.

"I'm going to change her soiled diaper now," Walter said, as he walked over to the dresser and pulled out a fair-sized white cotton sheet. He came back over to us, used the end of the bed as a table, and he folded the sheet into a diaper shape.

Oma and I watched him. I wondered if Walter might be the one my Matka had told me to wait for. Witnessing his devotion and love for his Oma confirmed he was for me. My heart melted. Watching him made me think about how my father had looked after my dear Matka. He bathed her, combed her hair, and changed her. What was most impressive was that Walter had the same loving feeling for his Oma that my father had while he tended to Matka.

"I'll leave you now. It was nice to meet you Oma." I watched her to see if she would react.

When Walter was looking away from her, she stuck her tongue out at me. At first, I thought my eyes were playing tricks.

I turned and started toward the door. "Wait, Stephanie." Walter came close to me. "Can we spend a little time together tomorrow evening?" he asked.

"I'd like that. Same place, on the porch?"

"Yes," he answered. Turning to Oma, he said, "Give Stephanie a wave bye for now." She didn't, so again Walter asked her, "Oma, give Stephanie a wave goodbye."

We both watched her lift her frail hand, and with a smile on her lips, she waved gently. I gave her a wave back. The minute Walter turned back toward me, she stuck her tongue out at me again. This time her beady little eyes were slits. I suspected this wasn't Oma's lack of sanity, but a dislike for me. Perhaps she had a mischievous nature that surfaced occasionally. Even though I didn't know for certain what it was, I knew it wasn't some sort of habit or twitch. She meant for me to see it.

Chapter 43

———◦∘⟨⟨⟩⟩∘◦———

WALTER AND HANK were waiting on the porch for me. It felt wonderful to sit down because I'd had a busy day making meals and cleaning in the kitchen. Lotte came bouncing out the door right after I sat down beside Walter.

"Lotte, why are you out here?" Asked Walter.

"Can't I sit with you and have a visit? The porch doesn't belong to you, Walter."

"Okay, Lotte, sit over there," As Walter laughed, he pointed to a lone chair on the other side of the porch. It was far enough away from us that Lotte wouldn't be able to hear our conversation.

She gave her brother an annoyed look, picked up the chair, and brought it over to us. "Don't let me interrupt your conversation."

Lotte was friendly, and her outgoing nature made her likable enough, but Walter and I both wanted to be alone. Neither of us would ever tell her to buzz off because her feelings would be hurt. She wasn't being nosy, but rather needing company.

After a few minutes of chit-chat about the day, Lotte asked me, "Have you met our Oma?"

Walter answered, "Yes, she has. Why are you asking?"

"When I went to Oma after supper to retrieve her dishes, she said, 'I want to see the new one.'"

"At first, I was puzzled, then it occurred to me she was talking about you," Lotte looked at me as she continued. "So, I asked her, 'Do you mean Stephanie?' She nodded, yes."

"I'm glad she remembered me, but I'm also surprised. I didn't realize your Oma could talk." All I'd ever heard were the strange noises she made when trying to get attention. I wasn't about to tell Lotte or Walter their Oma was spooky.

Lotte answered me, "She can talk when she wants to, but it happens rarely. Sometimes, her words are a bit jumbled, but we can usually figure out what she is saying. Would you like to take Oma some of her meals tomorrow? It would be a chance for you to get to know her, and she'd like that."

"Yes, I can do that." As I answered Lotte, I hoped my voice didn't show how reluctant I was.

Shortly after talking about Oma, we decided it was time for bed. We said our good nights at the top of the stairs.

The following morning, we prepared a hearty breakfast of bacon, sausage, eggs, potatoes, and toast. I was setting the table when Lotte said, "I'll take Oma's breakfast up to her. You can do dinner, or supper or both."

"Alright," I answered apprehensively, as I placed cutlery by the lovely bone-colored plates.

When Lotte returned, she mentioned that Oma had asked for me again. "My Oma is so determined to see more of you. I find it strange because she's usually only interested in seeing Walter. You know he's her favorite."

"Really, why is that?" I asked.

"Hasn't Walter said anything to you about his relationship with Oma?" replied Lotte.

"No, but when I went in to meet her, I could tell Walter and Oma have a loving relationship."

"Yes, they do. You'll have to ask Walter for the details on that one. He should be the one to share the history of their bond with each other." Lotte's words made me curious enough to press for more, but she changed the subject by asking me what she could help prepare for dinner. We worked together making a salmon loaf, mashed potatoes, carrots, and peas. Of course, dessert was a must. We made a delicious peach cobbler.

Ava was out helping in the field, but she returned close to noon to help us pack up the dinner to take out to the workers. Once we helped her load the truck with food, plates, and cutlery, it was time for me to take dinner upstairs to Oma. As I dished up the metal plate, I wondered what was going on between Walter and his Oma.

I headed up the stairs with the tray in hand. I could smell the delicious food under the metal cover used to keep it nice and warm. I set the tray down in the hallway outside Oma's door. It was clear she'd heard me because she was watching the door, and when our eyes met, I smiled at her before turning around to pick up the tray. As I approached her, I said, "Hello, Oma. Remember me? My name is Stephanie." There was no response. She watched me. "I see you're already sitting up, so I'll fix your bed tray and set your plate and milk on it." Still no words from her.

Her blank eyes followed my every move, with no face twitching this time. When I turned back and looked at her before leaving the room, she was starting to eat and paid no attention to what I was doing. Before I shut the door, I felt I needed to say something, so I smiled and said, "Oma, I'll be back for your empty plates in a while. Enjoy your dinner." She gave me the same blank glare.

Lotte and I cleaned up the kitchen; then she went outside to cut grass. I was going to bake cookies and oatmeal bread. Before I got started, I thought it would be best if I retrieved Oma's dishes.

When I entered her room, it appeared that she was finished eating. The metal cover was on top of her plate. Her cup was placed neatly on top of the empty dessert bowl. As I approached the bed, I asked, "Are you done your dinner?"

Oma answered with a nod of her head.

"Was it a good dinner?" I asked.

She nodded again.

As I bent over to pick up the tray, an offensive odor hit my nostrils. Oma had messed her diaper. The most I could do was to let Lotte know. It made me hold my breath until I was by the door. As I was pulling it shut, I heard her yell, "He's mine!" I didn't go back, to ask her who she was talking about because I already knew.

Walking down the stairs, I realized the odor was still there. When I reached the bottom of the stairs, I removed the cover from Oma's plate. And there it was. I couldn't take it. I quickly covered it back up and ran to the door. I flung the whole tray off the porch. I threw up and thanked God I made it outside before I did.

Lotte stopped cutting the grass and ran over to me in a panic. "What's wrong Stephanie? Why did you throw the tray and the dishes?" She shook her head in disbelief.

Looking up at her as I wiped my mouth on my apron, I screamed, "Go, look at the dishes. That's what your Oma gave me."

I didn't wait for Lotte to answer me. I went inside, and put my apron in the dirty clothes basket. Shaking my head, enraged, I couldn't believe what had happened. Tears of anger and frustration flooded my eyes. I wanted to be alone, so I started up the stairs.

Lotte came in, and before I could escape, she asked, "Stephanie, did Oma say anything to you?"

With a jerky voice, I answered, "As I was leaving her room, she growled, 'He's mine.'"

"Oh, Stephanie, that's horrible. I know why she did it, but Walter needs to explain it, not me." Lotte reached out to hug me.

"I don't care what your Oma's reason was. There is no excuse to justify such a disgusting act."

"I know, I know. I'm embarrassed by what Oma did to you, and Walter will be too. Please give Walter a chance to explain."

"Oh, I will," I answered. But nothing was going to change my feelings toward their demented Oma.

"Lotte, I almost forgot to tell you that you'd better go see her because she may need some cleaning up. I will get busy preparing supper." I watched Lotte head into the bathroom for supplies to clean up her Oma.

I worked away at preparing a potato salad for our supper. Thoughts about Oma came to me, the faces she'd made at me the night Walter took me in to meet her. Now this dirty trick, which tells me there is definitely something disturbing going on with her. Perhaps this is how a demented person acts. She lies there day after day, very little interaction with family, and no connection to the outside world. That would be reason enough for anyone to lose their mind.

Before we sat down to eat our supper, Walter came to me and said he wanted to talk. I could tell from the look in his eyes he already knew what Oma had done to me.

After supper, we had the porch to ourselves as Lotte stayed inside. I softened a little when Walter said, "Stephanie, I'm so sorry about what Oma did to you."

"It was disgusting," I replied.

"My Oma is old. She isn't mean, she just—"

"Oh no, don't you dare try to protect her." I felt the heat in my face. I yelled, "Who would put a pile of their shit on a plate, and let another person take it away?" I turned and stomped to the front door.

"Stephanie, no. Come back," pleaded Walter.

I ran up the stairs, tears streaming down from a mixture of anger and disappointment. Walter trying to make excuses for his stupid Oma wasn't the reaction I'd expected. Was I so unimportant to him that he could make light of my feelings?

Now, lying on my bed, not able to control my sobs, I questioned if I should stay here. What would I do? Go back to Adam? There was only one positive thought that came to me about our marriage—it was peaceful.

∾

I woke in darkness. Even though I'd cried myself to sleep, my demeanor had changed. It was like I had been wrapped in a cocoon, where only feelings of love could exist. My nightshirt lay at the end of the bed. I slipped out of my dress and fortunately, got my body covered back up in time before the door opened.

"Stephanie, Stephanie, it's me, Walter. Please let me come in. Can we talk?"

"Alright," I whispered back to him.

Standing beside my bed, in his pajamas, he asked, "Can I sit down here on your bed? I need to explain."

"Yes, sit down." I wanted to hear him out. I scooted back from the edge of the bed, making a spot for him.

"I'm sorry if I sounded unsympathetic or like I was siding with Oma because I'm not. This is embarrassing for me, and my whole family. I told Mama what happened. I asked her if I could share some of our family history with you. She told me I must explain the situation to you if I wanted to keep you by my side."

Walter spoke softly, "My mama fell in love at an early age. They dated for a couple of years, but when she told him she was carrying his baby, he left. Just like that, Stephanie, he ran out on her. There was no way she could look after her baby, so Oma and Opa took him. They loved him and raised him like they raised their only child who was, of course, Mama.

"A few years later, my mama met my father and they married. Right from the start, she was honest with him about having a son who was living with her mama and papa. It wasn't long into their marriage when both knew they wanted to have her little boy with them. Mama went to Oma and asked to take him, but Oma wouldn't hear of it. Opa was on the fence, but eventually, he reluctantly sided with Oma.

"Of course, this caused a lot of friction. Oma wouldn't give in, and Mama wouldn't let go of her boy. My mama and my father got a lawyer and fought Oma in court. After a year of fighting, and money being spent on expensive lawyers, Mama and Father were awarded custody.

"Are you following me, Stephanie?" asked Walter.

"Yes." I already knew what Walter was struggling to tell me.

"I was raised by Oma until I was seven years old. She considered me to be hers. She was broken when they took me from her. She resented Mama, and always called me 'hers.' Oma is very fortunate to have a daughter like my mama. Most would have turned their backs on her.

"Oma constantly looked for trouble. I was always in the middle of them. Loving both came naturally, but they made it difficult for me. Especially Oma, but in her defense, she felt I was all she had. It even got worse once Opa died." Walter's voice broke up.

My hand searched for his. When they joined, he turned toward me so I could see the tears sliding down his cheeks. Both of us were silent. I reached up to his shoulder and invited him to lie down beside me. We lay in each other's arms for what seemed like hours, neither of us saying a word.

I understood, then, why when I'd first met Walter, I thought he looked so much different than his father, siblings, and Ava too, for that matter. They only shared the same blue eyes. I wanted to ask him if he took after his biological father, with his fair curly hair and handsome, sharp facial features. But it wasn't the proper time.

The sun was starting to come up when we woke. Walter jumped up and bent over to give me a peck on the cheek before he hurried out of my room. This was the start of him coming to join me, once he knew everyone else was asleep; it became our nightly ritual. Life could be surprising. Walter's and my misunderstanding over Oma's nasty deed brought us closer. It would have happened eventually, but not as quickly.

Both of us feared not being able to have what was in our hearts and souls. We secretly thanked Oma time and time again for her jealous act (or her dementia). Whichever it was, gave us the push we needed to overcome our fears of being together.

Chapter 44

⟶○⟍⟋○⟵

I HADN'T YET thought about how or when I would tell my family about Walter and me. My first step would have to be asking Adam for a divorce. I planned to go home soon, and talk with him.

I was sure Walter's family had us figured out because of the way we looked at each other. He made me laugh, and I had never loved life more than I did then. Neither of us thought it proper to display our deep desires for each other in front of the family. We kept our romance private. Of course, we wanted reassurance and approval from Walter's mama and father, so we planned to tell them. Our chance came one evening right after supper.

"Mama, Father? Stephanie and I need to talk to you." Walter's voice was steady.

"Alright," answered Ava, "let's sit at the table and have a cup of tea."

Walter and I sat next to each other. As he started to talk, Walter put his arm around my shoulders. This was the first time we'd touched in the presence of anyone. They sat across from us. If they noticed Walter's show of affection, they didn't seem taken back or surprised.

"We have news to share with you," Walter smiled at me. "Stephanie and I are in love. We want your approval of our decision to marry. Stephanie will be talking to Adam soon and asking for a divorce. This will take some time, but under the circumstances, hopefully, it will be quicker than a typical divorce because their marriage should be annulled."

"And why is that? An annulment, I mean?" asked Arnold.

Walter looked at me. "Stephanie, do you want to answer, or do you want me to?"

"I can explain." There was no hesitation in my reply.

Both sat, staring at me from across the table, waiting.

"I was coerced into marrying Adam when I was fifteen years old. My family thought it was a wise choice because I'm crippled. Various other factors also played a role as to why my family thought it was the best for me. I made it clear to Adam if we married, I wouldn't share a bed with him. He agreed to that, along with a few other conditions."

Ava's sympathetic eyes watched me. "Oh dear, how sad. Why would your family do this to you? Do you think they regret it?"

"I don't believe that they do. They did it out of love for me. Adam is a good person. Our time together hasn't been horrible, but it hasn't been a marriage of love, but rather one of convenience."

"Arnold and I approve of your decision to marry one day. You need to tell Adam though, as soon as possible. It's not him, Adam, that I'm concerned about, but rather both of you. When you find true love, it's unfair to have to hide it." Ava smiled at me.

"Would you two mind if I talk to Stephanie alone?" Ava asked Arnold and Walter.

They looked across the table at each other, and at the same time answered, "No." Arnold suggested they sit outside on the porch.

"Stephanie, we would be pleased to have you in our family. You have a place in our hearts. We'll be here to support both of you. I'm curious. Has Walter shared his upbringing with you?"

"Yes, he has." I wasn't about to let on about Oma's shitty trick being the reason Walter had opened up to me. Although Ava knew about it, she never discussed it with me. I assumed she was too embarrassed.

"You know, Stephanie, life wasn't fair to Walter in his young years. Oma and I must take responsibility for a lot of the turmoil that accounted for the unhappiness he experienced in his childhood. But, he knows how much both of us love him. I'm sure it's helped him make peace with it.

"Our Walter will give you a good life. I don't imagine you'll have lots of money or material possessions. You'll have much more than money can buy. He'll make you laugh with his witty sense of humor. Stephanie … he'll never break your heart. I can see the love you share. I'm so delighted the two of you are together." Ava meant all her words. I could tell because Walter had the same honesty in his makeup.

"Thank you, Ava. We'll need your support. No one in my family knows about Walter and me. Telling Adam that I want a divorce will happen as soon as I can get over there to talk to him. Walter and I intend to keep our relationship private until well after my divorce. It's best that way, so the gossip doesn't get a chance to spread."

Ava replied, "I agree with you. Can I drive you over tomorrow? Rain is expected later in the morning."

"Sure, although with it being a Friday, I suspect Adam will be at work. If that's the case, I'll get the rest of my belongings, and leave him a note, telling him that I need to talk to him as soon as possible."

"Let's plan on leaving the house after dinner. How does that sound?"

"Yes, that'll be good. We can clean up dinner and be on our way." I was grateful for her wanting to take me over to Adam. Surely though, she wouldn't ask to come into the house, even if Adam wasn't there. I wanted to pack up my clothes on my own.

The next day, as we drove up the driveway, I spotted Adam's truck. He was there. Even though I was looking forward to getting it over with, my heart was pounding. It had occurred to me Adam might bring up Walter. I didn't want to lie, but I hadn't thought of a way around it.

We parked next to the walkway leading up to the front door.

"I think it best I go in alone." I had already opened my car door.

"Yes, but if you need me, wave, and I'll come in," answered Ava.

I smiled at her and nodded before I closed the car door.

I was halfway up the walkway when Adam opened the door. "Hi, Stephanie. I was expecting to see you today with the rain. Do you want me to go get your bags?"

"I didn't bring anything with me because I'm not staying." I made a point of not looking into Adam's eyes.

"What do you mean? Why wouldn't you stay home until the weather clears up?" Asked Adam.

Now I knew I had to face him. "Let's sit. I have to talk to you.

"Adam, I came today to get the rest of my clothes." I watched his mouth open, but I didn't give him a chance to reply. "I want a divorce."

With wide eyes and a look of desperation, he blurted out, "No, Stephanie, you don't mean it." Adam paused for a short few moments and watched me. Seeing determination on my face brought on the next barrage of questions.

"What is going on? Why now? Why would you want a divorce now? Does it have anything to do with Walter?" Adam's voice was losing its calmness.

"I don't have to answer that question. You know as well as I do our marriage was arranged, a marriage of convenience. I went into it with feelings of companionship for you. You understood and agreed to that."

"Have you thought about how this is going to affect your family? They're my family now too."

"You'll still be a part of my family. George would never give up his friendship with you. I will always care for you in a kind way. I wish nothing but the best for you."

Adam's cheeks turned a rosy color, "But Stephanie, we have a perfect life. I can't understand why you want this."

"My life is far from perfect. I was pushed into marrying you; we both know it. A divorce will be readily granted because we haven't consummated our marriage. It was an arranged marriage."

He shook, and his voice escalated, "No, I won't accept this. You need to think it through. I'm good to you, giving you anything you want. How can you not be happy with your life?"

I closed my eyes, took a deep breath and exhaled while thinking; *I want him to stop!*

Staring at him, through clenched teeth, I shouted, "Yes! I agree, your life is perfect. You have George as your best friend and me as your keeper."

Adam sat down at the table and buried his head in his hands. Nothing more had to be said. I went into my bedroom, packed quickly, and when I came out, I saw that he was lying on his bed with his back toward me.

As I was putting my suitcase into the backseat, a feeling came over me. I knew, before I even looked back at the house, he would be there, watching me.

Chapter 45

———⋙∘⟨⟨⟨⟨⟩∘⟫———

MY DIVORCE WAS granted quickly on the grounds of it being an arranged marriage. We had never even shared a bed. I was free to tell my family about Walter, but I held back.

Marie was coming to pick me up for a family supper she would be preparing for us all. Pete and Nelly were also invited. I was looking forward to seeing them. Maybe it would be a good day to tell them how much Walter and I loved each other.

Walter was always patient with me. It bothered him, I could tell by his quiet demeanor whenever I went to visit my family, and he couldn't join me. But he never pushed me. Many times, he would say, "When you're ready, my love, and only then. We have each other now. That's what matters to me."

When Marie and I arrived at the house, I noticed Adam's truck. "You didn't tell me he was coming."

"I didn't think I had to. You know Adam is a part of the family. It's going to happen, Stephanie. You're going to be around him, so you might as well get used to it." Marie's voice was filled with resentment. I couldn't understand why.

Shortly after we greeted each other, Nelly asked if she could speak to me in private. "Of course," I answered. Silently, I prayed she wasn't going to tell me any unwelcome news. We went outside and stood in the yard.

"Stephanie, Pete and I are moving into an apartment in the city."

"Why?" I asked. Due to Pete's declining health, I shouldn't have been surprised. He was becoming more and more crippled. Nelly had to do so much more work on the farm. It was taking a toll on her.

"It's becoming too difficult for us to keep up the farm. We'd rather spend our final years relaxing and keeping each other happy. The apartment we chose is near to the hospital and doctor's clinic." Nelly smiled as she carried on. "Shopping is within a couple of blocks. It's perfect for us. Both of us are ready for this, but we have one wish. It involves you."

"Me?" I asked curiously.

"Yes, you." Nelly's excitement escalated. "We want you to stay on our farm. We know how you'll look after it."

Looking down, shaking my head with disappointment, I said, "But Nelly, I don't have the money to buy your farm."

"I know. But your father does." She clapped her hands together. "He has already bought it. We offered him a lower price if he would buy it for you. He is pleased with the agreement. Will you take over our beloved farm, also the animals, including Blue and Meg?"

"This is a dream come true. I never dreamed of having my own house, let alone a farm. Are you sure about this, Nelly?" I had to ask the question but hoped there would be no changing of minds.

"Yes, my dear, we have never been surer. We thought you would be pleased. All we wanted was to hear your reaction. Our animals and farm will be in good hands. That gives us great peace of mind. Now, shall we go in and announce it?" Nelly led, and I followed her.

When she told my family the news, I could see they were happy and excited. Except Adam, who sat looking down at the floor, then he looked over at George's smiling face. Finally, he snapped out of his pouty mood. It was bewildering. Why wouldn't Adam be happy for me? I anticipated how Walter and his family were going to accept that I would be moving out. It filled me with excitement, thinking about how happy they would be for me.

My father never came out of the bedroom, not even to eat. I hadn't seen him in weeks. I had to talk to him. After everyone left and I helped Marie clean up the dishes, I told her I was going to Father's bedside. When I got close to him, I touched his shoulder softly. The feel of his bones made me choke up. He had nothing except his shirt to cover up the lack of flesh. When his eyes opened, he saw me, and I could tell, he wanted me there. His hand rested on his hollowed stomach. I put mine on top of it as I bent over and quietly said, "Hi Tata, I love you so much." Before he answered me, I gently kissed his cheek.

"Stephanie. I'm happy you came." His eyes looked cloudy. I thought back to Matka's last days.

"Tata, Nelly told me about you buying their farm for me. Thank you with all my heart. It means so much to me to have my own place."

"No need to thank me," said Tata. "I never knew that she was so cruel to you. I'm so sorry my dear child." The love in his eyes showed, but I knew they were also filled with submission. He was aware of what was coming.

My heart was pounding when I kissed him goodbye. His words put me into a tailspin. *I never knew that she was so cruel to you...*

Chapter 46

ALL MY LOVED ones were standing with me, except for Walter. That made sense, because I still hadn't told them about us. My eyes were red and excruciatingly sore from crying. Even though they felt better shut, I had to open them. I watched as the black dirt was being shoveled onto the casket.

A creature appeared. Red eyes flared. Its tongue whipped out of the black hole that encased it. While its ugly head pushed out toward me, the rest of its body twisted and flew up high into the air. It spun around and around, until it came back down, landing on long, spider-like legs atop of the casket. I watched in horror as its spindly legs turned into daggers made of fire and they burned through the coffin.

It pleaded, "Joseph, come be with me. We belong together." Then again, seductively, it said, "You know we should be together." Only then, when it was close to having him, did I realize the extent of my devotion to protecting my father. My body was filled with rage, which gave me physical strength.

I launched myself at it, screaming. "No! No, Father. It's her, Agnes. She wants you to join her in hell."

∾

I woke to Hank sitting beside my bed, howling. Nightmares could be so real. This latest one, the first I'd had since moving into my new home, had most certainly engulfed my inner being. *Why would this happen to me now?* I hoped it wouldn't become a part of me.

Hank had moved in with me because Walter thought I needed to have him for the company, and Ava had agreed. He was my dog now. Even when Walter came to see me, Hank greeted him but always wanted to stay close to me. I wasn't sure if my screaming had made Hank howl, but I was thankful he'd brought me out of my nightmare.

My father died two days after I talked to him. I was grateful I'd had the chance to thank him for buying Nelly and Pete's farm for me.

•

Marie found Father in the early morning. As always, she went in to check on him. She knew immediately he had slipped away. Marie would only say that his color wasn't right. Thank goodness it was she who found him and not Anna or one of the boys. She wasted no time in getting over to let me know. Marie and I comforted the young ones. When enough time had passed, Marie left to tell the others. We stayed back while she went over to Peter and Beth's.

Father was put to rest next to our dear Matka. Immediate family, including Adam, attended. Even though Nelly and Pete wanted to come, their health issues wouldn't let them.

Walter wasn't with me at the funeral. I still hadn't told my family about us. I'm not sure why, but maybe it was because I feared them not liking him. I was protecting him from their harsh judgment. Because of Adam's influence, I wasn't sure if they would give Walter a chance to fit in.

Even though Walter lived at his home, we saw each other often. He'd drive in before dusk and park behind the big spruce trees, out of view from the road. Marie rarely came over in the evening, but it had happened the odd time.

Walter and I had gotten to know each other on a level that set us free to be our true selves. We accepted each other's characteristics, even some of the quirkier ones, like when I discovered Walter didn't often change his socks. He would wear them for weeks at a time. At first, I never said anything to him, but I monitored the situation. Finally, when I asked him about it, he confessed the longer he wore them, the better his feet felt. It was peculiar. What made it even stranger was when he admitted that he would wear them for a length of time, and then he knew it was time to turn them inside out, which made them feel like new again. It seemed so important to him, so I never fussed. I let it be.

Without a doubt, he didn't understand some of my habits, but not once did he say anything. We were soul mates. Knowing we would be together for all time brought me a sense of richness and fulfillment that made me realize I would always be content. It was like my Matka had told me it would be, and I knew how fortunate Walter and I were to find each other. We shared everything—well almost everything.

My darkest secrets stayed locked up inside. My nightmare about Agnes calling for Father was not for anyone to hear, not even Walter. It was best that way. The payoff for not sharing how I was abused was the peace of mind knowing I could deal with my demons on my own time and in my own way. Never having to think about being unprepared or not being in the right frame of mind to answer questions, or listen to offerings of encouragement, or words of inspirations from others was empowering. I knew God was who I needed to confide in, and he wouldn't judge me, but rather he would bring me peace.

Soon I was to find out Walter didn't share all his thoughts with me. We were lying together in the comfort of each other's arms. It seemed like every other time, except I could feel Walter was tense. I brushed it off as being nothing and drifted off to sleep. Looking back, I realized it was the start of him knowing, but not sharing what he had already decided to do.

Chapter 47

⸺◦◦◦⸺

TWO DAYS AFTER Walter told me what he had been holding back, we married.

"I'm joining the army." Almost in the same breath, he said, "Steph, you know how deep my love is and if I didn't have to leave, I wouldn't. No matter where I am, you'll be with me, connected forever. There's something I want before I go," Walter took my hand and brought it up to his chest. "Will you marry me, before I go?" The tears filling his eyes made them even bluer.

"Yes, I will marry you." I felt joyful, but sadness was pulling me down. It was self-pity, and I asked myself, how many men and women are fighting in the war, away from their families?

I was relieved when my family accepted the news of Walter and me marrying. Marie confessed that, a while back, she and Adam had shared their suspicions with the family about Walter and my relationship. Even though I was surprised, I was thankful, because it made their reaction to our announcement less stressful. Marie and Ava agreed to act as witnesses for us at a civil ceremony. There wouldn't be a family celebration. Walter and I wanted to spend the rest of that day and evening alone. They understood.

One week after we said our wedding vows, Walter left for training to join the war. He'd thought it through before sharing his desire to help our country and all the people who deserved to live a life of freedom. I understood his need to go, but at first, I had a difficult time accepting his decision. He knew I would, and he gave me as little notice as he possibly could. Both of us had agreed we wanted to marry before he had to go.

We'd wanted to wait for the deepest physical intimacy until marriage. Kissing, hugging, and caressing had been usual for us. Many times, we'd had to pull away from each other before we had gone too far and there would have been no returning. Walter and I knew our sexuality and sensuality came from God, and we enjoyed and appreciated that our bodies were made to give and receive pleasure in many ways. Sex was sacred, and God intended it to be a beautiful union between a husband and wife. So, we waited until our wedding night.

Feeling him naked up against my breasts for the first time filled me with an uncontrollable yearning, and it spread to every cell in my body. He cradled my face in his hands while he gently kissed my lips. His hand moved down my back as our kiss deepened. We had waited forever, and now it was happening. Neither one of us was experienced, but I expected we would know what to do.

I became anxious when Walter's hand reached down to explore what was only meant for him. "Do you want me?" he asked.

"Yes, I do. I'm a little nervous. I'm sorry."

His soft gaze pierced my soul. "Don't be …"

Both of us knew the first time could be a bit painful. But neither of us had put any thought into another dilemma we would face.

"I can't move my leg very well," I said, hesitantly. I didn't want to ruin our first time.

"It's alright. Let's try it this way." Walter lay on his side facing me, and he gently moved me onto my side. He brought my leg up on top of his hip. "Is this alright? Can you lie like this?"

"Yes."

My arm lay on top of his upper back, and our faces were inches away from each other. He stared into my eyes. If I felt pain, I didn't want him to see it. I closed my eyes. My arm tightened around his back as he guided himself inside me.

"Are you okay?"

"Yes, keep going." I was feeling more tension than pain, but it was over quickly.

Walter had fallen asleep, I knew from his breathing. Later, I did too. Both of us slept through the night. Shortly after sunrise, he folded himself around me, and it was then when I rolled over and reached down. "Good morning," I whispered.

He chuckled. "Well, good morning."

I pressed his hardness up against my inner thigh. Teasingly, I moved him in small circular motions until I had him in the perfect spot.

"I feel so close to you right now," I murmured.

His gentle touch on my shoulder told me to lie on my back. He knelt over me.

The stiffness needed to penetrate me was against me now, and yet I felt the softness of him, rubbing me. "I love what you're doing right now. Don't stop."

Our warmth intensified. I watched him, wondering how he would taste. Imagining his sweetness, I was carried away with waves of pleasure, so intense that I wasn't aware of my surroundings.

Pleasing me excited him. His kisses were strong. Then, together we found our most satisfying way of lovemaking. We were filled with passion, so powerful that our souls were one. It remained our most treasured way of bringing pleasure to each other.

The week passed quickly. When we said goodbye, I fought like hell to hold back the tears. I wanted it to be as easy as it could be on him. Once he waved bye and the train pulled away, tears poured down my cheeks. It felt good to release it.

It couldn't have been a worse time for Walter to be gone. But is there ever a good time to fight a war? We wrote to each other, but I kept my letters cheerful, as I didn't want to cause any distractions that might affect his mental ability. Sad times weren't shared with him, and this wasn't unusual. For the most part, many wives and families kept their letters light and as positive as possible. We all knew our loved ones fighting the war didn't need more worrisome news from home.

Chapter 48

———⊸◦⟨⟨⟩⟩◦⊶———

IT HAD BEEN eight months since Walter left. At first, I had morning sickness. Finally, after the first three months, I felt healthy. The doctor watched me closely. He also prepared me for a challenging delivery because of my stiff hip. Walter didn't know we were expecting our first baby. Ava and I both felt we shouldn't tell him because there was no doubt in our minds he would find it difficult not being here with me.

The previous day, I'd received a letter from Walter, and I never slept well because of what he wrote. I grabbed it off the dresser and headed outside for a walk, knowing the fresh air would lift my spirits. I walked along the bush line, with Meg, Blue, and Hank following not far behind me. I chose a short grassy spot, where there was a stump I could sit on, and reread his letter.

My Own Sweet Stephanie,

I received your letter last night, and as always, was grateful to hear from you. I haven't written you or Mother for a while now. I see no reason for deceiving you about my last six days.

We moved in the dark and felt confident the Germans never saw us. I was on the front line, knee deep in water-filled trenches. Some degree of surprise was achieved, as we waited and saw them coming toward us. I was living in the seventh hell. We came out of it far better than the Germans. I have written enough for now. For most, it would be unimaginable, and it is best that way. We were replaced by fresh men the night before last. I pray for my comrades to return safely.

My sweetheart, my love, please write to me as often as you can. Hearing from you is what keeps me going. Trust I will return to you, just as I do. Holding onto thoughts of the day I see you again is what makes life worth living.

Please keep your love warm for me. Tonight, as every night, I imagine you are in my arms, and it's the only way sleep comes.

Your forever love,
Walter

Sitting there, crying out, "Oh, Walter," and not caring who heard me was all I could do because I was broken. Through my tears, I saw Hank coming toward me. He sat beside me and howled as loud as a coyote. Both horses headed away from me, across the field. "Oh, stop it, Hank. You're hurting my ears. I know, you miss him too." I gave him a pat on the top of his head. Silently, I thanked him as I got to my feet. Hank was my best buddy and always seemed to bring me out of a teary state.

He ran ahead of me, back toward the house. When I got close enough, I saw the smokehouse door was open. I could only see Hank's tail, his hind legs, and feet, but I knew he was up to no good.

My love for him quickly was masked by anger. "Hank—get the hell out of there." I took a couple of steps inside so I could grab him by his collar, but I stumbled and fell half on top of him, and onto the floor. "Damn you, Hank. You know better than to try and get at our meat." He sat down beside me, looking sheepish.

I put my hand on my stomach, even though I hadn't fallen directly on it. I felt the baby move, and I was thankful. My neck was a bit sore. As I sat there rubbing it, I noticed a board had popped up out of the floor. It must have been what I caught my foot on. I peered into the opening where the floorboard had been, and I noticed a little wooden box resting on the ground beneath the floor. Immediately, I picked it up, opened it, and removed its contents. My hands shook, and my heart was racing.

As I walked quickly to find Marie, I whispered, "Oh my dear Lord, oh my dear Lord." Even though I was afraid of what was clenched tightly in my hand, I needed answers.

She was hanging clothes on the line when I got close enough. I yelled, "Marie, we need to talk."

She turned to look at me, and I handed it to her. She went white. I could tell right then, from her wide eyes, and raised eyebrows, that Marie hadn't shared everything about Agnes's death.

"Where in the hell did you find this?"

"It was under a board in the smokehouse. The board popped out of the floor. I went in after Hank to stop him from trying to get the meat." We both stared at what was in her hand.

"Were you honest with me Marie?"

"I prayed this day would never come. There was no point in telling it all to you, Stephanie. You were hurt badly by that old bitch, and I didn't think you should suffer more."

"You need to tell me. Can we go inside?"

"No. The others are inside. You go home, and when I finish hanging these few shirts, I'll come over." Marie must have picked up on my reluctance to believe her, so she added, "Go, Stephanie. I promise you; I'll come over soon as I am finished here. It'll only take me another few minutes."

"Alright, see you in a few minutes." I headed back home, put on a pot of tea, and waited for her.

Chapter 49

MARIE LAID AGNES's ring and the note on the table. I got our tea and sat down, not saying a word, but waiting for her to start talking.

"Remember when I told you Agnes and Father were having many disagreements that seemed to escalate?"

I nodded.

"Father wouldn't tell me why they were fighting. I only knew bits and pieces because of what I overheard. I shared it with you at the time. On the day Agnes died, it was a battle right from the start of the day. I was outside and could hear them yelling. Father came out the door, and I watched him heading over to Nelly's. Agnes wasn't far behind him. I knew all hell had broken loose.

"I followed, and when I approached Nelly's, I could hear them shouting at each other even before I opened the door. They didn't seem to notice me at first.

"I heard Agnes accuse our father of seeing another woman. In anger, she removed her wedding ring and threw it at him. Father then took a piece of paper out of his pocket and held it up. I got close enough to him so that I could read it. Father said, 'Look what Agnes wrote to Stephanie as she left for the hospital.'

"Father found the note on one of our first visits to you. He never told me. I swear, Stephanie, I didn't know about it before that day. If I had, I would have handled things differently." She stared at the table. "My rage took over, and I told it all. How badly she abused you, and about Alex, and her affair with him. I didn't hold anything back.

"She kept denying and yelling that I was making trouble. Agnes came at me, so I gave her a good shove. She stumbled and fell, right over there," Marie said, pointing to the side of the stove. "There was blood pouring from her scalp. Father told me to get back to the house. I ran all the way home, so afraid of what I had done."

"Marie, did you kill Agnes?" I needed to hear her answer.

"I don't know. Father said I didn't. Both he and Nelly said Agnes was knocked out and she came around shortly after I ran home. They told me she sat on the floor for a few minutes, then got up and left without saying a word to either of them. They let her go. After, Father said how much he regretted not stopping her. No one expected she was going to commit suicide on the tracks."

"Marie, why didn't you tell the police exactly what happened?" I waited for her to give me an answer I hoped would make sense.

"Father—well, both Father and Nelly—said it was best to forget the fight ever happened. They didn't want anyone trying to accuse me of what I didn't do. At least that's what I was told at the time. I let some time pass, and I tried to question Nelly further. She got distraught and asked me to accept what she and Father said because it was the truth.

"Please, Stephanie, do not try to question Nelly about it. You won't gain anything other than causing her more pain."

I looked down at the ring and note. "So, do you think Father or Nelly, or both hid the ring and note, thinking it would never be found? Why didn't they destroy it?"

"I have no idea. Of course, it was planned never to be found, but why it wasn't destroyed is puzzling. Remember the police asked if we had seen Agnes's ring because they never found it on the tracks? We lied and told them no. The police also mentioned it was more common for males to commit suicide in such a violent way."

"I remember you were telling me about that," I answered.

"I live with this daily. Wondering if I did kill her, and now you'll be haunted by it too. We'll never be free of the old hag, will we, Stephanie?"

When I looked across the table at her, I realized how strong my sister was. I got up, went over to her, and as I bent down to hug her, I replied, "Yes, as of today we are done with the Devil. Now, what are we going to do with the old bitch's ring?"

"Let's throw it down the outhouse, where we know it'll sink into shit, and never be recovered." Marie laughed.

"Perfect, and we can burn the note," I replied. Finally, I felt set free.

We were already in the outhouse, and Marie was about to drop the ring down the hole when I stopped her. "No, let's not put it in here. I don't want to think about it every time I come to the outhouse."

"Stephanie, you're pulling my leg." Marie looked at me, and she could see I wasn't. I was serious.

"Well, okay. Where are we going to put it?" she asked.

"I'm not sure. The idea of it going into an outhouse is a good one, but not here, and not at your place either."

We stood there, inside the outhouse, trying to come up with a better place. "Oh, I've got it," said Marie.

"Where?"

"There's an old shithouse over at the cemetery. It'd be the perfect hole to hide it in. No one uses it, except for the people who clean up around the graves."

"I like that idea. Let's go for a walk this afternoon. We can visit Matka and Father's graves while we're over there."

Chapter 50

—————⋙⋘—————

MAY 15, 1945

It was exactly seven days after the war ended, and I knew Walter was on his way home. But I didn't know the exact day of his return. Every day, I thought about the first time we'd hold each other. Finally, we'd be together again. So much had happened over the past three years. I had fantastic news to tell him, and some that would hurt him deeply. The day Walter arrived home would be emotional; filled with excitement, happiness, and also some sadness.

It was mid-morning, and I was busy doing some mending by hand when Hanna opened the front door. "Mommy, a man is coming up the lane."

By the time I got as far as the front door, he was standing there in his uniform. Hanna moved from in front of me to behind me, where she could hide but still peek out at him when she felt brave enough. I didn't have to tell him. He knew. I could see it when he looked down at her. His eyes were teary, and with a hint of pain in his voice, he asked, "Why didn't you tell me?"

"Oh, my darling, your mama and I both thought it would make it tougher for you. We didn't want to distract you." I put my unsteady hand out to him. "Please understand, we wanted to protect you from the pain of knowing and not being able to be here for her birth."

He took my hand and pulled me into him. We stayed embraced, and our grateful tears didn't stop until Walter looked down at Hanna, who had got up the courage to poke him. She looked up at him with her bright blue eyes, and in her shy way, asked, "Who are you?"

Walter and I broke into laughter. He bent down to get closer to Hanna's little round face, and asked, "What's your name?"

"Hanna and this is my house. We cleaned it up because Mommy said my Daddy was coming home soon." Again, Hanna asked, "Who are you?"

"I'm your Daddy. I've been gone a long time, but now I'm here, and I don't plan on ever leaving. You and your mommy,"... Walter paused as he rubbed his eyes, before starting over again. "You and your mommy are the reasons I fought so hard. I needed to come home to you."

It wasn't as though I hadn't told Hanna all about her daddy and that one day soon he would be coming home to us. Even with all the talk about him, Hanna in her three-year-old world, acted like he was a total stranger to her. I quickly realized we were all going to need time to adjust. Many families would have to go through the same.

Telling Walter what we'd kept from him wasn't going to be easy. Waiting to do it another day or a better time wasn't an option. It had to be now, so we sat at the table, and with Hanna up on my knee, I told him the news I thought would rip his heart out.

"I have some sad news for you. Oma passed away in the fall of last year."

"How did she die?" Walter seemed to remain calm.

"She passed away in her sleep, and your mama found her in the early morning. She had a tiny smile on her lips, and her hands were crossed over the top of her chest." It was all true, but I wasn't about to tell Walter how his Oma called out for him days before she passed.

"Oma had a long good life. Now she is with Opa and at peace." Walter handled the news without emotion. I expected it to be difficult for him.

We talked for hours about his family and mine. Walter didn't have a lot to share, but he was full of questions. He was anxious to see them but needed a day or two of rest first. Supper was going to take a while to prepare, and I could tell he was worn out, so I told him to sleep, and I would wake him when it was time to eat. Hanna played with her doll, and periodically she would stop and stand in the bedroom doorway. Silently, she watched her daddy sleep. None of this was what I had expected upon Walter's return. I had changed, and so had he. Hanna was going to have the biggest adjustment because, to her, a stranger moved in.

Both of us were nervous when it came time to get into our bed. I didn't know what to expect, and I am sure he didn't either. We embraced each other until I knew he was asleep. I wiggled free and turned onto my side, thinking, *this will be the best sleep I have had in a long time.*

I woke. "Ouch, oh ouch!" Pain blossomed on the back of my shoulder.

"What's wrong?" asked Walter in a worried voice.

"I don't know. My shoulder's hurting badly." Crying and afraid to touch it, I asked Walter to turn on the light.

"No, oh God, no. I'm so sorry, Stephanie. Oh, God." Walter was shaking.

I went over to the dresser mirror. When I saw the blood coming from what was unmistakably a human bite mark, I knew what had happened. Walter was sitting on the edge of our bed, with his face buried in his hands.

I sat beside him and cradled him in my arms.

After a few moments, he explained, "Horrible nightmares come to me. I prayed that they'd stop once I was home. Sometimes, I wake in a sweat, remembering the horror that came to haunt me. This time, like many occasions, I have no recollection of my dream."

Listening to him made me wonder if what he had been through was ever going to ease up haunting him enough to allow him a normal life.

"I'm sorry, Stephanie. God knows, I never want to hurt you." Walter was filled with sorrow. "Do you have any antiseptic? We need to clean it up."

"Yes, it's in the bathroom. I'll get it."

Walter followed me, and he tended to the broken skin.

Once back into bed, Walter suggested I should start sleeping with Hanna.

"No, never will we sleep in separate beds again. It'll take time, but we'll get through this, my love." My thoughts turned to Hanna, and how she would come into my bed when she was having a bad night. I'd have to let her sleep on the edge and me in the middle.

Chapter 51

⚯

THE WAR AFFECTED everyone. We all handled the uncertainty and fear in sometimes unexplainable ways. Many of the wives were unfaithful to their men, who were fighting not just for their own lives, but for ours too. I heard gossip about women attending dances and socials so that they could have some normality in their lives while their men were gone. It became common behavior for some of those women to have affairs with whoever struck their fancy. The excuse for their cheating was hearing about the soldiers sleeping around while on leave. Some wives permanently replaced their men with new lovers and gave birth to their babies.

Fighting men arrived home with the thoughts of making love to their wives and holding their children. Instead, some found another man had replaced them, and now that man slept beside her. The wife they left behind and expected to be there when they returned had started a new life. They had no idea until they returned that their home was occupied by another man and perhaps his child.

The lives of many returning men were in turmoil, and they were in disbelief. After all, promises had been made, and men had gone away feeling secure, thinking their relationships were for eternity. While some of the marriages were broken, surprisingly, some survived the infidelity. Walter was never going to have to deal with this deceit.

Friends sometimes invited me to join them for a night out of dancing and socializing. I always refused their invitations. I blamed my lack of interest on being crippled. My love and devotion for Walter were strong. There was no desire to be with people who chose to gallivant around having fun. The pain of Walter being gone was intense and real. It had become part of my love for him, so why would I want to mask it?

Walter had been back home for more than two months. He held me, caressed me, and kissed me but would never go any further. He would only say that he couldn't do it. He couldn't take it any further. I never asked why, but rather, I assumed it was because of the trauma he had been through, and his nightmares were a testament to the horror he experienced. Kicking, slapping at me, and cursing happened too many times to count. The biting only happened the first night he came home, and I was thankful for that.

As much as I wanted him to make love to me, I was patient with him. His love for me was obvious, and I never questioned it. He always put my needs first. Even before he committed to help his father build a new barn, he asked me if I was okay with it. His father was going to pay him, and the money he earned was needed. I had saved a little nest egg for us from the money Walter had sent home when he was away, but it wasn't going to last.

Hanna and I went with Walter to his mama and father's most of the time. There was always work to be done over there. Hanna loved spending time with her Aunt Lotte.

One day, I asked Lotte and Hanna to take some fresh cold lemonade out to the barn, and even though they yelled that they would, they never came downstairs to do it. Lotte was no child, so I was annoyed when I realized she must have forgotten about it. *Easier to do it myself*, I thought as I headed across the yard to where the new barn was being constructed. They weren't there, but I knew they were close by because I heard them talking. I went toward the voices coming from the old barn.

They never saw me. Walter's father said, "Son, you need to tell her. If it's bothering you this badly, telling her is what will make your guilt go away."

I stood outside the door and waited to hear more.

"I know, but I'm so afraid of losing her. She means the world to me, and I know it'll break her heart. I love her so much. If she leaves me, my life is done." It was Walter's voice, and I knew he was talking about us.

"Here, please, take the letter. Hopefully, this will be the last one she writes. It should be. I made it clear in my last letter to her how much I regret being with her. When I read what she wrote back here, I believe she's accepted I don't want her in my life."

"I'll put it back in our dresser drawer for now. Your mother destroyed the others. She made it clear she didn't read them. Both she and I agree on what you must do to make this right. Walter ... Mama hasn't changed her mind about not wanting to talk to you regarding this. She says it's too painful, and it won't change how she feels."

I turned away, walking back to the house with the full jug of lemonade. Shortly after, Arnold came into the house and went into his bedroom. I knew what he was doing, and I had already decided I was going to get the letter.

When he came into the kitchen, nonchalant as ever, he asked, "Stephanie, is the lemonade for Walter and me?"

"Yes." I had my back to him. I never turned around to look at him. I heard him leave.

Their dresser only had three drawers. I found it in the first one. My hands were shaking as I looked at the envelope, which was addressed to my father-in-law. I opened it and read with speed.

My Dearest Walter,

I will keep this short. When I read your last letter, it made me give up any hope of us being together. That is what you wanted from me, I am sure. All along, you made it clear, and I knew your heart belonged to her. I thought when you found out I had come back to the United States, carrying your baby, you would change your mind. I suppose, for you, my next letter that announced my miscarriage was a blessing. This was when I had to admit you would never want me.

You will always be in my heart. If not for you, I wouldn't have been able to bear the pain of losing Douglas. He was the love who took me there, and you were the love who got me through all the hell. Now we, like many others, must put it all behind and try to live a normal life.

Forever grateful to you. Letting you go forever,

Sadie

I replaced the letter in the exact place I found it. My head was pounding, and I needed to get outside. Quickly, I left the house, quietly pulling the front door closed. The road was dusty, and when vehicles passed, I ate it. Walking gave me time to think about what to do. I was a fool, a broken-hearted fool.

Chapter 52

OVER THE NEXT two weeks, I waited and pondered how Walter was going to tell me about his love affair. From the onset, even in my outraged and broken-hearted state, I had decided what my reaction would be. I never wavered from my decision because I felt my response would be the best for keeping our marriage intact. Did I still love Walter? I couldn't answer that question, and I knew it was too fresh, so I chose to not think about it.

When the day of truth arrived, Walter was eating breakfast before leaving to work on the barn. "Stephanie, I need to talk to you when I return. It'd be a good idea if Hanna stayed overnight with her Oma so that we can be alone." Walter wasn't asking, he was telling me.

"Alright with me. Hanna loves spending time over there, especially when she gets to share Aunt Lotte's bed with her. She'll be thrilled. I'll wake her, and help her pack a little overnight bag."

I went into Hanna's room and saw her eyes were already open. "Mommy, do I get to go stay at Oma's?" It was clear she'd heard Walter and I talking.

"Yes, you do, baby. Let's get your overnight bag out, and I can help you pack. Daddy is eating breakfast, and soon as you are packed and eat a little something, you'll leave for Oma's."

"Can I take my dolly with me, mommy? Aunt Lotte lets her sleep in her bed with us."

I loved her with all my heart, my darling child. "Of course, you can take her," I answered, as I admired her smile, showing how overjoyed and excited she was.

I waved and blew kisses to them as they drove away. My mind needed to be occupied until Walter returned. If I finished all my chores in a reasonable time, I'd walk over and have a visit with Marie. Walter's mama and father knowing about the infidelity wasn't ideal, but at least my family would never have to know. Especially Marie. If she knew how hurt I was, it's hard to say what she would say and do to Walter. Recalling the day when Marie went after Agnes with the piss pot, made me reflect on how protective she was. Marie was the softest-hearted, most giving person you could meet. She had a long fuse, but if provoked long enough, look out. She was like a wildcat protecting her kittens.

By the time I finished washing clothes, tidying up, and getting the vegetables ready for our supper; I had no time for a visit with Marie. It was just as well because I would've been taking a chance by seeing her. Even though I was good at keeping my feelings hidden, she could pick up on my mood most of the time. It wasn't a time for Marie to get involved, and I wasn't sure if I would ever tell her. Then there was Alice, our know-it-all sister. I could imagine her reaction: *Stephanie, well, you should have stayed with Adam. Never, ever would he have done this to you.* Not what I wanted to hear from anyone.

Walter walked in, and it was evident he was upset. "Stephanie, do I have time to clean myself up before supper?"

"Yes, go ahead. I'll wait a few minutes before mashing the spuds. Everything else is ready and can be kept warm."

We ate in silence. Walter helped me clear the dishes and I made us some tea before we sat back down at the table.

Nervously, Walter started, "I haven't been able to make love to you since I came home, and you need to know the reason. There's something I should tell you before you give yourself to me. I want you Stephanie, and it's been hard for me not to have you, and make love the way we did before I left." He hung his head, and I saw when a tear fell onto his pants.

"Go on Walter." I could feel my throat tightening.

"You can't imagine what it was like, fighting for my life and watching my buddies die right next to me. Some days I wished it was me, instead." He paused. "Stephanie, at times, I was living worse than a dog. I'll never tell you all the horror I went through because it would devastate you."

"This is what you wanted to tell me?" I asked him.

He put his face down, and I thought to myself, *You'd better look at me when you confess what you have done.*

He did. His eyes were filled with fear, and he sounded sorrowful. "There's no easy way to say this. I was with another woman. She worked for the army. It started innocently. We were there for each other. If we hadn't been in so much pain, it wouldn't have happened. Please believe me, Stephanie. Let me explain."

"Stop, Stooop." I held my hand up. "Don't you dare say another word. You're not going to make this any better or make it go away by torturing me with details of your affair. Fuck you, Walter!" I almost added, "And your mistress, Sadie, and unborn child," but I stopped myself in time. I planned never to let Walter know that I'd read the letter.

"Do you think my life was a real joyful time when you were gone?" I never waited for him to answer. I continued, "When the doctor questioned if I'd be able to carry the baby to full term, or if the baby would be healthy because of tuberculosis I'd had and the medications I was on, it was hell for me. I had to go through it all on my own."

"I'm so sorry, Stephanie. Please, I beg you, let me explain it to you."

"No, no you don't, Walter," I screamed. My fist hit the table. "You're not going to use me to help you work through your guilt. Keep it to yourself. What you need to do is pray to God and ask for forgiveness."

"Are you going to leave me?" His sobbing and his questioning eyes infuriated me.

"This is my house. If anyone leaves, it'll be you." I jumped up and went outside. I couldn't look at him anymore.

I walked down the road in the opposite direction of my old house. Running into Marie right then would be the worst because I knew my thoughts would spill out.

When I got far enough down the road, I veered off into the bush and sat on a stump. I cried. I screamed. I yelled profanities. When I needed to take a break, I did, but then it would start all over again.

As dusk was approaching, I headed for home. Walter was still sitting at the table when I got back. "Where did you go?"

"I needed to get out of here. Now, I need to sleep. You sleep in Hanna's bed tonight." I closed the door to my bedroom, changed into my nightgown, and laid on the bed in the fetal position. Over and over in my head, I heard, *Fuck you, Walter, how could you?* Had I gone crazy, or was it anger controlling me? I didn't know the answer.

The next morning, he was sitting at the table when I came out in my nightgown.

"Sit down, and I'll fix your coffee." Walter got up and poured me a cup and topped up his. His body showed how tired he was, and I was sure he'd never slept because of his swollen red eyes.

We sat across from each other and drank our coffee until I finally broke the silence. "Hanna will be back today, and it would be best if we keep it as normal around here as possible."

"Yes, I agree."

"You can come back into my bed but only as an attempt to hide this from Hanna. You'll have your side, and I'll have mine. Don't ever make the mistake of touching me." I watched him to see how he was taking it.

"Sweetheart, seeing you like this, makes me want to hold you … to make all the pain go away."

"Walter, don't. It's going to take time if this is ever going to work. Let me work through it on my terms. Part of it will be waiting until I'm ready if ever, to have you in my bed as my husband. Don't ask me stupid questions, such as how long it'll take because I can't answer you."

"I understand," Walter mumbled, in a soft voice.

Chapter 53

———⊶◦⟨⟩◦⊶———

AVA AND I were close, and our conversations were usually light and fun. When I told others I had the best mother-in-law in the world, I meant it. She was usually relatively quiet, but when she decided to share her thoughts, we all knew hearing her out was our only choice. It was perfect that Ava was the one who chose to tell me about Walter and Sadie because had it been anyone else, I wouldn't have given them a chance to talk. My respect for Ava was what made me listen to her.

She started by saying, "Walter has been home for six months. Stephanie, I would never interfere in your and Walter's lives. But I love both of you and little Hanna so much. I feel the need to help the two of you get through this.

"I didn't want to hear all the details either, but Arnold said I needed to. He sat me down and told me what Walter had already shared with him. Walter doesn't know that his father told me, and it should stay this way. You see Stephanie, what our son went through over there is horror that he doesn't want to share, and especially not with the women in his life. Walter feels strongly about protecting those he loves. His father kept at him until he finally broke down and shared the worst of it.

"Both of you are hurting. I'm disappointed in what Walter did. Please don't think I'm making excuses for my son when I tell you what happened to drive him to infidelity."

"I'm not sure it's a good idea for me to hear this right now. I told Walter to never talk to me about his affair." I calmly answered.

Ava persisted. "Stephanie, you need to know how, why, and when it started before you can forgive Walter if that is ever to happen. Wait here. I have something to show you." Ava returned with an envelope, and I knew it held the letter I'd found and read.

As she opened it, our eyes locked and she handed the letter over to me. "You need to read this Stephanie, and when you are finished, I'd like to tell you what I know."

Looking at the letter for the second time was even more painful than the first. As I read again about Sadie's love for Walter, I thought about how she'd held the letter in her hands and licked the envelope before sending it. I hated her.

When I got to the second part, I realized there was something new there, words I hadn't read. *How could it be I didn't remember reading the part about some guy named Douglas?* That puzzled me. I handed it back to Ava.

"Walter made friends with a soldier named Douglas Watson. They became best buddies, looking out for each other when on the front lines, and confiding in each other when not fighting the Germans. Douglas told Walter he was in love with a woman named Sadie and said they'd both joined the army at the same time. Neither one of them was married, yet they kept their love for each other private because relationships were frowned upon. It was thought to be a distraction from duty. Douglas introduced Sadie to Walter, and on occasion, the three of them spent time together.

"They were on the front line, and in a fierce battle. Walter didn't realize his shoulder was bleeding through his uniform. Douglas saw it, though, and waved the medic over. The medic assessed him and determined it was only a superficial wound, but still needed cleaning up to avoid infection and further complications. Walter went along with some of the other injured soldiers to the camp, which was a couple of miles back from the frontline. As soon as the wound was cleaned up, Walter started back to his infantry unit." Ava took a deep breath before going on.

"They had gained ground on the Germans, and their battle position had advanced a short way from where it had been before Walter went for medical attention. Walter never made it back before he heard artillery shells being fired. He stopped and waited, and when he saw the medic coming toward him with an injured comrade, he asked what he had already suspected. The medic told him there were at least six dead and twice as many injured. Walter pushed toward his infantry. His comrades were on the ground, either wounded or lying there, lifeless. The medics and men still standing were loading the injured onto stretchers and some over their shoulders.

"Walter heard a yell for help. He went over and picked the soldier up. He had a wound in his abdomen, and the medics had it tied off to stop the bleeding, but some was starting to leak through. Walter carried him back to where they had set up a makeshift triage camp to quickly assess the wounded before going on to the camp where there were doctors and nurses. The whole way back, Walter told his father how the soldier he was carrying kept on repeating, 'Fucking Germans, they got me.'

"Walter returned to look for Douglas. He was almost ready to give up, and then he heard a rustling noise. There was movement in a tree, only thirty feet away." Ava stopped, and I knew it was because her pain kept her from talking. I put my hand on top of hers and waited until she was ready. Finally, it came out.

"Stephanie, it was Douglas. His mangled body fell from a tree." First, Ava hung her head, pausing before looking back at me. Shaking her head, she asked, "Do you understand why Walter tells us that what they went through would be unimaginable to us?"

"Oh, dear God," was all that came out of me. We embraced and cried.

Still holding onto me, Ava said she needed to tell me the rest. "The following day, Sadie asked Walter if he saw Douglas get killed, or if he knew how it happened. Of course, she would want to know, and Walter understood, but he never told her the truth. He said when he got back from getting his shoulder patched up, he found out Douglas had been killed but didn't see it happen or see his body.

"As I told you before, it was no excuse for Walter and Sadie's intimacy with each other, but knowing what he experienced helped me understand why it happened, and I hope it'll help you too. Walter losing Douglas and seeing the horror of it was too much for him. Sadie, well, she cried on Walter's shoulder and needed to be rescued. Their grieving is what brought them together. It wasn't because of love, for sure not on Walters's part. I know my son, and right from the time he met you, he fell in love with you."

Ava stood, and with pleading eyes, asked me, "Are you going to let the war rob you of your happiness? Are you going to let it take away any chance of living a normal life?" She walked across the yard, put the letter in the burning barrel, took a box of matches from her pocket, and lit a fire. She came back to me, and I knew she intended what she was going to say as her final words on the topic. Ava wasn't one to repeat herself. "I pray for you and Walter to have the strength to get through this. I love you both."

Chapter 54

———⊸∘⟨⟐⟩∘⊷———

55 YEARS LATER, 2000

Our lives had many changes over the years. Mostly, the people have gone. I was the only one left. I'd outlived all my brothers and sisters, even the younger ones. Thomas and Annie both passed away from cancer. Then, the twins died a couple of years apart, both from heart attacks. Years before that, we lost George, Alice, and Adam, who had eventually moved in with them. They died in their sleep when their house caught fire. It was an awful tragedy, and the community was devastated. Peter and Beth were gone too, and my closest sister, Marie. When she passed on, a piece of me went with her. She was special.

It was no different for Walter. His mother passed away years ago, then his father. Walter was the oldest, but despite that, he outlived both Karl and Lotte. We were fortunate to be able to help each other through the pain of each loss.

My aging body had started to let me down a couple of years ago. Now in a wheelchair, I consider myself fortunate that I am still able to draw on my memories. A large part of my day is spent reminiscing about all of the events in our lives. Walter no longer had this ability, because for the past few years, his mind was failing him. It started happening in his late seventies, and at the age of eighty-two, Walter lived in the moment. When it became impossible for us to look after ourselves, fortunately, Hanna asked us to come live with her. She was alone, her husband, Tony, had died in a car accident, and her grown children had moved on with their own lives.

Now, as I sit with Walter beside me, both of us watching Hanna work the dough, how she moves her hands, and the way her little smile comes when the dough sings, makes me realize how much she is like me. Not being able to work the dough anymore is alright because I feel the same peacefulness watching her. She gave it a flip and a punch, and when it made its unique squawk, her smile spread, and the fine lines around her eyes showed her age. It is a passion, getting our hands into the dough, and making all sorts of different sweet treats. Yes, in so many ways, Hanna carried on with our Polish traditions, and I was grateful.

She has some of her father's makeup too, which he inherited from Ava. All three of them were straight shooters, and because of it, they sometimes came off as downright rude. Their words were direct and honest to a fault. Fortunately, they all had a witty sense of humor that made up for any mis-understandings. People warmed up to them quickly, and soon realized they meant no harm with their awkward abruptness.

Often, I reminisced about Walter, and how he made me laugh. Even though this part of him was gone, up until the visit to his doctor, I never let myself fully accept how bad it was. It all changed, a month ago, with that doctor's appointment. Our hearts broke as our state of denial was no longer able to protect us.

The doctor's first question to Walter was, "Is it daytime or night-time?" His answer, "Night-time."

Hanna and I looked at each other in disbelief.

The next question, "Who is this sitting beside you?" The doctor was referring to me. Walter looked at me but didn't answer.

The last question, "Is this person sitting beside you important to you?" Walter nodded his head.

Both Hanna and I were in tears. The doctor handed us a tissue as he expressed his sorrowfulness. He explained his concerns about Walter's safety and strongly suggested we put him into a care facility. That same day, we agreed to let him go. The doctor expected a wait time of a month before Walter would go to his new home.

Hanna and I hadn't shared with the doctor what our home life was like at times. It didn't matter if it was day or night to Walter because there was no schedule with him. Some nights he awoke, yelling out in fear. We knew he was reliving events from the war. When these flashbacks occurred, we were by him, but our fear made us keep our distance.

Two weeks had passed, and we got the phone call. There was a room available at Walter's new home. For the next couple of days, Hanna worked getting the room ready.

Today was our last day spent together as a family. My emotions were running wild. It was a beautiful summer day for sitting out on the patio, so Hanna wheeled us both outside to watch her while she worked in the garden. We were fortunate to have her. As I watched her, kneeling with a bucket beside her for the weeds she was pulling; my mind wandered back to when Walter and I had troubles that almost tore us apart.

It took several years before we got through the worst of it. Ava played a huge part in helping us because it was her talk with me, so many years ago, that made me want to have back what had once filled my heart. My love for him has changed over time but is still alive and stronger than ever. We have had many happy times, and a few trials that would tear most apart, such as when we almost lost our Hanna. It was a painful memory, especially because I knew I was the cause of the accident that almost took her life.

It was a day I'll never forget. We were out in the field, working long days while the fall weather cooperated. Hanna came with me on the tractor to head out to the field where Walter, his brother, and their dad were combining.

The baler was hitched on behind the tractor. I misjudged and turned too sharply on the approach into the field. The tractor flipped, and Hanna was pinned underneath it. I was lucky to be thrown far enough to escape with only a few scrapes and bruises.

The men were working close enough for me to see them, but they couldn't hear me screaming and yelling for help. Only when I started out into the field, waving my arms, did they notice me. They rushed over and started talking about how they were going to free her. They decided to use some pieces of lumber and a jack. By the time the ambulance arrived, they had freed her.

I went in the ambulance with her, and the fifteen-minute ride to the hospital seemed endless. A quick assessment by the doctor found Hanna had broken ribs which were causing issues for her left lung, along with a broken collarbone, broken shoulder, and wrist. She was rushed to the city for further tests and surgery.

Walter and I drove up to the same hospital where I'd had my hip surgery so many years prior. We waited for hours before the doctor came to let us know what was happening. It was then we were told Hanna needed multiple surgeries, and next came the most shocking news. The doctors discovered that Hanna had also suffered a heart attack. That news hit both of us hard. I blamed myself, and even though Walter tried his best to convince me otherwise, I couldn't shake it off. The guilt stayed for many years. We never talked about my guilt, but I felt it, and a piece of me carried the shame of my poor judgment that caused Hanna so much pain.

It took the passing of Ava, years later, before Hanna shared what had happened to her when the accident occurred. We were told Ava didn't have much time left, and we wanted to be with her when she passed. Hanna and I were in the room when Ava started crying, and we could see the fear in her eyes. Hanna's talk with her Oma and myself remained with me, and it was she who confirmed what I already knew from my own experiences. Hearing what Hanna had to say prepared me even further for my challenges yet to come.

She asked Ava, "Why are you crying? Are you afraid of dying?"

Ava nodded.

Tears welled up in Hanna's eyes, and she spoke of her accident for the first time, or at least it was the first time I'd heard it. She eased into it, and I'm not sure if she did it to protect us, or if she was preparing herself by slowly letting us in on what she referred to as her most precious blessing. Holding her Oma's hand, Hanna let out the truth that she'd kept inside for all those years.

"The white curtain that blinds us represents hardness of mind and heart. The hardness is formed by our sins and fears while we are here on earth. When we go beyond the white curtain, we go on a journey to heaven. Then, we realize how close Heaven is to us, and how God is right here. Sometimes, it takes dying before we realize this because the white curtain does such an effective job of separating us."

Hanna, with tears streaming down as she looked over at me, choked out her secret. "Mama, when I was hurt in the accident, I died."

I froze. Hearing this for the first time made my guilt surface in full force. "Hanna, I'm so sorry it happened. I've never forgiven myself for causing you so much pain."

Hanna came over to where I was, by Ava's bedside. I'll treasure her next words forever because I went from feeling guilty to being set free. While hugging me, she said, "Mama, please don't feel bad. You must understand. What happened to me was a blessing. I have been blessed, Mama."

I asked, "Why haven't you talked about this before?"

"How do I explain it? I can't put into words what happened to me because it's not of this world. I kept it from you and Dad because I didn't know how you'd feel about it, and mostly because I was protecting you from hurting. Mama, neither you nor anyone could ever see it in the same way as me.

"Even when I first told Tony about it, he just listened. He never asked me any questions, up until when he was passing away. Then he asked me to describe it again. Of course, I did as best I could. When I say it is the most glorious feeling, the most beautiful, or the most magnificent feeling, it frustrates me and makes me feel sad because no words can do it justice. There are no earthly words that can ever describe my gift of leaving this life behind, as brief as it was, and the remorse inside of me when I was told I had to go back."

She directed her words to Ava. "Oma, don't fear death. Death is a gift. It doesn't separate us. Trust what I am telling you, and let go of your fear. Let God fill you up.

"I'm at a loss about part of what happened to me when I was told I had to go back, and I can't let it go." Hanna's confusion came through in her tone.

"What is it, Hanna? What's troubling you?" I asked.

"Mama, did I have a sister or someone close, who was stillborn or died when they were still an infant?"

I froze. Looking at Ava, and trying to avoid Hanna, I answered, "No, why would you ask me that?"

"When I went beyond here to be with God, all that happened to me was very real. At first, when I was told I was coming back, I felt sadness. I am calling my feeling 'sad,' but there is no earthly word for how I felt. To begin with, I didn't want to come back, but eventually, I became alright with it. The last part of what happened doesn't make sense. It frustrates and bothers me."

"What happened?" I asked.

Hanna continued, "A voice said to me, 'Take my hand, come with me,' and I was guided back. I never saw her, but I heard her, and I felt a pureness about her that I didn't understand. She knew my questioning thought, 'How can you be so pure?'

"She answered me, 'I have only been held by two. Under her heart, and now in His hands.' There's no mistaking what happened. I think about it often, and I know she is in God's hands, but who is she? Do you know, Mama?"

I hung my head, and with a heavy heart, I answered, "No." Then it came to me, "Yes, I lost a brother. He was stillborn. He's buried at the old farm."

"No, it wasn't him. This was a girl. Was there anyone else who lost a baby girl? Someone, who I share the same blood with?"

I shook my head. "No."

Ava asked me to stay when we were about to leave her. Hanna left, and I already knew what I would be told.

"Stephanie, you need to tell her about Walter fathering a baby when he was away at war." Ava sounded determined. "It's not fair to Hanna. She's troubled. You need to tell her so that she can put her mind at rest."

"I will, Ava. In time, I will let her know." My answer was an honest one.

"What do you mean in time? There's no better time than now, and to think anything different would be selfish." Ava was very annoyed.

Even though I wasn't sure, I nodded my head. Ava didn't need that stress, not when she was so close to leaving us. How could I tell Hanna about her father's affair? It would break her heart. The following morning, Ava passed away. All these years later, and I'm still waiting for the right time to tell Hanna about her father. Something always tugged at me, holding me back.

Hanna interrupted my thoughts when she asked me, "Mama, will you wash up these potatoes for our supper? I can wheel you over to the patio table, and you can still enjoy being outside while working."

"Yes, I can do that. Put your dad over beside me, and he can watch in-between his naps."

We went back inside, and Hanna packed her father's clothes so we wouldn't have to do it in the morning. I was nervous, and I knew Hanna was too. Not by anything we talked about, but rather the opposite. We were both quiet.

Hanna cooked ham and baked potatoes because she wanted her dad's last home-cooked meal to be his favorite. Not that he could tell us it was his favorite, nor could we see it in his expression, but because we knew. I asked myself, *How are they going to know what his favorite food is, or that he loves his back rubbed but not too hard, and that he wears his socks to bed?* Those were my worries. Walter and I had never been separated since he got back from the war, and I prayed for the strength to do what was best for him. I knew I had to let him go.

Chapter 55

⸺⊸∘⟐∘⟞⸺

THE NEXT DAY, we arrived at the care center mid-morning, as the manager had requested. A couple of the nurses came out to help Hanna, first to get Walter into a wheelchair and inside, then myself. Neither Walter nor I could walk any distance, but we could still stand, and with some help, transfer into wheelchairs. A caregiver took us to Walter's room, which we had previously viewed. Her name was Carrie, and she was a favorite right from the first day. Hanna made several trips out to the vehicle to bring in her father's clothes and toiletries. She and a friend had brought in a chair and dresser previously, and the center provided a bed. So, by dinner, we had Walter's room organized. Hanna pushed her father down the hall to the dining room, and I stayed in his room and waited for her to return to me.

Carrie asked if we'd like to have dinner, and we gladly accepted. The homemade soup was delicious, and the buns were still warm from the oven. Walter ate his usual amount, and it didn't appear he was anxious. We went back to his room, and a different caregiver came in and asked if Walter would like to lie down. We explained this was his routine at home, and so she removed his shoes and put him in his bed. He napped most of the afternoon.

Hanna and I stayed with him the first day, right up until he was put to bed for the night. It was all going well enough, so we left, feeling relieved and thinking he would be alright.

That night, when I went to bed, I let my heartache surface. Hanna heard my sobs, and she came in and lay down beside me, in what used to be her father's spot for all those years. She put her arm around me, and I knew her tears were silently flowing. This first night was when I let myself admit it. I had lost him. Hanna was feeling the same.

The following morning, we headed back in to see how Walter was doing. Carrie approached us as soon as we entered and informed us that Megan, the nurse who was on duty, needed to talk to us about Walter. We only waited a few minutes, and she called us into her office. We didn't expect what she told us, nor did we like it. She said that Walter had been up all night, and when the caregivers tried to get near him, he had become violent. He wouldn't let them change his soiled underwear, and he swung his fists at them.

Believing that she was done talking, I told her we wanted to see him, and maybe when he saw us and realized we would be coming to see him, it would make him feel better about being in here.

She said, "I am certain he won't be awake. The doctor was in early this morning, and when we talked about his behavior, he thought it was best to start him on a medication used for Alzheimer's patients. The medication is to help him remain calm. A side effect is drowsiness, especially when first introduced to the system. He slept through breakfast, and we will see how he is by dinnertime."

Nurse Megan was right about the drug making Walter drowsy. We shook him gently, trying to wake him, but he was in a deep sleep. It was like that for a week, but then we saw a change, and he started to stay awake for longer periods of time. The caregiver knew how concerned Hanna and I were, so she explained that the dose he was on would be adjusted because Walter's initial dose had been too high. She asked us not to tell anyone what she had told us because legally, it wasn't right for her to give us the information.

We thanked her, and it was the start of me realizing that once you were in the system of care, you had to rely on the professionals. I reminded myself that we had a caring, wonderful doctor who I trusted would do the best for Walter. Letting go was difficult, even when it was all going well. Hanna and

I were doing better as we watched Walter becoming more acceptant of his new home. Then the unimaginable happened.

Three weeks had passed since we took Walter to live in the care center. Hanna and I went to see him daily. Sometimes we brought in Walter's favorite food, or we would stop and pick up an ice cream cone, which he loved. On that day, we arrived mid-afternoon with a piece of apple pie. I held onto the pie and Hanna pushed me down the hall toward Walter's room. His door was always kept open.

As we approached, we heard voices, so we knew the caregivers were with him. We got to the entrance and couldn't see them because there was a partial wall and they were behind it, by Walter's bed. Both Hanna and I heard them say, "Walter, bark like a dog." Again, the same voice repeated it, only more demanding, "Walter, bark like a dog." We heard him. He made the sound of a barking dog, just like they asked. Both laughed hysterically.

Still laughing, they came around the wall to where our eyes met. Their faces went straight. Hanna backed up the wheelchair so the caregivers could come through the doorway. They never said a word, nor did we.

We sat in silence, looking at him, my darling Walter. Hanna turned to me, and with tears in her eyes, she said, "Mama, I'm going to talk to the manager. I need to report this."

"Please don't do that Hanna. Not right now, not until we think about it."

Later, when we returned home, Hanna asked me why I didn't want her to report them. I asked her what she expected to gain by reporting them. She never answered me. Hopefully, I gave her enough reason to stop and think about, and she would work through it like I would have to.

I thought back to my abuser, Agnes, and how she influenced the way I was digesting this cruelty brought onto Walter by practical strangers. Seeing this kind of shared behavior made me afraid. It was difficult, witnessing people doing such cruelty together.

If they only knew the man sitting in the wheelchair was a brave man who'd fought in a war for their freedom. Walter had told me how he'd lived no better than a dog when he was away at war. Asking him to bark like a dog, when he was in late Alzheimer's, was adding insult to injury.

When Hanna asked me again, "Why don't you want to report those two she-devils?"

I answered as best I could. "Hanna, I don't see it changing anything. What's done, is done. You need to understand. It's not our job to try and change people. Furthermore, we don't know why they did it. Maybe they are naïve enough to think it wouldn't matter because your dad is in late Alzheimer's and he wouldn't know anyway.

"With what you've told me about your own experience of crossing over, you should understand better than any of us. We saw their cruelty, but it doesn't matter. They think it does, but it doesn't count against them. We're all God's children, and he'll deal with each of us in his own way. We don't need to carry that burden. Please, Hanna, let it go." I wasn't convinced she was ready to give in to my wishes. At least she never argued, but she made it clear how it offended her.

"Mama, because I was blessed with the wisdom of knowing there's much more for each of us once God calls us home doesn't make me a saint. It's not fair for you to use it against me. Of course, I know deep down inside all that you're telling me is true, but I'm as human as the next person, even with the blessing God gave me."

What I told Hanna was only part of how I felt, but I never shared all my thoughts with her. I didn't want her to have the fear that I had to deal with: if we reported the abuse, I doubted they would lose their jobs, and Walter could suffer more harm from them. I suspected it would only make the matter worse. They'd been cruel for no reason. I shuddered when I thought about how they'd treat him if they were out for revenge.

We visited Walter regularly, and it was a week later when we passed the one abuser in the hallway, not too far away from Walter's room. I looked at her, in a friendly way. To my surprise, she was glaring at us.

Hanna bent down and whispered to me, "Shouldn't we be the ones glaring at her? She's messed up, Mama."

"Yes, she sure is. Best not to make eye contact." But the day would come when she would be in Walter's room when we were there, and it would be awkward.

Chapter 56

AFTER ONLY A couple of months of Walter being in care, we could see he was getting worse. He'd dropped weight and was in another world. His blank eyes showed nothing. The nurses knew, and they tried to prepare us. They said Walter eventually would stop eating, and the end would be close.

It was the kind of day where you didn't want to go outside. About three inches of snow had accumulated. I was feeling my own aches and pains, and I wanted to rest. Hanna made a chocolate cake in the morning, and she cut a piece to take to her dad. Before leaving, she got me settled on my bed and said she would be back in about an hour. I told her to kiss her dad on the cheek for me.

I was lying down on my bed when I heard her come back in. It had been longer than an hour because it was starting to get dark outside. She knocked on my bedroom door and quickly opened it. Her worry showed on her face before she even spoke, so I knew there was a problem.

"Mama, Dad isn't doing very well." She sat down on the bed.

I gasped, "Hanna, what's wrong?"

"They got him up this morning, like usual, but he wouldn't eat his breakfast, and he slumped over in his wheelchair, so they put him back to bed. They never got him up for dinner because there was no point; he wouldn't have eaten. I tried to wake him, but he wouldn't even open his eyes."

"Please take me to him."

"Of course, Mama."

The nurse was in Walter's room when we got there. She was checking him to see if there was any change. There wasn't. He was lying there, as if in a deep sleep. Hanna pushed me close to him so that I could hold his hand. I knew my Walter was going on his journey. God was calling him home. He looked peaceful. That was all we could ask. For many, many years, part of my daily prayer had been that God would call me home before him. I realized then that wasn't in his plan.

Hanna sat on the other side of the bed. I thought back to what Hanna shared so many years ago about her own afterlife experience. She handled death differently than most people, and I understood why. For many years, I cursed the unborn child Walter had fathered. After Hanna told Ava and I about her dying and how she was helped back, my feelings turned from anger to gratefulness. She must be Hanna's angel.

"Mama, what are you thinking about?" Hanna's question interrupted my thoughts.

"Nothing, I'm resting, and praying for your dad."

"Are you alright?" Hanna got up and came over to me.

"Yes, I am. It's alright if you want to go home. But I'd like to stay for a while longer … you can come pick me up."

"I want to stay too, Mama. We need to eat. I'll go get us a sandwich."

Hanna left the room, and I closed my eyes for what seemed like a couple of minutes. Walter made a small noise. It was enough to make me look at him. I watched him as he took his last breath. It was as peaceful as I'd prayed it would be.

A nurse came into the room, and I said, "He's gone."

She bent down and hugged me. Hanna returned.

"Is Dad gone?" she asked. We both looked at her, and she knew the answer.

She came over to her dad's bedside, held his hand, and kissed him on the cheek. "You're alright now, Daddy. I know you're with God."

Chapter 57

————∘◦⌘◦∘————

LATE SUMMER, 2007

Walter had been gone for seven years. During that time, I stayed with Hanna up until my mishap. I had stood to transfer into my bed from the wheelchair, and I fell. Hanna was right there, but she couldn't stop me from falling.

The doctor told us the fall more than likely didn't cause the break. But rather, when I stood up, my hip broke and it caused me to fall. They repaired my hip as best they could during surgery, but the doctor said because of my bones being so weak, and my age, I wouldn't be able to walk or stand again. It meant I needed specialized equipment to transfer, and staying with Hanna wasn't possible.

I would be released from the hospital and put into the same care center as Walter had been—there was no other choice. Hanna was having a harder time with it than I was. At eighty-three, it didn't appear to be such a dire situation. I hadn't been able to look after myself for years, and Hanna couldn't look after me any longer. No one ever wanted to be put into care, but I was thankful for a place to go.

The first day in the care center, Hanna stayed with me. I saw her worried eyes, and I told her, "It's alright."

My room was large enough for a kitchen table, chairs, dresser, television stand, and of course my bed. Hanna set my room up in advance and did a fantastic job. She felt it lacked that personal touch, so she planned on bringing in some silk flowers and ornaments over the next few days.

Judy, a caregiver, came in to give me my night medications which were locked up in the bottom drawer, over by the kitchen sink.

I woke up several times during the evening, especially when they came into check on me. In the middle of the night, I was awake with my eyes closed when I heard someone opening my medication drawer. I opened my eyes. It was Judy, the caregiver. I had a nightlight plugged in by the cupboards. She took out my pills, and I heard her remove some from the package. Next, she popped it in her mouth and drank from her water bottle.

She jumped when I spoke. "Judy, I don't need my medication until morning."

"I know," she answered. "I'm checking to make sure I gave you your night medications. For some reason, I thought I forgot. From looking here, I see I did give them to you." She left my room.

The next evening, Judy was back on duty. After my supper, she got me into bed. She went into the medication drawer and brought my pills over to me with a glass of water. The other caregivers put my pills into a small cup, and I took them out myself, one at a time, so I could take my time swallowing them.

Judy had the pills in the cup, and when she handed me a glass of water, she said, "Open your mouth for your pills."

"I like to take them separately," I answered, holding out my hand.

She bent down close to my ear. "Why are you so difficult? Take your damn pills."

I opened my mouth. I looked into the cup as she brought it up toward my mouth. My pain pill was missing. Then I knew for sure Judy was taking it. No way could this go on.

The following day, having dinner, I realized many issues were going on in my new home. Four of us sat at the same table for our meals; me and two women and one man, who never talked. The one lady was so tiny, and she reminded me of a kewpie doll, one that had seen a lot of years. The lines on her face were so profound and saggy it made you wonder if the skin was still connected to the skull underneath. She was friendly enough but had a difficult time even saying hello because of the rattling noise coming from her chest.

I was expecting her to have a coughing attack when she started to eat her soup because it had happened at breakfast. A caregiver came over and told her to relax and breathe. She coughed up some thick phlegm, and the caregiver wiped it away from her lips.

Sure enough, it was happening again, after only her second spoonful of soup. When the coughing started, I thought she was going to choke. I looked around and saw a nurse at the other end of the dining room giving out medications to residents. She looked over at the little kewpie doll and kept on with what she was doing. The coughing went on for a while longer, and thankfully, the phlegm came up and landed on the table in front of her.

When the nurse came to give us our medications, she saw the phlegm. "Stop spitting! You know better. How many times do I have to tell you?"

Kewpie doll started to cry, and she was struggling to breathe. Watching her was difficult. Her tears, her eyes, her shaking hands; she was scared to death. The nurse hovered over her, showing no sign of regret. The others at our table watched in silence.

Up until then, I was capable of putting a Kleenex up to my mouth, but the nurses didn't know me that well. I coughed up what I could and spit it on the floor.

She caught it out of the corner of her eye, and she turned her tongue on me. "You can stop spitting too." She glared at me. "What's the matter with you people?"

I knew I didn't dare ask her what I was thinking, *Do you swallow yours*? It was on the tip of my tongue, but I kept it in.

The little kewpie doll had stopped crying and was sitting across from me, smiling. Right from the first time, I think she had it figured out. Now she had a friend. So, I became a spitter, and I know my little friend was grateful. She was an easy target, and it seemed as though she was constantly breaking into tears because of her feelings of helplessness. When I could, I created a distraction. What I didn't realize was how attentive some of the other residents were.

Chapter 58

JUDY WAS WORKING nights, and I planned to talk to her about my pain medication. When she wheeled me up to my room, I asked her, "Judy, can I talk to you about something?"

"Sure," she said, flatly. "What is it?" We were waiting for another caregiver to help put me in the lift sling.

"I know you've been taking my pain medication. You should go for help." I said.

Both of us were facing the window. "Oh, you're crazy. How dare you accuse me of taking your pills." She shook her head. "No one is ever going to believe you."

"I will." Judy turned to see who was talking. I didn't need to because I knew the voice. It was Hanna.

The other caregiver came into the room, and all of us were quiet. As soon as they got me into bed, Hanna told them she would be staying to do the rest of my night care.

Hanna wasted no time. "What was that all about, Mama?"

"Judy's been taking my night pain medication. She did it twice that I know of." I knew Hanna would be mad at me for not telling her.

"Mama, you should have told me. I heard her. I heard her call you crazy. I'm going to the manager."

"I wish you wouldn't. Don't make trouble in here."

We heard a little knock at the door, and Hanna went to answer it. I couldn't see who it was, but I knew it was a female voice. Hanna brought her into my room, and I saw it was a resident who sat at the next table to me in the dining room. I had to strain my ears to hear them. I know I didn't catch it all, but it was enough.

"I want to tell you about your mama," was how she started out, but next she asked, "Does she talk?"

Hanna answered, "Yes, she talks, but she is a quiet person."

"Has she told you that some of the ones working in here aren't nice to us?"

"No, she hasn't told me that. Can you give me some examples of what you mean?"

"There are a couple of them here who yell at her for spitting up. They yell at another lady sitting at the same table as your mom, and she cries so hard, she can't catch her breath."

"What does my mama do?" I heard Hanna ask.

"Never says a word. She doesn't even look at them."

"The same ones are mean to me. Some of us talk about them, and their meanness. Don't let them fool you. They act differently when you're visiting."

"Have you gone to the manager?"

"No, we are all too afraid. If they're allowed to stay on, think of how they'll treat us. I don't want you to say anything about what I told you."

"Thank you for telling me. We'll talk again soon." Hanna said to her as they walked to the door.

"Yes, and I don't want to get caught talking to you because they'll know, and I'm afraid of them."

They were around the kitchen corner now. I couldn't see them, but I knew there was more said. I could only hear mumbling.

I knew what was coming, before she even started, "Mama, is any of this true? What's going on in here? You need to tell me, right now."

"Hanna, don't get so upset. Yes, there are some of them who aren't nice. Most of them I call my earth angels. They work so hard and try to make my life and the other residents' lives as pleasant as they can. They talk to me and tell me about their own lives. Some of them bring in their children and their pets to meet me. I'm blessed to have them looking after me."

"Mama, remember the two who were abusive to Dad? Remember how hurt and upset we both were?"

"Yes, I'll never forget it," I answered.

"Well, you must be able to understand how I feel right now. The ones who are abusive need to be reported. I'm so worried about you right now, and I don't want to leave you in here." Hanna's eyes were filled with tears.

"It'll be alright. Leave it be, Hanna," I said in a stern voice.

She sat there for a few minutes. I could tell my words weren't going to be enough for her to drop it. "Okay, I won't go to the management, but I need to know what's happening in here, behind closed doors. Leave it up to me."

"You should go home and let this go out of your head so that you can get proper rest."

She bent down and kissed me goodnight before leaving. I couldn't blame her for wanting to protect me. What worried me was that Hanna was so much like her late Aunt Marie. Both were soft as an angel, but they protected their loved ones with the fury of a demon. I needed to protect both of us. I didn't want to get kicked out of the care center, nor did I want Hanna stopped from coming in to see me.

Hanna returned the next day, in the afternoon, before my nap.

"Well, Mama, have they been kind to you?"

"As I told you, I am very fond of most of the nurses and caregivers. Please don't keep asking me about how they treat me. I talked to you many times about when my Matka passed away and what she had to say to us kids. Be kind, and keep God in your heart. That was part of her last words, and I expect the same from you. Now, I don't want to talk about it, and I don't want you dwelling on it."

"Alright, Mama. Does it mean we can't protect each other?"

"Hanna, there is only one way to protect yourself from an abuser. Walk away from their venom, and don't be tempted by your fear because it will breed and spread. Eventually, it will take away your innocence, and you will be left powerless."

"Take away my innocence?"

"It'll take away your pureness, which is your strength. Don't lose sight of why God has put you here Hanna. He has a purpose for you."

"I know, but what about you?"

"Me?" I chuckled. "I've lived a long life and faced many challenges. I'm not afraid of them. I pray to God to help me forgive them. I pray for them to find their way out of the hell they are living in. Don't worry about me. My faith is strong. An abuser will never break me. I focus on the good ones. When I drift off to sleep, it's them that I think about, no matter what happens during the day."

Hanna screwed her eyes shut before answering. "I know you're right, but I need to know you are being cared for properly, and you asking me to ignore abuse is something I don't know if I can do. I'm not making any promises."

Unfortunately, a couple of days later, Hanna walked in on a caregiver who was moody, not just with me, but the other residents too. She had me strapped into the lift that was controlled by her. She stood next to me, watching me and knowing how afraid I was of this contraption, which lifted me up into mid-air. "Smile, Stephanie. Smile, or I'm not going to put you down." I was hanging in mid-air, very close to her face. It wasn't anything I wasn't used to with this caregiver because she did it all the time. She saw the fear in my eyes, and for whatever reason, she enjoyed it. The other one helping her was standing alongside the bed, facing me.

I caught Hanna, out of the corner of my eye, standing behind them, watching, and listening. They couldn't see Hanna. I smiled at the caregivers, and she gave her usual laughter in response, the other one joined in with a weak chuckle. It was how it always worked with her. Hanna said nothing, but the hurt and disappointment showed on her face.

When they turned and saw Hanna, you would think they would have been afraid of the fact she saw their behavior. That didn't appear to be the case, though. They put me in the wheelchair, and left the room, knowing Hanna would finish getting me ready for my dinner.

"Mama, I had a tough time not saying anything to her. What is wrong with her and the other one? She had a little chuckle too."

"I am proud of you for not reacting, Hanna. That's the first step in realizing how forgiveness sets us free. Her purpose in life is to help us get there."

Hanna, knelt beside the wheelchair, "That's so ignorant of her, and the one chuckling along with her is a lost soul. One day, she'll realize how she was snatched up and used to feed the abuser's cravings. It makes me feel nauseous thinking about them."

"Oh, Hanna. Just leave it alone. I don't want to talk about it anymore." She got behind me, and quickly pushed me toward the door. Her sighs were deep and repeated, and while I ate my dinner, it carried on.

One day, the following week, when I woke from my afternoon nap, Hanna and another lady were in my room. The lady was up on a step stool, looking at my hanging silk plant. Neither of them saw I was awake, until I spoke, "What are you doing, Hanna?"

They turned, and I saw they were both spooked. "Nothing, Mama. I brought a friend in to meet you, and she was admiring your silk plant."

I pursued it further, "Can't she admire it from the floor? Why is she up on a step stool?"

"Oh, yes, she was looking at it from the floor but wanted to feel the leaves. She thought it was a real plant." Hanna looked back at her friend, who was now off the step stool.

"Well, are you going to introduce us?"

"This is my friend, Carol." Hanna appeared nervous.

"Hello. How are you?" Carol asked.

"I'm fine," I answered. *Carol must be a new friend of Hanna's. I've never seen her before or heard Hanna talk of her.*

Hanna's friend wasted no time visiting. She had to get back to work, so she grabbed a black bag and left.

"Hanna, what was she doing in here?" I tried again for an honest answer.

"Nothing, Mama. She stopped in for a visit. We decided to meet here because it's on her way to work."

Chapter 59

———————⊸•੦⫸⫷੦•⊷———————

I HEARD A favorite caregiver calling the nurse. I wished it wasn't she who'd found me. She had a heart of gold.

Frantically she yelled into her phone, "You need to come into Stephanie's room. I'm not sure what's happened to her. She isn't responding in her usual way." She paused, listening to the nurse on the other end. "No, she seems to look alright, but she isn't talking. It's like she's lost her voice."

Within minutes, the nurse arrived and started doing a test on me. She asked, "Stephanie, can you hear me?"

I gave her a questioning look, and she came close to my ear, and yelled, "Stephanie, can you hear me?"

I nodded.

"Can you talk, Stephanie?"

I shook my head; then I stared at the glass of water on my bedside table. Both tried a few more times, asking questions that I would usually answer. I couldn't give them anything.

"I'll leave a note for the doctor to visit her," the nurse told the caregiver. "I'll also make a call to her daughter, and let her know." They both left my room.

I was having dinner when I saw Hanna come in. She went directly over to the nurse's office. She wasn't there long before heading toward me.

"Mama, what's wrong? The nurse told me you aren't talking." Hanna bent down, so she was close to my ear. "Mama, are you feeling alright?"

She got right up in front of me, where I couldn't avoid her worried eyes. By nodding, I hoped I put her mind at ease.

242

It took longer than I expected for the nurses and caregivers to find out I had no voice. I suppose part of the reason was there were so many of them working in here, and I was one of many residents. Various ones, right in front of me, debated about whether I could hear, or talk. Often, one would say to the other, "She can talk. She just doesn't want to. I think she has selective hearing too."

When all of them finally concluded I wasn't going to talk anymore, they got more comfortable around me. It was a turning point in my life. My days were more fulfilling and exciting when I had no voice.

The kind ones, when in my room together, would talk about the same people who were abusive to us. In one way or another, those same ones got under their skin too. When I realized they created anxiety for their co-workers, I didn't feel alone anymore. Their frustration of having to work alongside them came through in the stories they shared with each other. I got to know which ones did most of the talking and venting, and those who were good at listening. Some of them played both sides.

They talked with each other about their relationships with their husbands, children, mothers-in-law, and the stories were always entertaining. The young one, I called "spunky," was full of mischief. She reminded me of Nurse Viviana, from all those years ago. Mostly because she was Italian, but also because she had the same golden-brown eyes and skin tone as Viviana. When she came into my room, I knew it would be a wonderful day filled with the most unusual stories. She didn't disappoint me that day, during my bath.

Spunky said to the tall blonde, "Let me tell you what happened to me when we were doing it last night."

"I'm not sure if I want to hear it." She chuckled.

Spunky knew it really meant that the tall blonde was all ears, so she continued. "My butt cheeks hurt."

Then, chuckling even louder, the tall blonde asked, "What do you mean?"

"Honestly, it's not a joke. After we have sex, my butt cheeks cramp up, and they hurt. It goes on for a day or so after we do it. I get him to massage my butt, and it helps but doesn't take it away. Have you ever experienced this?"

Laughingly, the tall blonde asked, "Are you sure there isn't some spanking going on?"

I had to turn my head away and fake a cough, to disguise the laughter building inside my chest.

"No, no, nothing like that. I move around a lot when we do it. I don't know if that's the reason. When I orgasm, my butt clenches tightly, so I'm using those muscles. Hubby and I think that's what causes it."

I loved the tall blonde's next question. "Why do you do that? Maybe try and not clench your butt."

"I have to. It makes my orgasms so intense."

"I can't help you," answered the tall blonde. She was still chuckling when she reached for the shampoo.

The two of them put me back into my bed, and I was alone until they returned to get me up for dinner. Their discussion triggered my memory of Walter's and my intimate times. We often would go for a walk on our land, and if the bushes could talk, I would die of embarrassment. It reminded me of my own butt incident.

I recall it was the kind of fall day we all hope for. The air was crisp and calm. By afternoon, Walter and I knew it would be warm enough to enjoy the outdoors. We were both in the kitchen. I was washing the breakfast dishes. Walter came up behind me, wrapped his arms around my waist, and pressed himself into me. He stood there until I acknowledged him in my most usual way. I turned to him, not saying a word, but our eyes teased each other. He nestled his lips on my neck, and I can still hear his tempting words, "Soon as the air warms, let's go for a walk."

Walter laid the blanket down amongst the trees. Because of my frozen hip, I couldn't get onto the blanket by myself. He gently picked me up and placed me so carefully on it. Time went by, and we undressed.

While arousing each other, I screamed. Walter misunderstood, and kept touching me. Both of us spotted the buggers, swarming around us. Realizing now, we were on top of a wasps' ground nest, Walter jumped to his feet, picked me up, and ran. When we got to the house, Walter examined my backside. He washed me with soapy water to remove as much of the venom as possible. It helped, but the swelling and pain persisted for a couple of days. Months passed before we were able to joke about it.

Chapter 60

————◦◦◦◦◦————

ON OCCASION, THE lady who'd told Hanna about the abuse came into my room. It was because of her that Hanna started to doubt me.

"I heard your mama talking last night," she told Hanna in a matter of fact tone.

"What?" Hanna was shocked. "My mama hasn't talked in months."

"Well, I heard her more than once. Last night, on my way to bed, as I walked past here, I heard her again. To make sure, I peeked in, and she was praying, out loud." Both were sitting on my sofa, staring over at me lying in my bed.

Hanna didn't believe her. Unfortunately, I'm sure that was why the lady had to share more.

"You've heard the workers talk about there being a ghost who lives on this side of the building, right?"

"Yes, they talk about it often," Hanna replied.

She leaned into Hanna, "It's your mama ... that's who they hear. She's their ghost." It was clear; she was certain she'd figured out the big mystery. I could see their fondness for each other when they hugged before she left.

It was after that talk when Hanna changed her ways. She would pop in at the oddest times. I even think she sat in my room where she wasn't visible from my bed, being quiet, and just waiting. I couldn't see her, but I could feel her presence.

One day, she came around the corner of the kitchen area and pulled up a chair alongside my bed. She sat there for what seemed like hours, watching me so intently, before deciding to tell me what was bothering her.

"Mama, I don't know what to believe. The lady who comes to visit us told me she's heard you talk more than once. If this is true, why would you want us to think you have no voice?"

I stared at my empty water glass and touched it.

"Oh, you need me to fill up the glass." Hanna took my empty glass into the kitchen and returned with it full of cool water.

"Mama, I have to tell you what happened to me. It's going to be hard for you to hear it, but it is best that I tell you about it now. I don't want you to feel any guilt or pain. You couldn't have known.

Because of my experience of leaving this earth, and coming back, I know from what happened to me that you'll eventually find out what I'm about to tell you. As difficult it may be for you to understand, believe me, when you are there—meaning between here and before you reach your final destiny—all that is important to you and to those that are close to you is revealed. I want you to be aware of this now before it comes to you in your transition.

I watched her. She had to wait, and I knew she needed a bit of time. When she finally spoke, I didn't want to believe her, but deep down, I knew she would never make up something so horrifying.

"Mama, remember the old man who moved in across the field from our place? Harvey? When I was a little girl, you sent me over there many times with food for him." She paused, "Your heart was always in the right place."

Hanna looked away from me before she could carry on. "When you go into transition, you'll find out what he did to me. You'll know that I heard him when he was dying, and I never told anyone. I stood at his door, and I heard him moaning in agony. I ditched the food on the way back home, and I chose not to say a word to you or dad.

"Days later, when you sent me back with more food for him, I knew when I approached his door, and the stench of his rotten body hit my nostrils that

I was safe. Only then did I return home to tell you that I thought there was a problem with him."

I could feel my own tears, but as difficult as it was for Hanna to tell me this, she wasn't crying, not even a single tear.

"Mama, I had to tell you this because when it's your turn to go, you'll find out. I 'm trying to protect you from the guilt and sadness you would've felt. You see, Mama, there's no need for guilt on your part. I've made peace with it. Hopefully, by me telling you about it now, you can do the same. I pray for you to make peace with it now." Hanna sat beside me, in silence.

It took months before I could come to terms with it. There were times when I wished Hanna hadn't told me. Nightmares haunted me, but one kept repeating. When I sent Hanna over with food, I saw her frightened little face, and her pleading, "Do I have to, Mama? Can't I go later?" I would wake with such guilt and shame for my naïveté. I should've picked up on her nervousness.

It was a process I needed to work through. I understood how it was necessary to be thankful for even the cruelest events we endured through our lifetime.

Chapter 61

———————————⇒∘ᴄ⌇∘⇐———————————

MY TIME WAS nearing, and I was ready. No words were spoken, but Hanna knew it too. She called the nurse in to see me, and to confirm my tired old body was giving in. Both left the room, whispering.

Hanna returned in a few minutes. I was on my side, and with God's help, I lifted my arm and held my hand up to her. It was my way of letting her know how grateful I was to her, and to say my final goodbye.

She saw my hand, came to me and gently held it for a few seconds before she placed it on my chest. "Oh Mama, I love you." Those were her last words to me, but not the last connection. I knew she was sitting there, and even though she cried softly at times, I felt her peace. She knew when I took my last breath.

I watched, and when I saw her pulling the white sheet up over top of my empty shell, I knew what her thoughts were, clearer than if I were physically still there.

Mama, you have gone beyond the white curtain, yet remain closer than ever.

ꙮ

Her curiosity and fear of the unknown taunted her, as I knew it would. Ultimately, she gave into it. As she sat and watched the secrets captured from behind the silk plant, the tears streamed down from her swollen eyes. I felt her gratefulness, her sorrow, her anger, and the turmoil it created within her.

My earth angels and all their pure loving energy to make my life peaceful, were part of her now. But so were the others, Satan's servants who created a hellish reality for me.

Now, she had to decide. Which one was going to feed her soul?

249